Current

Abby McCarthy

Published by Abby McCarthy, 2016.

Copyright © 2016 Abby McCarthy

This is a work of fiction. All characters, organizations and events portrayed in this novel are either products of the author's imagination or are used fictitiously. The author acknowledges the trademark status and trademark owners of various products referenced in this work of fiction, which have been used without permission.

All rights reserved. This book or any portion thereof may not be reproduced or used in any manner whatsoever without the express written permission of the author, except for the use of brief quotations in the book review.

Cover design by Hang Le

Dedication

For Nicole. I appreciate you more than you know
For: Louisa, Nicole, Kerry, Jade, Kristine and Dawn- Love my BBAUAN Bitches

current

{noun}

a body of water or air moving in a definite direction, especially through a surrounding body of water or air in which there is less movement.

{adjective}

belonging to the present time; happening or being used or done now.

PROLOGUE

"Jake! Where the hell are you? We should've been out on the water by now!" Shit, Jake thought. The old man didn't sound good today. He wondered if he even slept. When Jake left early this morning, his old man hadn't come home yet which could mean so many things.

Jake looked over to June who was decent and breathed a sigh of relief as his dad walked through the clearing. If his dad was just minutes earlier he would have seen June. The thought sickened Jake.

June stood up as soon as she saw Mr. Daniels, her cheeks flushed pink from embarrassment and she hoped he had no idea what they had been up too.

"Hi, Mr. Daniels," she said.

"You again, huh? You're the reason Jake isn't where he's supposed to be, aren't you?"

June didn't know what to say. She heard Mike Daniels say unkind things to Jake, but he had never been rude to June before. Jake reached June and slipped his hand in hers and gave her a look that said don't answer him.

"I'm coming now, Dad," Jake said. June was instantly sad that she had to leave Jake.

"I'm good at cleaning fish. I bet I'd be a great help on the boat Mr. Daniels," June offered up ignoring the glare Jake gave her. She knew he didn't want her around his old man, but she also knew her time was coming to an end.

Mr. Daniels was quiet and thought for a moment and said, "Fine. Let's go."

Jake felt it low and in the pit of his stomach that something about this was a bad idea, but when June squeezed his hand and said, "Please," he couldn't deny her.

The fishing boat was not a luxury boat. It was a dirty, slightly rusty boat, with large nets hanging off the front of it, and other fishing contraptions off the back that June had no idea what they did. When she thought of fishing, she thought of how her dad did it with a pole, a couple of beers and a day out with friends. There were poles attached on the side of the boat and baskets attached to the opposite side. It became very clear to June that this was not a leisurely trip down the river.

Jake cringed when June sat on the bench that he knew had dried fish guts staining it. He hated that her pretty dress was going to be ruined before the day was over. He hated even more when he saw his dad take the whiskey bottle to his lips before pushing off their small dock. He never wanted June to be around his dad, and for once, he instantly regretted giving in to her quiet plea to go with them. He was shocked his dad agreed in the first place.

The boat pushed off the dock and Jake dropped cages to catch crawfish and he explained to June that they would sweep back around and grab them on the way back.

"Less talking. More work," Mr. Daniels yelled more angrily than necessary at the young couple.

June quickly asked, "What can I do?"

Jake tensed at his dad's tone and then tensed even more when he watched him take the fifth of whiskey to his lips again finishing the bottle.

Eventually, they reached a spot on the river where Mr. Daniels swore the fish would be biting. Jake showed June how to bait and cast out a line, taking his time in making sure she learned it right.

"If I'd thought this was going to be a day of you trying to get in your girlfriend's pants, I'd have thought twice about letting her tag along," Mike Daniels spat at the two, jealous that they had each other and angry that he no longer had his sweet wife. She was always the only person who made him good. Without her, he had nothing. He never felt connected to Jake. Jake always occupied his wife's time and Mike resented that. He hated Jake even more for it when he no longer had her.

Jake cringed again at the vulgar words his dad used around June, mouthing, "Sorry," to her.

June responded by squeezing Jake's hand and for the first time she got a small glimpse at what Jake went through on a daily basis. Her heart hurt for him and she was going to do her best not to let Mr. Daniels harsh words get to her.

Mr. Daniels pushed past the two and intentionally shoulder-checked Jake. Jake knew not to stand up to his old man, especially not when June was there, so he gritted his teeth and tried to check his temper. Jake was angry that his dad was acting like this in front of June. He could take it, but didn't need for June to put up with it.

Mr. Daniels threw a line out, stationed his rod and then cast another, doing it all rather clumsily. The boat swayed side to side and Jake thought there would be no swimming for the pair tonight, the river was far too choppy. It was one of the reasons he didn't rush to the boat. He never thought his dad would want to fish in this.

June squealed with excitement when she felt a tug on the line. Jake told her to reel it slow at first and let the fish think that he was getting the bait, that way the fish would really get hooked. She did as instructed and after a few minutes of give and take on the line, she reeled in her first fish. It was small, too small to sell, and so Jake showed her how to unhook it and then he threw it back in. Jake caught several large fish while his dad had yet to catch one.

The clouds looked heavy and low, signaling to Jake that a bad storm might be coming.

"I don't think we should stay out here, not if we're going to pick up our baskets on the way back," Jake said to his dad.

Mike Daniels looked furiously at Jake. He knew when to call it quits. It was his boat. He'd been fishing on this river since he was a boy. Maybe he shouldn't have had that extra fifth of whiskey with breakfast-who was he kidding-for breakfast, but it didn't matter he knew when to call it quits and that wasn't yet. He needed more fish. He needed a bigger haul. He lost big on the tables last night and if he didn't come up with money to pay Mr. Stevens there would be hell to pay. He'd already lost the farm and that shit son of his couldn't even catch enough fish to help pay his debts. What good was he, anyways?

"The fuck did you say, boy? I'll tell you when we're ready to go."

June flinched at Mr. Daniels tone but tried to not let Jake see it had affected her. She also tried not to flinch when Mr. Daniels threw out his line and snagged his rig against a bunch of turned up branches that the coming storm was pushing down the river.

"That's a fifty dollar rig. Get your ass in the water and go get it," he said to Jake. Jake wanted to argue about the fast current and how dangerous it was. He also hated the thought of leaving June alone with his old man even for a second, but he could tell by his old man's tone that today could get even worse than it already was. Jake stripped off his jeans, into his boxers and quickly jumped into the murky water, looking back at June once before plunging under the water.

June's stomach tightened. Every second Jake was in the water was a second she felt like she couldn't breathe.

It happened fast. Mike Daniels was too close to June for comfort.

"You know I saw you two together. I didn't figure you for a whore, but at least my boy is getting some. I'm thinking I should get a taste. See what all the fuss is about that's been keeping him so busy."

June froze. She didn't want Mr. Daniels to come any closer to her, but she needed to make sure that Jake was okay.

Jake emerged from under the water near the brush. The water was choppy, and there were more limbs below the surface than above. He reached out and tried to unhook the rig, but the tumultuous waters pushed a sharp jagged stick into his ribs. He felt it cut his skin, but he had to go on.

"Stop!" he heard the faint cry from June, and turned his head back to see why she was yelling. His dad had his hands on June and was groping one of June's breasts.

"No!" she yelled again and he watched as she struck out and smacked his dad. He needed to get to her, he knew what happened when he tried to fight back and. Fighting back only made it worse.

He couldn't swim back fast enough to the boat. His arms burned with how hard he was trying to get to her. The sky opened up and sent large pellets of water everywhere. Jake could barely see through the dense rain. He pushed himself as hard as he could but felt like he was failing when he saw his dad grab her by the back of her hair and force her to her knees, with his other hand around her throat. He knew his dad was sick, but he never imagined him trying to do something as vile as this.

Jake reached the boat just as his dad's belt buckle was being undone and his world went black.

CHAPTER ONE

"I'm low on funds Liz and if we're going to get in before they start charging the five dollar cover we have to go," I say tugging on Liz's purse trying to break the locked gaze she has with the beefy blonde. She shoots me a sideways look with a slight grit to her teeth that tells me without words, she isn't ready to leave.

"Just tell the guy at the door you're writing about the band for *The Scene*. He'll totally be cool with letting you in for free," Liz says but doesn't take her eyes off of Blondie.

"And you know I can't do that. The band isn't supposed to know I'm there."

"Fine, fine," she says dismissively, "You mind if I meet you there in ten?"

"Whatever," I say annoyed with Liz, but not surprised. This is typical Liz behavior. A cover charge doesn't make a difference to Liz, but it's the difference of me eating more than Ramen Noodles tomorrow. I am the typical broke college student, hence why I need to pay zero for a cover.

I grab my coat that's hanging on the back of the barstool and holler over the music which has suddenly increased in volume, "You better not ditch me," I say waving over my shoulder. I leave the bar, exiting into the chilly air, throw my coat on and walk the three blocks to Parrot Blue's.

Two weeks ago, I stopped in Parrot Blue's just as a band was leaving and I swore for a moment that it was him; the one I've been searching for, but before I could catch up to him, he was gone. I'm not even supposed to be covering tonight's show, but I took on Andrea's articles covering the local swap meet in exchange for her giving me the show to cover.

The bar is a dive in the best possible way. Old license plates and bumper stickers from long since forgotten radio shows cover the ceiling. On one wall is the first dollar they earned and the subsequent first dollar spent on the day of each of their anniversaries- forty-eight dollars total. I know this because one night, the most dreadfully boring band was playing and I managed to count all forty-eight.

I was able to beat the crowd tonight and find a seat at a freestanding circular table with several bar stools around it. Ash, a bartender that is covering the floor until his late night staff gets in stops by the table.

"All by yourself tonight, June?" he smiles a warm friendly smile.

"Hopefully not for long, Liz should be meeting me. Been slow tonight?"

"Not too bad, besides the night just got better."

"And why is that?" I ask knowing that Ash is a flirt.

"Well, you walked in for one. Whatcha having anyways?"

"Water for now, I need to watch myself."

"At your service," he says dramatically then walks away. Ash is harmless and has always been a gentleman to me. He might flirt from time to time, but it's all in good fun.

The bar pays a crew to help set up. They're overweight guys with torn shirts willing to do any grunt work for the fifty dollars or so the bar is paying them. These guys are fairly efficient in placing the large speakers, amplifiers and running all the wire for the sound equipment. I sip my water steadily until and Ash brings me a refill. Liz isn't here yet and I'm getting annoyed.

I shoot her a text message.

Where r u Liz?

The bar begins filling up with patrons and I hope to God Liz gets here soon otherwise I'm going to have to throw down for these seats. The drummer comes out and starts doing a sound check. He is wearing a Slayer t-shirt. His face has a full beard and a baseball cap covers his eyes. I hope like hell this isn't death metal. I have little tolerance for that.

"Check, check," he says into the mic.

The lead singer is wearing black motorcycle boots, a pair of jeans with a chain attached to his wallet that is tucked into his pocket, a white t-shirt and has a pretty boy face with dark hair styled on top begins to adjust the mic. The lights go dim and I know the band is getting ready to do their thing. I'm straining to see them, I need to see if it's him.

"There you are!" Liz scoots past me and slides onto the stool against the wall. I purposely sit on the edge facing the band so that I can see everything. Across from Liz, Blondie grabs a seat. Next to him, a nicely dressed man, and by nicely I mean khaki pants and a long sleeve button up shirt with frosted tips on his hair and dark beady eyes sits down across from me. I catch Liz's eyes and silently tell her I want to strangle her if she is trying to set me up with this guy. He is not my type. At all.

"Hi, I'm Allen," the guy in front of me says and stretches out his hand. I reach my hand out and meet his. He shakes my hand, by barely holding it and moving it up and down way too fast. It speaks volumes about him. I wonder if he fucks like he shakes hands. I shudder at the thought. He is nice enough looking, if you like the preppy type. Liz likes any type, me not so much.

"June," I say as uninterested as I can.

"Can I get you something to drink?" he asks.

"No, I'm drinking water right now. Pardon me," I say not explaining myself to him or why I need to pay attention to the band. He already distracted me while the rest of the members joined the small stage and I really need to see if it's him.

"How's everyone doing tonight?" The lead singer shouts into his microphone and the room responds with several hoots and hollers. "A big thanks to Parrott Blues for inviting us back tonight. We're Silent Tides."

Opening keys on a keyboard start to play. The keyboardist is turned away from me, so I can't see his face. I immediately recognize the song as Brian Adams Everything I Do I Do It for You. Oh no, not another eighties cover band. The bassist joins in. He has long straggly hair, is slim and wearing red skinny jeans. The singer starts singing. His voice is soothing. It has a nice raspy tone to it. I close my eyes for a second to absorb it.

"You really get into this stuff don't you?" Allen asks me, trying to get my attention. I open my eyes and give him a glare.

"Don't mind her. She's writing about the band," Liz explains to Allen.

"I love this song!" Blondie shouts.

I take my attention away from the distractions at the table and I listen to the music. They are all playing well. I haven't gotten that "wow factor" yet from them, but as far as covers go, it's nice. The singer ends the first chorus, and then everything changes.

The keyboardist stops and adjusts a microphone. The singer picks up a trumpet from the case and starts playing. The entire tempo changes and the keyboardist starts singing in a fast upbeat Ska/Punk kind of way. He sings the lyrics, "Look into my eyes and you will find…"

The energy in the entire room has shifted. Maybe the regulars were expecting this shift because the crowd moves right into it, dancing and singing along. Heads start bobbing, but a magnetic pull brings me center stage. No one moving around me matters because my eyes are fixed on the man singing. His eyes are so familiar. It can't be him, can it? They look so much alike. I've been searching for so long. So many years have passed. Maybe I am imagining what he would look like. This has to be a figment of my imagination. I want it so badly. All of these years I've needed to see him again, but could my mind be playing tricks on me. I wish it was him, but I'm also afraid that it is.

I'm mesmerized. His eyes lock onto mine. I'm hopeful that he recognizes me, but if he does, he doesn't give anything away.

Song after song our eyes remained locked. His eyes are the lightest shade of blue-green. Liz and the two guys join me on the dance floor and attempt to dance with me, but I can't be bothered. I probably look strange just standing here staring, taking him completely in.

"Your eyes remind me of the sea," I say. *He links his fingers in mine.*

"You know I don't like compliments."

"That's just 'cause you're not used to hearing them, but I'll tell you again and again. They are the most beautiful shade of blue-green I've ever seen."

"June," his voice is filled with emotion as he says my name.

"Do you know how special you are?"

"June, stop."

"No. I wish you'd see what I see, Jake."

"You don't stop, I'm going to kiss you, June."

"Then kiss me." He doesn't delay. Not even a second. Jake is two years older than my fifteen-year-old self. His lips are tender as they press against mine.

Sweet.

Simple.

Perfection.

He pulls away all too soon and my lips tingle from his touch. I press my fingertips against my lips. "Kiss me again."

"Not much of a dancer are you?" Allen says in my ear all too close. I ignore him too entranced by the stage, too entranced by those eyes. He switches with the lead singer. Some songs are his to sing, others are not.

Blue-Green Eyes finishes his version of Every Rose Has Its Thorn, brushes his hand through his hair and says into the microphone, "Going to slow it down a bit with a Silent Tide

original. It's called Ripple. Then, we'll take a small break. If you'd like to purchase CD's or any merchandise, there will be a table set up after the show."

The keyboard starts a slow, steady pace. It's followed by the gentle beat of the drum, next the bass and guitar. It still has a punk feel to it, but it's a ballad for sure.

A small bump
In a series of bumps
On the surface
You changed it all
Everything was one way
Until my ripple
You passed through me
For a moment in time
Changed the flow
When you were gone
You left
A ripple
The way you moved in
It'll never be the same
You left
A ripple
Driving me insane
Faster and faster
It all fell apart
When you left a ripple
You stole my heart
I'm left with little waves
You tore through me
The ripple

I'd never change

The music stops. The crowd is in quiet awe. It's a second of silence; a second for the crowd to get their bearings. My heart is beating.

Thump, thump.

I barely register the applause.

Thump. Thump. They're setting their equipment down.

Thump.

Thump.

He's getting closer.

"Hey," he says, his eyes locked on me.

I'm suddenly shy. I'm never shy. Could it be him? Does it matter with the way he has entranced me? Of course, it matters. I nervously fiddle with a strand of my black shiny pixie cut, suddenly nervous if my recent trip to Sally Beauty Supply was a good idea. He reaches out and tucks a tiny piece behind my hair and I have the overwhelming need to dye it back.

"Hi," I finally say staring back into his eyes.

Thump. Thump. His eyes are exactly how I remember. Could my mind have altered it to fit? Am I so desperate that I would do that?

"I'm June." I want to see if recognition flashes in his eyes, but I see nothing.

That's not exactly true, I see so much. I see the beautiful eyes I've dreamt about, but I also see a man. The eyes I fell in love with belonged to a boy. His dark hair has a slight curl that hangs over his forehead. He has a small scar along his angular jaw and I itch to reach out and touch it. I want to know how it got there. A black t-shirt that says. "Are you looking at my wiener?" with a picture of a wiener dog hugs his chest. I can see that he's in shape, but he doesn't look like he's overly buff. His Levi's are faded with a tear in the knee and his Chuck Taylor's tell me he is laid back.

"June," he says my name, letting it roll around his tongue, "Have a drink with me." He doesn't ask. He commands in a soft voice that leaves no room for no.

I follow him to the bar through the throngs of people. Liz catches me by the arm and whispers in my ear, "He's hot. I got dibs on our place tonight." I nod at her and shake off my shivers as I see Blondie lick her neck.

Allen must have gotten the hint because I walk by him, he's chatting with a table of women. Thank god.

Ash quickly makes his way to us. "Jameson straight up, and whatever she's having."

"Water for you then, June?" Ash asks.

I shake my head, "Tequila."

Ash raises an eyebrow at me and goes about pouring us drinks.

"You're here a lot?"

"Enough, but not like you might think." I can't tell him I'm writing about the band, it would ruin the integrity of the piece.

"Care to elaborate?" He has to almost shout to be heard over the crowd of people.

"Not really."

Ash sets our drinks down in front of us. Blue-Green Eyes hands him a bill and tells him to keep the change. "Are you good, June?" Ash asks me. I can tell he's concerned. I don't normally drink if I'm here to write about the band.

"Yeah Ash, I'm good." I get a head nod from him as he takes his next order.

"Let's go to your table; it's quieter back there," he says grabbing our drinks.

Again, I follow him. It's strange, I haven't even gotten his name yet, but somehow it feels like I would do whatever he asks of me.

"What's your name?" I ask taking my seat. He stands next to me; his drink on the edge of the table; he's in my space.

My heart is beating, hard. Please say Jake.

Be him.

Don't be him.

I'm indecisive on what I want.

"Lucas," he says sliding the glass to me. My face falls a bit, let down that it's not him. It will never be him. Sometimes, I think I imagined him. The good times, a memory; the bad, a nightmare. Still, there is something drawing me to Lucas. I shift my eyes away from him,, not wanting to give too much away. He grabs my chin between his forefinger and thumb and turns my head to look at him. "Did I say something wrong?"

"No. You just reminded me of someone." I smile at him, not wanting to take away from the undeniable attraction between us.

"Are you disappointed I'm not him?"

"I think I'm exactly where I need to be with exactly whom I'm supposed to be with."

"You don't seem like you belong here. Yet, the bartender's looking out for you. What's your story?"

"I don't look like I belong?" I ask pretending to be affronted.

"It's not that you don't belong. Most of the kids here look like they're all about the cliques, and you look like you don't care about what anyone is doing but June." God, the way he says my name.

"I'm a college student at Cleveland State. Just the same as most of this crowd."

"That's not true, June. Not at all. There is nothing like you that's the same as everyone else."

I feel my face grow warm and I know I'm blushing. I never blush anymore. Why is it that Lucas brings this out of me?

"We haven't touched our drinks yet." I want to take the attention off of me so I grab my glass.

"To new acquaintances," he clinks his glass to mine. I put my glass to my lips and drink half of the small rocks glass. I watch as he does the same. His lips, a light shade of pink are wet as he pulls it away. I lick my lips and relish in the tequila burn.

The lead singer walks over and throws his arm around Lucas' shoulder. "Hey brother, five more minutes. You sounded great on the last one. The crowd really dug that shit. We should totally do more originals. Hey, I'm Dietz," he says to me and I watch Lucas's body shift so that he is blocking me a little from his friend. It's not blatant, but I can't help but feel like he subtly claimed me to him.

"June," I say raising my hand doing a small wave.

"Dietz, I'll be over in a minute," Lucas says to him and downs the rest of his drink. I follow his lead and finish mine as well. "Will you stay for the next set?" he asks. Besides my obligation for The Scene, there is no way I would leave.

"I'll be here," I say and Lucas brushes his fingers over my short strands of hair across my forehead then walks back up to the small stage. His touch still feels familiar. Even though I know they're not the same person, I can't shake this feeling.

CHAPTER TWO

The next set is just as good as the first, if not better. The crowd is definitely into it. I'm finding their original music to be better than the covers. They all have skills, especially Lucas and Dietz. I sit for the first few songs and then before I know it, Lucas's eyes have drawn me close to the stage again. Liz takes a break from making out with Blondie and starts to dance next to me.

"Damn, I haven't seen two people eye fuck each other like you two ever," she says over the music. Liz is wearing a red strapless fitted dress. Her long blonde hair falls down past her shoulders but sways and bounces as she moves to the music.

"Where did your blonde toy go?" I ask.

"He's getting us drinks."

"Allen? Seriously?" I ask.

Liz cringes, "Sorry about that, but Mark wouldn't leave the other place without him."

I shudder, "Next time tell them I'm gay."

"That will just turn them on," Liz laughs and I can tell she is fairly inebriated.

"Maybe you're right. Make something up that will turn them off the trail then; I don't care what it is."

"Fair warning, remember you said this. If a guy thinks you're into baby play, you'll know why."

"You wouldn't," I giggle noticing that the tequila must have affected me, since I hadn't eaten dinner. Liz winks at me, throws her hands up over her head and starts to bounce to the upbeat song. I laugh at my best friend and dance right alongside her, until Mark joins her, followed by Allen. I roll my eyes. I was hoping I was rid of him. Allen puts his hands on my hips and tries to dance with me. I shake my head at him, and tell him I'm not interested.

"Oh, come on. A pretty little thing like you would have so much fun with someone like me."

I peel his hand away from me, "Allen, I think you're a douche. I've been trying to be polite, but don't touch me."

"You don't have to be such a bitch," he says rather loudly. My eyes are fixed on Lucas. His brow furrows and the tone in his voice while he is singing changes. The song has natural anger to it, but the anger in his voice just kicked up about ten notches. Again with his anger, he looks so much like I would imagine Jake to look like.

"I can't believe he just talked to you like that." Jake runs his hands through his hair, taking a deep breath, "I hate him, June. I hate him so fucking much."

"You don't mean that." I wrap my arm around his waist and pull my head onto his chest. We're standing in the back of the empty, dirty barn and his dad just left. He caught us kissing. He wanted Jake to help him clean the fish he just caught, but he couldn't find him. When he found us in the barn with our lips locked, something we'd been doing a lot of lately, he called me a whore.

"I mean it, June. I don't want you anywhere near him. Maybe you should just stay away from me. I'm no good for you."

"Jacob Daniels, don't you dare talk like that. I don't care what he calls me." Jake is angry; angrier than I've ever seen him. His brow furrows. He shrugs from my embrace and punches the tall wooden pillar. Blood drips from his knuckle and he rears his fist back to punch it again.

"No, stop!" I latch onto his arm and do my best to stop him from hurting himself. "Jake, no. Look at me," I plead trying to get him to let go of his anger. I stop him from hitting the wood again, but the anger is coming off him in waves. "Please don't let him hurt you any more than he already has."

"Don't call my friend a bitch, you asshole!" Liz yells breaking me from my quick memory. Allen flips her off and storms towards the bar. "You okay?" she asks me.

I do a whatever motion with my hand, flipping it around in the air, brush off the bitch remark and pump one arm up over my head with the beat.

I take my eyes off of Lucas for a moment and look at Liz. Marc is mouthing "I'm sorry," to her and pleading with Liz not to be pissed. Maybe Blondie isn't so bad after all; at least he didn't chase after the douche bag.

I return my attention to the band. I know I need to watch all of them for my article, but it's hard to avoid the vibes coming from Lucas.

I can tell Dietz and the bassist also can feel Lucas's anger and they try to draw him out of his mood by playing around him. It works and Lucas is smiling and back to playing the keyboard with the same easy flow.

Before long, Dietz is at the microphone. "Thanks for coming out tonight. We'll be around for a while. We have CD's and other Silent Tides merchandise available at the table by the door. If you enjoyed the show, buy that shit!" The crowd is clapping and whistling.

I'm nervous and excited. I look down at my watch, it's just past twelve-thirty. I've been so engrossed in everything that is Lucas that I haven't used the restroom and decide that now is a good time. I'll give him a second to get off stage and do what he needs to do. There is a line with at least three women ahead of me. I check myself in the mirror while I wait. My hair is still in place after all of my dancing. My blue doe eyes are lined with a charcoal smoky eye that's slightly smeared. Sweat sticks to the back of my neck, from dancing so I grab a paper towel, wet it, fix my make-up around my eyes, then press it against the back of my neck while continuing the perusal of my outfit. I have a t-shirt that hangs off one shoulder, it's black and reads, punk's not dead. I'm wearing a jean skirt with little black boots that are barely laced.

I get it, next to Liz I don't look like I fit in. I'm not one to really care if men like me or not. Either they do or they don't, but I want Lucas to like me. I know I'm small. I'm petite. Always have been. *"You might be small, but you got fire,"* Jake's words resonate through my mind and briefly I wonder if they will ever go away.

I leave the restroom and notice that the line has doubled. Lucas is standing by my table with a few of the band-mates. They have drinks in front of them and a small group of women surround them. I feel like an intruder, but my coat is on the stool. Lucas laughs at something one of the girls says and notices me approaching. His smile brightens.

Dietz calls my name loudly, "June!"

I laugh and watch Dietz throw his arms around a woman's shoulders with long curly dark hair. "Where the heck have you been?" Dietz asks jovially.

"There was a line," I say and notice that Lucas pulled out my stool.

"I got you a drink," Lucas says. It's another round of tequila. Normally, I would never take a drink from a guy like this, but I'm slightly buzzed and I oddly feel like I can trust Lucas.

"Thanks," I say and do a double-take as a girl with large breasts, even larger fluffed out blond hair and even fewer clothes takes a seat next to me. "I'm Bernie; Eric's girl," she says righting herself in her spot.

"Eric?" I question.

"I'm Eric," The bassist with the red skinny jeans says as he sits down across from Malibu Barbie.

"Hi," I say to the both of them, but am cut off by Eric when he asks, "Where's Rhett?"

I lean in and ask Lucas who is standing on the edge of the table, "Who's Rhett?"

"He's our drummer, and dude I have no idea. He grabbed his sticks and was all like, 'I'm out.' as soon as our set was over. Anyone know what's up with him?" Lucas asks the guys.

"I think he is ticked off at Joey," Dietz says. I surmise that Joey must be the guitarist. I look around for and see that he's by the front door selling merchandise.

"Those two have more drama than any chicks I know. If they're not fighting over the same girl, or griping about a song, then they're generally inseparable, but seeing as they have the same taste in women and bump heads over music, it hasn't been fun lately," Bernie says.

"She's right. Those two are full of so much bullshit," Lucas agrees and takes a sip of his dark amber liquid.

"So Bernie, that's an unusual name?" I ask.

"So is June," Eric says. He has a slight attitude about him, but I'm guessing it's the fact that he is coming down from a show. I've been to enough of these to know that the adrenaline from performing can make them act differently.

I see Bernie give a kick to Eric's shin with her white stilettos under the table. "It's short for Bernadette."

"I like it," I say and decide that I like Bernie.

"So, June. What's your gig?" Dietz asks.

"Good old C.S.U. student," I say with mock enthusiasm.

"What's your major?" Lucas asks me. He's quieter than the rest of the guys. But it seems like he really wants to know my answer.

"English," I say taking a sip of my tequila.

I see Liz on the other side of the room headed towards me. Her hair bounces from side to side as she sways her hips. Mark follows behind her as if an invisible leash has him tethered and that's how she likes it.

"Hey chick!" she says as she approaches the table.

"Everyone, this is Liz." I introduce her, my voice coming out louder than I meant to and I know that must be the tequila.

"Dietz. My pleasure," and happily gives a side hug with Liz, obviously checking her out.

Marc scowls and grabs her close. It's nice to know he has a backbone. At Marc's blatant claim staking, Liz squints her eyes and says, "Hey, Dietz. Everyone, great show. We're going to take off. Are you good?" I don't miss the look Liz gives Dietz; I'm just unsure what it means.

I look around the table and feel Lucas' fingertips trail lightly up my arm. It feels so familiar. "Yeah, hon. I'm good." Then, I pull her close and whisper in her ear, "Be safe and keep your cell on."

"Marc?" I ask.

"Yeah, what's up?"

"I need to see your license?" I tell him. He gives Liz a confused look. Then, I add, "You don't want me to see it, that's fine; but Liz will be staying a while longer to hang out with me."

"Give her your license, Marc," Liz demands.

Marc pulls his license out, hands it to me, and I slide my phone from my jean skirt pocket and snap a picture of it, then explain, "Just gotta make sure I know who my girl is taking home."

A few of the guys laugh at the table, but for some reason Lucas doesn't seem that amused. Liz and Marc leave and I join in the conversation with the table.

"Is that something that happens a lot?" Lucas asks me.

"What? Liz hooking up?"

"Yeah."

"Yeah, I guess it kind of does. She's Liz. It's just who she is. Has been that way since the day I met her, and Lord knows I'm not changing her."

"But she's your roommate?" Lucas asks.

"Men always with the double standard. Look at Dietz, he'll fuck anyone, anywhere, no one questions him, but the second a woman is doing it, look out," Bernie adds.

"I'm hurt," Dietz says in mock horror. "I wouldn't sleep with just anyone. They have to have a vagina."

Eric coughs and mumbles under his breath, "Vegas".

"That didn't happen," Dietz denies. "And with that, I'm getting another round. Who wants one?"

The entire table places their order. Before long, I'm doing another shot and laughing with Lucas.

"SO, THE BAND? IS THAT a full-time thing?" I ask drunker and more outgoing than I normally am. Eric and Bernie took off a few minutes ago, and Dietz is entertaining a crowd of women.

"I have a regular job; the band is for fun. Some of the guys take it more seriously than others."

"What else do you do?"

"I'm at a body shop. How about you?"

"School is kind of it for me," I say and then hate that I'm lying, so in my inebriated state I come clean, "Shoot, that's not the truth. I write for *The Scene*."

"Why? Is that a bad thing?" he asks.

"No, but I might be here sometimes writing about local music."

I see it dawn on Lucas that I'm writing about the band. I shrug then say, "Don't tell anyone because I'm suddenly finding myself a little impartial."

"Is that so?" he flirts.

"Perhaps," I smile and coyly take a sip of my drink.

Ash stops by the table and removes a few empty bottles, "We're getting ready to call last call. You still good, June?"

"I'm freaking awesome, Ash. This is Lucas. Wait a minute, you know who he is. He's in the band." I sloppily hit myself on the forehead then shake my head as if everyone should know that was a silly statement. "How did you do tonight? Make some big bucks?" I ask with a slight slur.

"Are you drunk?" he asks ignoring my question.

"I am slightly buzzed, but it's all good Ash."

"I got her man, everything's cool," Lucas says. I can tell Lucas' body language has changed and that if Ash doesn't back down this could turn into a pissing match. So I do what a horny, drunk, college girl does, I lean into Lucas and say loud enough for Ash to hear, "I'm not ready for the night to end yet. You?"

Ash's shoulder's slump like he's disappointed in me. "See you later, June," he says and walks away, clearly getting the point.

"I like the way you think, June. Let's get out of here," Lucas says, his pupils dilate as he takes my hand and helps me shrug my coat on.

His thumb strokes my hand and he links his fingers with mine and I realize that in some way, he's been touching me since his set ended. I like this. It's soothing.

"I don't have a car here. Maybe we should get a cab?" I ask.

"We haven't decided where we're going yet. Are you up for a little adventure?"

"It depends on what you have in mind."

He leads us towards the front door and asks Ash if he'll sell him a six of PBR to go. Reluctantly, Ash agrees and Lucas stuffs the six pack into a backpack that he grabbed from the stage before the stagehands said goodnight.

"A couple blocks from here, there's a cemetery where some president is buried. I used to work on the grounds and have a key."

"You want to bring me to a cemetery?" I ask, thinking this just got a little weird.

"It's not that morbid, I swear. There is this spiral staircase to the top and you can see the whole city from up there. Plus it's only a few blocks from here and I think it's too early for us to walk to my place."

I had no idea if he meant too early in the night or too early for us meeting each other to walk to his place, but I oddly respected that.

"Are you close to here?"

"Not far. So, are you okay with checking out the city?" His hand is still holding mine and I realize we were already walking along the metal gate to the cemetery. I knew where he was talking about. How could I not? You can see the peak from various points in the city and I know it isn't far from the bar we were at.

"Isn't the front gate going to be locked? It's nearly two A.M."

"I know a spot," he says as he flashes a smile.

"I should be concerned. Middle of the night; hot guy asks a girl to go to the cemetery. If this were fiction, I would be screaming, "No, don't go there," but since it's reality, I'm strangely okay with the idea of breaking into a cemetery and breaking into our dead president's holy sanctuary," I laugh as I say the last part.

"Good, I'm glad you trust me enough to commit felonies with me."

"Oh hell, are we going to get busted?" I ask as he stops us at a spot on the fence where the gate changes from old to new. An overgrown tree is nestled just enough in the opening that it makes climbing easy.

"Not if you're really quiet and really fast. Shit! Cops! Quick, kiss me." He pushes me against the wrought iron fence as I barely register the police car driving past. His lips crash down on mine immediately begging for my mouth to open. When his tongue hits mine, I can faintly taste whiskey.

This isn't a light, get to know you kiss. No, this is a desperate, I'm pulling at his hair and grinding my hips into him kiss. I lift on my tiptoes and he bends into me. My nipples are hard and I wish I were free of my coat so that I could be closer to him. His tongue swirls against mine and then sucks it deep before breaking away. Immediately, I mourn the loss of contact.

"Damn June, that was..." He grins and shakes his head. I'm not even sure what came over me; that was more than I could have hoped for, and it was everything that I'm not. I'm not carefree, let go, and kiss wildly on the street. I'm in control, often spunky, but I rarely do things with abandon.

"I think they're gone."

"Who?" I ask.

He laughs at me and it's a deep beautiful rumbly laugh. "The police."

Oh right, that's why he kissed me.

"Here, let me help you," he says lifting me up then instructing me to use the tree to climb over. My boots are thick and slightly clumsy, but he's right behind me guiding me up, making sure I don't fall.

Once I am up and over, he easily climbs the gate making my strained effort seem foolish. I smack him on the arm, "That was so easy for you."

"I almost have a foot on you, it should be easier."

"Okay, but nobody likes a show-off," I tease.

We walk down winding trails; tombstones and mausoleums flank each side of us. "This place is huge," I say in wonder. It's dark and eerily quiet. Some people might be afraid of sneaking into a cemetery at night, but it doesn't bother me.

I can see our breath in the cool night air. Perhaps it's the adrenaline from sneaking in here, maybe it's the unbelievable sexy kiss or our undeniable attraction, but the cold isn't registering with me. All I can think about is the company I'm in.

"It's huge. You can get lost in here easily. Trust me. It only took about six weeks for them to can my ass because I got lost so often."

"Really?"

"Yep, but I managed to get a key in that amount of time."

We approach the monument from the backside. I have to tilt my head completely to see the top. As we walk around to the front, at least thirty stairs made of stone lead you up to the front doors. Wow. Even in the dead of night, the monument is impressive. We climb the stairs hand in hand and then move to the large, oversized doors. Lucas looks from side to side to make sure no one is watching, then he grabs a key ring from his pocket sifting through them until he finds the one he needs.

"Careful, I need you to follow me in and walk exactly where I walk. Any odd moves could get us in deep trouble. There are motion sensors all over the place," he warns me.

"Really?"

"No," he laughs, "only by the gate leading to his body. Relax, I've done this before," he says and I hate the idea of him doing this with another woman.

He unlocks the door, it's dark. The moonlight filtering through the windows is the only light we have. There is a marble staircase leading to the basement. I can tell that's where his tomb must be evidenced by the large American flag and plaque.

"This way," Lucas says grabbing my hand and leading me to another wooden door. A thin, spiral staircase awaits us once the door is opened. "After you," he whispers. I begin to climb with Lucas right behind me. Once we reach the top, I'm met with another door that is thankfully unlocked.

I step outside into the cool night air. There is a large balcony made of sandstone. Behind me, a cylindrical pillar continues to show the great expanse of the building. I walk close to the stone edge that only comes up to about mid-thigh on Lucas but closer to my waist for me.

"Lucas, it's amazing! You can see everything. Is that the Terminal Tower?" I ask pointing to my left.

"It is. And over there is Severance Hall."

"Oh wow, I can't believe how clear everything is even at night," I say and fall back into Lucas's arms as he folds them around me.

"Want a beer?" he asks after we stand silently and take it all in.

"Sure, PBR me." I reach out my hand ready for the beer as he unzips his bag and hands me the Pabst Blue Ribbon. I crack the can open and we both take sips.

"Let's sit," he moves against the building and scoots down to the ground. I follow suit and we stare out at the skyline. The stars and moonlight are enough light for us. Little sparkles illuminate the sky.

We drink and talk. He tells me more about the band and funny stories about Dietz. We both crack jokes and our humor matches each others. I still can't shake this feeling that he reminds me of Jake, but I think it must be how much I miss him.

I open my second beer, Lucas his third. I drink it fast and he does the same. I shiver because the cool night air combined with my skirt is finally getting to me. "You're cold, come closer," he says taking off his coat.

"You're shirt's funny," I joke.

"You're cute," he says back. My smile is so big it almost hurts.

I inch close to him.

He moves closer.

The air feels like it changes and it's suddenly warmer, but maybe that's just his nearness. Our bodies are touching; my bare leg against his jeans. My black boots press against his Chuck Taylor's. I think about his kiss earlier and I want another.

He moves to put his coat over my legs. I lean in for a kiss. I want it more than I need warmth. I want to feel his lips again.

We move simultaneously in and our heads barely miss.

"That could've been bad." I try to laugh it off feeling rather foolish.

"You don't need to be embarrassed with me, June," he says tucking a small piece of hair behind my ear. It's such a simple gesture, but it's so incredibly sweet.

"I'm kind of drunk," I admit.

"I kinda am too," he laughs. His gaze moves to my lips and his expression completely changes. "I want to kiss you again. Can I kiss you, June?"

I nod my head, too turned on to let any words escape.

"Say it, June. Say you want me to kiss you."

Without hesitation, the words come out, "I want you to kiss me."

And then it's on. Right on top of our dead president.

I lean over Lucas so I'm slightly on top. His lips brush my neck first. I arch, then moan. On instinct to straddle him. Our lips finally meet. My breasts harden and feel full. Our kiss is hard, then soft, sweet then supple. My body is responding to him. My hips begin moving as he thrusts his tongue around my own. I can feel him begin to grow with excitement and it's a marvelously, beautiful, exciting feeling. Our lips break apart. Fuck my coat is bulky. I'm aching to let his hands get at my breasts.

"It's too cold out here for you, let's go to my place," he says.

"Yes," I whisper. I'm in college and have had one night stands before. Not a lot, but a few. None felt as right as this. And I want this. "Yes," I say again, "Take me to your place."

He doesn't hesitate. He stands and I watch as he adjust his dick in his pants, obviously pained from stopping.

"Let's go, June."

CHAPTER THREE

We open the door to his apartment in a rush. The alcohol hit me on our walk making my bladder scream, "I gotta pee right now-you shouldn't have put that much liquid in me, and if I was a little drunk now I'm really drunk," kind of way.

"Hurry!"

"I'm hurrying, I swear," Lucas laughs as he unlocks his door, "It's the first door on the left."

I race to his bathroom, in too much of a hurry to take anything in. I shrug off my coat, pull up my skirt, pull my panties down, not wanting to spend a second more on buttons and finally, relief.

I finish and quickly make my way back to the living room. It's a wide open space with high vaulted ceilings. The floors are unfinished giving the apartment a rustic feel. Two of the walls are exposed brick. It's not trendy, but I like it. The apartment is sparsely decorated with a navy blue couch under a window, a small table with a lamp, and an old box TV on the ground. Other than that, the only other furniture is a freestanding keyboard with a stool behind it.

I walk over to the keyboard and run my fingers over the keys. It's not on, so it doesn't make a sound. "How did you get into music?" I ask.

I'm suddenly aware of Lucas' nearness to me. He takes off his shoes and is barefoot, which strangely turns me on. He looks so casual as he walks behind me. He begins trailing his fingers down my arm until they hit the keyboard. Boxing me in, he turns the keyboard on with his other hand. "I had good inspiration and a good teacher."

"Were you young?" My breath hitches on the last part as he places a kiss on my exposed shoulder.

"I was seventeen," he answers and then starts to play a few notes on the keyboard. He hits more keys, faster and faster. His fingers begin to dance over the zebra pattern. He strikes the keys hard, and each time the tempo changes. I feel like my heart is going to beat out of my chest.

"Who was your inspiration?" I ask, trying to break myself from his spell.

"A girl who made me believe in myself," he whispers and kisses my neck again at the same time hitting the keys passionately.

"Should I be jealous of this girl?"

"Hardly, June. She was a girl, you're so much more." I pull in yet another breath, letting it seep into my lungs. I can't take it. His keyboard playing foreplay has gone on long enough.

He chuckles.

"Drats. I said that out loud, didn't I?"

"You did," he confirms hitting one final key.

I turn so that I'm facing him, no longer wanting to wait any longer. "I want you to kiss me."

"Here," he says and kisses my shoulder again.

"Everywhere, Lucas. I want you to kiss me everywhere."

As if I didn't think I could get any more lost in the depths of his blue-green eyes, I completely lose myself when I see his expression glaze over with what could only be described as hunger.

"LUCAS!" I SCREAM AS he has me leaning over the arm of the couch, his beautiful cock is filling me up. Hitting every part of me. Deeper and deeper each thrust pounds. I stretch my arm out to grab on to something. Anything. I don't know. I'm lost as each wave of pleasure consumes me.

Crash.

His light hits the ground making the room dark.

I laugh, because I'm drunk and too intoxicated by Lucas to really care. The last however-long since I told him to kiss me everywhere has been a-freaking-mazing. He did that. He kissed me everywhere, and I mean everywhere. I was stripped of my clothes and pulling at his until he was naked. His body? Oh Lord, how beautiful it is. His abs sculpted masterpiece; his thighs the perfect amount of muscle; and don't even get me started on how hard his ass feels beneath my tight grip. I got on my knees and took him into my mouth, sucking his length and cupping his balls until he positioned me on the couch and began to eat me from behind. My pussy clenched and throbbed each time he sucked and then when he added his fingers, wow. Oh, how I wanted his glorious dick inside of me. It was wonderful, thrilling really, to let myself go so much with someone I hardly know but have this amazing attraction to.

And then he entered me. It is by far the best sex of my life. A little clumsy because we're both a little drunk, but "Oh, my right there!" I scream as he hits that spot inside of me."

"Fuck, June! Your pussy's so wet for me. God, how it clenches around my dick."

My hands bump the table again and I almost knock the whole table over this time.

"Oh yes!" I breathe out and Lucas pulls out of me and flips me over. His eyes are dark and look so much like Jake's. A pang of hurt spreads through my chest. Jake would hate that I'm having a one night stand.

"I want you to ride me. Sit on my dick and work it, baby." The sound of that brings me right back into the moment.

Lucas lies on the ground and I glide myself on top of his slick cock.

"The way you feel, Lucas," I say as he reaches up and pinches my nipples between his thumb and forefinger. "Yes, that's it. It's amazing."

He bends curling his abs and claims my mouth. It's intense, like everything and then it's so sweet again. I lift my knees and take over a steady rhythm. I move at a gentle pace not wanting this to end. His teeth tug at my lip as I pull up and rock my hips.

I pull up a little too far. Lucas slips out of me and before my drunk mind catches on to what I'm doing I move back down and hit his unaligned dick right against my pubic bone.

"Ah, fuck," he hisses.

"Oh my God. Are you okay?"

He winces and I could curse myself for being clumsy during drunk sex.

"I'll be okay, just slide down gently," he says grabbing his dick in his hand, so that I can slide down it and make sure he's intact.

He enters me slowly and his expression changes from one of pain to complete pleasure.

"I'm sorry. I'll be more careful," I rock my hips forward. I should be humiliated, but any embarrassment is washed away as soon as he thrusts his hips upwards and he hits that deliciously wonderful spot inside. I moan and throw my head back, rocking back and forth as he simultaneously bucks his hips.

"Lips," Lucas demands wanting to kiss me. I lean forward and give him what he needs. It's soft; tender almost.

Our lips break apart and I watch his eyes. They still remind me so much of a past I can't help but wonder about. For a second, I close my eyes and pretend that it's Jake. His body pumping into me, the way we never did. I picture his eyes getting soft as he looks at me and then I move my hips faster and faster picking up the rhythm. I open my eyes and see Lucas staring at me, and I swear it's Jake, but my mind's playing tricks on me.

Our bodies are both slick with sweat. My legs are starting to quake with exertion. Lucas feels me losing my rhythm and puts a hand on my lower back to hold me in place and then in a fluid motion flips me to my back. My small breasts shake and then he is close and our bodies are friction. Everything moves, and I mean the earth, the room, it spins as my muscles climax again and again. I grip his back and feel him jerk inside of me over and over as he too finds his own release.

It's late, or early depending on how you look at it. After we have sex, we have another drink, this time, laying in his bed. I shrugged on a t-shirt of his and he strode happily around naked. I don't mind the view one bit.

His room is exactly like his living room, empty. He has a mattress and box spring that sit on the floor and his clothes are on hangers in a doorless closet. It's not messy, but it also doesn't scream 'I'm planting roots here' either.

"Have you lived here long?" I sleepily ask.

"Maybe six months or so. Why do you ask?"

"It's just so empty," I observe.

"I guess I don't really need a lot of stuff. I never have been one for things. I just need food in my belly and a place to lay my head at night."

"It's that simple for you?"

"It can be, yes. How about for you, June? Is it simple for you?"

"Right now, this right here feels very simple," I yawn.

"You're exhausted. Come here," he says taking the nearly empty glass from my hand and sets it down on the ground next to his, and I'm out.

I BLINK AND THE ROOM is dark. The curtain covering the window has little lines of light seeping in. There is a weight around my waist and I suddenly remember all that is Lucas and the wonderful things he did to my body last night. He must feel that I'm waking up because suddenly I feel a very hard, very ready penis prodding my backside.

I move on instinct, still half asleep. I push my behind into him and his hand moves up and under my shirt grabbing a hold of my breast, tweaking my nipple. I open my legs and let his silky skin fall against my sex. He begins to slide his hard cock over my very wet pussy, up and down my slick folds until finally I can't take it anymore and I arch just right so that he is pressed right against my opening.

"Need you," I say sleepily into my pillow. That's all it takes for him to slide into me again. It's slow and lazy, both of us still tired from not enough sleep. His hand lets go of my nipple and plays my clit, and by play, I mean exactly what a talented pianist should be able to do. He moves it in a way that wakes me right the hell up. No longer am I sleepy, but I'm craving more. I push my ass into him and meet him as much as I can from this angle. It's good. No, that's not right; it's great. I feel myself start to spasm. Already. So quick. I quiver and shudder faster than I ever have, but he's not done with me.

Lucas removes his hand from my clit, bites me gently on the shoulder, then pushes my back forward.

"I'm going to fuck you hard, sweet June. Can you take it?"

"Yes," I whisper.

"Good." He continues to push me forward so that my face is next to my knees. He slides in and out, gently at first. I clench in anticipation from what he promises to come. My body is still so sensitized from my release moments ago. His hands are on each side of my hips, he pulls me forward and slams me back onto his hard thick length. He's relentless.

"Fuck," I hiss out, in pain and in bliss.

"You okay, June?" he stills for a moment.

"More," I pant out, "I need more."

"You're perfect," he thrusts with even more strength. I feel pure euphoria as the warm- I'm about to come- sensation rolls through me again. His hand grips me hard on my hip and I realize that he has lifted me up an inch or so off of the bed. I'm still in the spoon position, just a really bent spoon. This time when he finds his release, I am right there with him, only he comes on the shout of my name.

"Morning," he pulls me upright and tucks me into the crook of his arm.

"Morning," I goofily smile back.

"What time is it?" I ask.

"I think it's early. Why do you have somewhere you need to be?"

"I should write my article today. I like to do it while everything is fresh in my mind, but I can't seem to want to get out of bed. So sort of, but nothing that can't wait."

"Stay with me, then. Just you and me in this bed. I'm not done with you, June. Not by a long shot."

I'm not sure why his words make me giddy, but that's exactly how I feel and so for some reason unbeknownst to me, I tell him. "You make me giddy as hell."

"Are you still a little drunk?"

"Crap, I guess I am. Things still feel a little hazy." I put my hand over my mouth and smell my terrible morning after drinking breath, then excuse myself to use the restroom. I go to get up from the bed and he pulls me back down to kiss me. I put my hand up to block him, whispering, "Dragon breath."

He laughs and moves my hand. "I don't care about that. Give me your lips, June."

I let him have my lips because how can I argue that. I head to the bathroom to do my business, brush my teeth with my finger and a dab of toothpaste. The bed is empty when I return. I lay down and pull the blanket over me, feeling my eyes flutter closed.

"Juniper," he whispers, "I brought you water and a couple Excedrin."

He called me Juniper. How could he call me Juniper? My name is June. Only one person has ever called me Juniper and that was Jake. My heart begins beating wildly and I sit up and in an accusatory tone, "What did you call me?"

"Whoa, June," he says throwing his hands up in surrender, "I just said I brought you water and a couple of Excedrin, June. What did you think I said?"

I blink at him a few times. Could I have imagined that he called me Juniper? Yes. Yes, I must have. That is the only thing that explains it.

"Sorry." I take the water and Excedrin from him. "Thank you, maybe I just need more sleep." Lucas pulls me back into his hard naked body then says, "I checked the clock. We've only been asleep for about three hours. Let's rest more."

"Okay," I relent and lay there for as long as I can trying to figure out if I imagined him calling me Juniper or not. How I could do something like that? How desperate am I? How wrong is it of me that no matter how beautiful Lucas is, there is still a part of me that wishes he was Jake?

I wake up again, this time feeling more alert. Light kisses are pecked across my belly. I look down and smile when I catch Lucas's eyelashes flutter, followed by a mischievous smile. He continues a downward path until his kisses are more like licks and those licks are followed by a finger, then two. Damn, I'm already so wet. Am I that wet from just this? It's possible, but...No! Holy shit, we didn't use a condom last night or this morning. I should've thought about it. How could I be so dumb? I'll need to get Plan B and ASAP.

Lucas pinches my clit bringing me out of my panic and suddenly all I can think about is what he's doing to me. It's abrupt, when it hits me. I'm surprised at how quickly he is working me there.

"Oh my," I scream out and throw my head back. My body is still spasming. I feel like the most incredible spark has been lit inside of me.

"Wow," I say as Lucas looks up at me with a cheeky grin. His blue-green eyes sparkle in the light and I realize he pulled the drapes open. "That's quite the wake-up."

"That last good morning wasn't half bad either," he says and pulls me up to his arms. "I could stay in bed with you all day, but I'm starving and have no food in this place. There's a diner practically across the street, let's get up and grab something to eat."

My stomach does a rumble at the mention of food, "I could eat. I only have last night's clothes, though."

"You can borrow a t-shirt, but I'm sure it will be huge on you."

"I think I'll pass, I'd swim in it. Besides, what a better way to say punk's not dead than by wearing the same outfit two days in a row? Seriously though, my place isn't far. After breakfast can we stop there?"

"So you're really going to spend the day with me?" he asks hopefully.

"You really want me too? I mean we hooked up, but it doesn't have to be anything serious," I say hoping that he actually isn't only looking for a one night thing. I know he said he wanted to spend the day with me, but maybe he was just trying to be nice. Then again, men who are only looking for a one night stand don't usually wake you up by going down south.

"June," he says my name sternly, "I don't have a ton of one-night stands. Do you? Is that what you think this is?"

"Well honestly, I'm kind of hoping it's not."

"It's not," he says quickly and adds, in an it's not up for discussion kind of way, "Well, do you?"

"Do I what?"

"Have a lot of one-night stands," he seems irritated by the thought of this, but it doesn't really make sense. We did, after all, meet in a bar, have drinks, and stay up most of the night screwing each other's brains out.

"Not a lot, but I'm in college. Has it happened? Sure, But it's not the norm for me, if that's what you're asking. Frankly, I don't feel like I should have to defend myself to you considering we were both in this together," I finish by getting out of bed in a huff and walking to the living room to retrieve my clothes. I'm pulling my skirt up when Lucas walks in wearing black boxer briefs.

Damn him and his sculpted chest. It's a freaking beacon waiting to be touched. Seriously, I'm annoyed with him. I need to stop drooling. "Have you seen my shirt?" I ask.

"Come here," he walks towards me with open arms, "Don't be mad at me. I didn't mean to offend you. It's just that I like you and I feel like we could have something. I know we got together fast last night, but it felt right. It feels right."

With his words, I curl into him. I can't stay mad at him. After a few minutes, I look up at him, "Let's get something to eat."

He grins at me. I grin back. We separate, get dressed and make our way to the diner.

THE DINER IS A GREASE pit. It doesn't seem like the cleanest place, but the food must be good because the entire dining room is full. We put our name on an list and stand shoulder to shoulder with people in the waiting area . It's a complete clusterfuck. After ten minutes or so, a waitress who is also acting as a hostess calls our name. There is a small booth that's opened up.

Lucas sits down and I sit across from him. Plastic menus are set in front of us and a waitress with bags under her eyes says in a rushed voice, "What can I get you to drink?"

"Coffee and a water for me," I say.

"I'll have the same," Lucas adds.

The waitress nods then walks away as I look over the menu. "What's good here?" I ask.

"Pancakes, waffles, omelets, eggs benedict. Their hollandaise sauce is amazing," he tells me.

"Sold," I set down the menu, not needing to look at it any longer. "What are you going to get?"

"Bacon pancakes." He places his menu down on top of mine and sets them on the edge of the table.

"Bacon pancakes, seriously?"

"Yup."

"That can't be good for you," I shake my head and smile at him.

"Everything's better with bacon," he deadpans.

The waitress returns, sets our drinks down and takes our order.

"Ever have a bacon milkshake?" he asks after she walks away.

"No, that sounds disgusting."

"It's not. It's amazing.

"Only you would like bacon on everything." Those words slip past my lips and I freeze.

"What did you pack?" Jake asks me as he pulls his foil wrapped sandwich from his backpack.

"Mom made me a BLT," I say sitting down on the bank by the water.

"Let me see your sandwich."

"Why?" I ask.

"Just let me see it." He sits next to me and reaches out his hand waiting for me to hand it over. I am amused with what Jake will do next so I pretend to hand him the sandwich. As soon as he reaches for it, I pull it back and giggle.

"June, sandwich," he says again a smile dances all over his face.

I hand him the sandwich and watch as he opens it, snags off two pieces of bacon, opens his peanut butter and jelly sandwich and places the bacon right in the middle of his sandwich.

"Jake, that's just gross!"

"It's so good. You should try it."

"There is no way I will try that!"

"Your loss," he says with a mouthful of bacon and PB&J.

"Only you would like bacon on everything."

He grins at me. There is a smudge of peanut butter at the corner of his mouth. I want to wipe it away with my thumb, but I'm still too nervous.

"June?" Lucas asks. Oh shit. I must've gotten lost in the memory. My heart beats rapidly and I feel the beat behind my eyes all the way to my fingertips. I blink once, then twice. I need to get a grip. It's not him. He's not Jake.

"Are you okay?"

I realize I still haven't answered him. He grabs my hand. I wonder if he can feel how rapidly my heart is beating. "I'm, I'm okay." I inhale deeply steadying my nerves, then take a sip of my hot coffee.

"What was that?" concern lacing his voice.

"I'm not really sure," I lie. I don't want to admit him how much he reminds me of Jake. I like Lucas. I like Lucas and don't want him thinking that the reason I'm with him right now is because of the similarities. Yes, that's probably part of it, but Lucas is sweet, funny and there is this unbelievable connection.

Lucas squints his eyes at me. He is trying to read my face to see if he can decipher my lie.

"So, what's on the agenda today?" I want to change the subject.

"We can go back to my place and I can take advantage of every beautiful inch of you," Lucas says low and seductively.

I blush thinking about how much he has already taken *advantage* of me.

"That's very enticing. I do have a request, though."

"I take requests."

"After we stop by my place and I shower, change and make sure everything is good with Liz. I also need to stop by the drugstore."

"Everything okay?"

"Yes, I need to pick something up, that's all. No big deal."

He looks at me concerned for a moment, then brushes it off when I smile brightly at him.

When we walk into my dark apartment Liz is on a purple yoga mat, watching a DVD, and mimicking the slender woman's pigeon pose.

"You're up early," I flip on the light switch.

"You're not alone?" she says accusatory.

"Hey, Liz," Lucas says with a short wave, his eyes roaming over our small eclectic apartment. Liz switches poses in sync with the instructor on the television. Lucas doesn't pay her much mind, which is a feat in itself since she is gorgeous and decked out in yoga gear.

Our apartment has a nice flat screen TV, courtesy of Liz. The sofa has a bold flower print and on each side of the sofa there is a small armchair that tends to act more like a catch-all for me. The small coffee table has since been pushed against the wall to make room for Liz's yoga. Incense sticking out of the house plant in the windowsill above the sink, mixed with Liz's freshly shampooed hair makes the apartment smell like clean hippies, if that's even a thing.

"Where's Matt?" I question, surprised he isn't still with her.

"Ugh, Matt had too much to drink and had some issues." She scrunches up her face as she shifts into downward dog.

"That bad, huh?" I ask.

"So bad, I needed to relieve some pent up energy."

Lucas is still taking in the apartment, when he asks, "Which room is yours?"

"Last door on the left," I explain to which he replies, "Mind if I check it out?" This might seem strange to some, I mean how often does your one night stand come home with you and check out your room? I can tell by the way Liz is looking at me that she finds it peculiar, but for some reason it seems natural to me.

"Go right ahead. Just don't mind the mess." Lucas kisses me tenderly on the shoulder and then walks into my room.

"Wow, so you had a better night than me, I take it?" Liz asks switching positions again. She's talking to me with her head between her legs and I can't help but laugh.

"I had an amazing night. We're going to hang out today. Mind if I borrow your laptop, so I can get my article done today?"

"Not at all. Have fun." She stretches her arms up over her blonde head.

"I intend to." I flash a huge grin as I walk away and into my room with Lucas.

My room is a mess. Being neat and tidy has never been my thing. Clothes from last nights 'what do I want to wear' are in huge piles on my twin bed. On the floor is a pile of laundry I need to wash and sitting right next to that is a basket filled with clothes I need to put away. When I walk in, Lucas is standing in front of the tall dresser. He's looking at something that I can't quite see. The look on his face is tender. I get closer to see what he is looking at and my breath hitches. Of all the things he singles out in my cluttered room, he's looking at the one thing that means the most to me.

It was the last morning I'd ever spent with Jake. Of course, I didn't know it at the time. I thought we would have more time together.

I slip on my flip flops and have one foot out the door to head to the river when Mom yells, "Don't forget your camera, June." She knows me so well. I keep telling her how I want more pictures to capture this summer. She thinks Jake and I are cute. Whenever she says it I laugh at her and tell her cute is for babies, but what I really want to say is that what we have is so much more than cute. What we have is once in a lifetime and I'm just lucky enough to find it when I'm fifteen. I thank her for reminding me, grab the camera dangling from the short black rope on her hand and make a mad dash to meet Jake. He's in a bad mood, kicking dirt when I sneak up on him. I hate to see this side of him. It truly breaks my heart. I hate his dad. He can destroy the best days for Jake in minutes.

"Jake!" I call out and take a picture of him as soon as he looks up to meet my stare. He hates getting his picture taken. His face breaks out in a silly grin when

he sees me. "You know I hate that. I'm going to get you for it," he says and chases after me.

I'm laughing hard as I dart in and out of trees trying to evade him, but it's useless. He's quick. In seconds, he grabs a hold of me and begins tickling me. Before I know it, we are both on the ground and he has my hands pinned over my head. He grabs the camera from me and begins snapping shot after shot. I turn my head away from him laughing, "Stop Jake! I want pictures of you, not me." I squirm and buck under him. For the first time, I feel him grow hard against my body. It shocks me, and the air instantly changes. He's embarrassed. I can tell by the way he quickly gets off of me and lets go of my wrists. I'm not embarrassed, though. I'm curious.

"Don't do that, Jake. Don't you dare shy away from me." I don't like when he hides any feeling from me.

"Sorry, June. I didn't mean for you to feel that," he puts space between us.

"Why? It's part of who you are." I'm still on the ground. Jake is on his knees. I crawl to him and get close again.

He moans, "Don't do that, June."

"Do what?" I ask flirtatiously.

"Crawl to me."

I can't take it. I've been curious about him and what he looks like, what he'd feel like. "Can I touch you?" I ask.

With my question, it's like everything has changed. The air is thicker, or maybe I am just more aware of everything. My heart is beating hard in my chest and I'm so close to Jake now that I can smell his Ivory soap.

"Oh my, Juniper," he groans, "I've been trying so hard to go slow with you. You're so young. I don't want you to do anything you're not ready for."

"How about we stop if it's too much?" I ask seeing the war rage in his eyes. I decide for us as I reach my hand to his zipper, unzip it and slip my hand inside feeling his hard length against his boxers. His eyes widen in shock, but I know he won't pull away. He grabs my chin with his thumb and forefinger and lifts my eyes to his.

"You sure?" He asks leaning in and pressing his lips to mine. His tongue glides into my mouth and I feel my panties begin to dampen.

I answer his question by finding the opening in his boxers and gliding my hand against him. He groans in response. "Can I touch you too?" he asks breaking the kiss.

I only got my period about six months ago, and I've only recently touched myself for the first time. Jake makes me feel comfortable like I'm the one with all of the power. I nod my head yes, both excited and nervous.

"First, let me show you what I like," he says and undoes his belt buckle and slides his pants over his hips. I let out an audible gasp when I see him. I've never seen one in real life before and his is pretty. I giggle and tell him this. "It's pretty," I say.

"You can't call my dick pretty," he sucks in my earlobe suddenly I'm serious again.

"What do you want me to do?" I ask wanting to please him and do it right.

He grabs my hand and wraps it around him, sliding it up and down his silky shaft. "Move your hand up and down like this," he commands.

I do as he says and I hear his breath quicken. He looks into my eyes as he trails his fingers up my thigh and under my dress.

Jake's fingertips trace the outline of my white cotton panties. I want this. I want his fingers touching me. He pushes aside the soft cotton and slides one finger in between my folds dragging my wetness to the top and circling it with his finger tip. It feels good and a moan slips past my lips.

"Faster, June."

I do as he says and move my hand faster up and down his length. Jake's finger drags back down my slit and pushes in my small tight hole. I gasp. Even when I've done this, my small finger felt nothing like this. His palm presses against the top of my privates while his finger pumps in and out of me. "Oh, God," I moan.

"Yes, June. Keep it up just like that," he says his eyes fixed on mine. "My God, you're so pretty. I'd do anything to keep you with me."

"Shh...," I tell him. Any talk of us not being together will dampen what we have going on here. "It feels so good," I gasp as he somehow adds another finger.

"One day, I'm going to be inside of you so deep you'll never get me out," he tells me as his body begins to shudder.

"You're already that deep, Jake. There's no getting you out," I tell him not talking about his finger inside of me.

Warm liquid spurts onto my hand and Jake pulls my forehead to his pressing them together while he catches his breath. He's pulled his finger from me and in a faint whisper he says, "God, I hope so."

Lucas is staring at the picture Jake took of me, I'm laughing hysterically in it. The camera is angled over me and my long auburn hair is fanned out around my head. I don't want that picture in his hands. That's my moment with Jake and although the two men share the same eyes, they are not the same; and that smile belongs to Jake.

CHAPTER FOUR

I stride over to the dresser and grab the photo from Lucas' hands, quickly open a drawer and set it inside.

He looks taken aback for a moment. "The photo?"

"Is private," I say curtly feeling like he had no right to look at that even though it was only a picture that I left out in the open.

He raises a brow at me, then backs down and changes the subject by flopping down on my bed. "You weren't joking when you said not to mind the mess."

"I warned you," I wink flinging a hot pink bra at him that is hanging on one of the knobs of my dresser.

"Don't mind if I do," he laughs and slips his arms through the bra.

I laugh at his playfulness. "You're silly, Lucas. I'm going to take a shower." I start to walk out of the room when Lucas all but growls, "Lips."

I walk back to him lying on my bed, thinking how fantastic he looks sprawled out over my things. I lean down and press my lips against his meaning for it to be a quick, I'll be right back kiss. Lucas doesn't do the sweet, I'll be right back kiss, because as soon as his lips touch mine, it's no longer me kissing him gently before I get in the shower. No, this is me giving him my lips. He takes them, sucking and pulling, his tongue sliding in and moving against my own. My body is pulled down on top of his firm chest. This kiss, oh this kiss. How it's making my nipples react instantly. My laugh and my heart might be Jake's, but at this moment, Lucas owns my body.

Lucas' hand pulls at my short hair, and I do the same to him. My legs move to each side of him and my skirt hitches up and over my hips. I moan as I rock with him, feeling his cock press against me.

"You're so fucking beautiful. I want you," he says pulling my shirt and bra down and sucking in my nipple, twirling his tongue over the hard bud and pulling it taut with his teeth.

I moan again, "Yes, that."

Bang, bang, bang. Three loud wraps hit my door. "I'm home remember," Liz shouts from the other side of the door. I pull back from Lucas and he groans in protest.

"Can't we ignore her?" he asks hopefully.

I pull my shirt up and over my breast and begin to get off of Lucas, he stills my hips and looks at me with a pout. "No, we can't. Liz and I have an agreement that we don't do that while the other person is home. These walls are paper thin." I slide off of his lap and pull down my skirt.

"Well, hurry up so we can get back to my place," he throws his head back in frustration. I notice his cock is still straining against his jeans.

"Sorry," I mouth as I grab my robe and leave him alone.

I return to my room in a robe feeling surprisingly amazing given the amount of alcohol, sex, and sleeplessness that I endured last night. Lucas has his palms over his eyes. I conclude that he's either sleeping or in deep thought, so I do my best to be quiet. I rifle through my laundry basket that I've yet to put away and pick out a pair of black lace booty shorts and slide them up my legs. I look back to Lucas and it seems that he is still asleep or whatever so I take off my robe and put my bra on. I'm petite in stature so my full B cup is very proportionate. I'm bending over looking for my favorite jeans, the ones with the tiny black gemstones in the shape of a skull over the left back pocket when I hear, "You're killing me, Sprite."

For a moment, I freeze. That was something I've heard Jake call me too, but I quickly shake it off. With my pixie cut and tiny frame, it's not the first time I've been referred to as some type of faerie.

"Relax, Lucas. I'm almost done," I wink finding my jeans and pulling them up my hips. He groans in response, I laugh at him.

I grab a soft pink blouse with small cap sleeves. It's the polar opposite of my punk rock vibe I had going on last night, but I don't care. It's pretty and it makes me feel pretty. I begin buttoning the shirt, starting from the bottom and working my way up. I'm on the third small button when Lucas commands, "Come here."

I do as he asks and stand in front of him as he begins pushing each tiny button through the hole. He is slow and deliberate. His fingertips brush over my skin as he moves upwards from button to button. When he is between my breasts, he gently outlines the edge of my bra. I can't help the heated look my eyes give him. These are very calculated touches. He is at the top button when he leans into me and whispers into my ear, "There. All done."

My breath hitches again and I move away before I say to hell with Liz. I grab a light gray sweater that has tiny skulls on each arm by the wrist and slide my feet into my Chuck Taylors that are very similar to the ones on Lucas' feet.

"I'm just going to grab Liz's laptop and we can get out of here," I say applying a tiny amount of blush to the apple of my cheek. Besides a small amount of mascara and the little bit of blush I just applied, I barely have any makeup on.

Lucas follows me out of my room and into the living room where Liz has cotton balls wrapped between her toes and she is brushing on a dark red polish.

I grab the laptop and slip it into a bag. "Sorry about before," I giggle and kiss Liz on the top of her head.

Lucas and I get into his car and I remind him that I need a drugstore. His phone rings as we are pulling into a spot in front of the store.

"Yeah," he answers, then says, "It's Dietz."

I get the hint and start to get out of the car, "Hang on," he says to Dietz and then gives me a look that says you better not get out of the car without kissing me. I lean in and give him a light kiss that is returned with a smile. Lucas returns to the phone call and I hear him say before exiting the car, "What did you tell them?"

I brush it off as I walk into the store, thinking that Lucas sounded frantic, but maybe it's nothing?

I search the aisle for the Plan B and it's not there. I check with the pharmacist and she tells me that they are out, so I quickly grab a box of condoms and decide that we'll just have to stop at the next pharmacy we see.

I get into the car, and immediately notice that the atmosphere has changed. Lucas seems to be anxious.

"Is everything okay?"

"Yeah, yeah. Just some band stuff. Did you get what you needed?" He seems distracted as he nervously runs a hand through his dark hair.

"They didn't have what I need. Maybe we can stop at another store?"

"Can it wait? I really want to take you somewhere,"

I mentally go over what Liz told me about Plan B. She said she had seventy-two hours after unprotected sex to take it so that she didn't get knocked up. Not the best birth control, but it's there in case of any accidents.

"Yeah, um, I guess we can wait. Are you sure everything is okay?" I eye him, getting a feeling that the call he took from Dietz was anything but good.

"Relax," he smiles at me trying to reassure me.

We drive north for twenty-minutes until we pull into a practically empty state park on Lake Erie. "Come with me. I want to show you something."

I follow him out of the car and he takes my hand guiding me when I'm in reach. The park looks like it's used as a Marina in warmer months. There are two large piers that lead out onto the choppy waters of Lake Erie. The water splashes ferociously. There is a man sitting on an upside down white bucket with his fishing poles all in a row, just waiting to catch a bite. Woods line the large parking lot with over-sized spaces meant for boats.

Lucas leads me to a bridge that crosses over the mouth of the river. We stop in the middle of the bridge. Lucas stands behind me, wrapping his arms around me. To my left is a raging river. To my right, an even angrier lake. The moist air covers my face with a light sheen of water giving me a chill. A single seagull squawks then lands several feet away from us. The lake is vast and never ending as it bleeds into the horizon, while the river is backed up with fallen trees and branches tangled on top of one another, not sure if they are headed in or out, but fighting for a place to settle.

"I love it here," Lucas says close to my ear. "When it's warm, it's filled with fishermen, but right now is when I like it the most. See how the water rushes together? The current from the river is so strong wanting to get out and be free from the narrow banks, but the lake fights back. It's bigger than the river, stronger. When the water is turbulent like this, it's as if the two sides go to war, but you know what I love the most?"

I shake my head, loving the sound of his voice and how he can make this sound almost poetic.

"I love that the current is strong enough to let the river break free even though it's up against something so vast."

We stand for a while silently watching the turmoil. I only just met Lucas last night, but I feel like he has an uncanny ability to make me feel at ease.

After some time, we walk over the bridge to the sandy beach area. Besides, the fisherman on the pier, we are completely alone.

"What are your dreams, June?" Lucas asks me as we sit close together with only a hint of sand separating us.

I could tell him about my journalism dream, but I feel like I need to be completely honest.

"I lost someone once and my biggest dream would be that I'd find them again, and that maybe I'd live happily ever after. I guess that sounds more like a fairy tale, though."

He gulps. If I wasn't staring so hard at his beautiful features while he stared out at the water, I would've missed it. "It's okay to believe in fairy tales. Maybe you'll find them. Besides Juniper, I think you deserve a happy ever after."

My heart is beating wildly. Juniper. He said it again. I wasn't imagining it before. I stare at him. His eyes are so much like Jake's, it hurts. This hurts. How can there be so many similarities? Have I somehow tainted my image of Jake?

"That's the second time you've said that," I accuse.

"Said what?"

"Juniper. Why did you call me that?" My hand is shaking and I feel like I'm betraying Jake somehow by letting Lucas call me *his* names.

"Sorry, I just figured June was short for Juniper," he looks at me and moves his fingers through my hair trying to calm me.

"Well, it's not. Please don't call me that," I snap. I need to get a grip. This is not his fault, it just feels so similar.

"What about you, Lucas? What are your dreams?"

"I'm not so sure that I'm not living it right now," he flirts and then leans in and kisses me. Damn this man and his kisses. Every time, they completely distract me. No, it's not that they distract me, more like enrapture me. Each pull and tug at my lips has me begging for more. More of his tongue. More of his hands on me. More of him. I find myself on my back pressed against the sand with Lucas hovering above me. My hands inch into his jacket and under his shirt coming into contact with his smooth, warm chest. I inch higher stroking my finger over his nipple. He roams over my jeans his hand stroking me between my legs. I'm so wet and turned on.

"Shit, June. We need to stop or that guy is going to get quite the show," he pulls away from me and I can see by the bulge in his jeans how hard that was for him to do.

"Let's go to your place," I say breathlessly wanting more of him.

He doesn't hesitate to grab my hand again and lead me back over the bridge and to his car. He takes shortcuts trying to avoid any lights so we can get to his place sooner. He strokes my thigh and occasionally rubs his hand over the inseam of my jeans, keeping me exactly where he wants me.

When we get back to the apartment, we have wild, undeniably hot sex. It's amazing and if I'm honest, it's the best I've ever had. I make Lucas wear a condom and explain to him that we recklessly had sex without protection and that we should've used something. For a moment, he's panicked and then I tell him about Plan B and that I'm going to buy it right away. After napping from having spent all our energy on each other, I sit and work on my write-up of the band. They really are original. When I finish, I let Lucas read it, and he smirks at me when he reads how I think that the heart of the band's talent lies within the keyboardist.

"Hey, I told you I was partial," I joke.

He smirks at me and says, "Dietz might die a little at the news, but I think he'll have to get over it."

He's still reading and hasn't gotten to the end yet so I decide to mess with him, "Well you haven't gotten to the part yet where I say how panty dropping hot Dietz is."

His face is unreadable when he asks, "Panty dropping hot?"

"Oh yes, the last paragraph goes into great detail about his swagger."

Lucas finishes reading as quickly as he can, and then when he is done I give him the biggest smirk, "You," he says tackling me back on the bed and immediately finding my most ticklish spots.

"Say, uncle!"

I scream, but he doesn't relent. He eventually grasps both of my wrists in one of his hands. I squirm and buck until the tickling stops and it turns into something else entirely.

I STAY OVER AGAIN WHICH is unheard of for me. Liz calls me at seven in the morning waking me up shouting about where am I. I sit up. Being woken up by Liz is not something I'm used to. "Shh," I tell her still half asleep. "I stayed at Lucas' again."

"No shit, two nights in a row. You should've called a sister," she scolds. I instantly feel bad because she's right, I should've called. I would expect her to call me.

"I'm sorry, it was late and I wasn't thinking. I'll make it up to you. Meet me at Starbucks in forty minutes, I'll buy."

"You'll buy? Yeah right. I know how broke you are. Meet me in thirty and I'll buy."

Fine, see you soon," I say hanging up the phone.

"Lucas," I nudge him and he hardly stirs.

"Lucas, wake up."

He mumbles again this time hooking an arm around my waist and pulling me backward. He pushes his shirt up, that I slipped on last night to sleep in and starts kissing my stomach.

Heat instantly pools between my legs, but I have to go.

"I can't. I have to meet Liz in thirty minutes for coffee and then I have class."

He rolls on top of me and sleepily kisses my neck, "Skip?"

"I can't miss my classes."

Another kiss, a little harder. He's trying to persuade me with his mouth.

I want to stay, but I struggle to pay for school and it's important. "It's important. School's important," I tell him.

He stops kissing me and jokes, "Why didn't you say so?"

I fix myself the best I can in the bathroom moving about at a lightning speed. I come out and he is still lazily lying in bed.

"I think I'm drunk off you," he tells me then gives me a smile that could melt any woman's heart, but it especially makes mine do weird flippy things. "I want to see you later. What time are you done with class.

"Today's no good. I work at the bookstore on Mondays and Wednesdays as soon as I get out of class. What time do you work?"

"In a few hours. The shop is pretty lax with hours, but I would've taken off for you. I'll tell you what. How about you come over after work. I'll make a late dinner."

"I highly doubt you've ever cooked a meal in your kitchen. I wish I could tonight, but I have homework that I should've gotten done this weekend and didn't."

"Tomorrow then, come over after your last class."

"Tomorrow my schedule isn't that bad. I have to go to The Scene for a little while, but after that I'm all yours,"

He smiles warmly at me. "All mine," he mumbles and then without any thought I lean down and give him my lips, kissing him goodbye.

Liz is waiting for me, double fisting two steamy coffees.

"Hey, hooker. I brought you a shirt so you're at least wearing something clean. I can smell your sexing from here." Liz is dressed very meticulously. Her wool coat, that is unbuttoned showing off the white designer shirt and thick wool pants that are hidden under her tall brown boots, screams put together.

"Shut up, you cannot." I sit down beside Liz and take the first sip of coffee savoring the rich aroma.

"So, you've had an eventful weekend."

My cheeks flush at Liz's accurate description.

"It was so good Liz. But oh fuck, we didn't use a condom and I totally need to get that pill you told me about."

She looks at me with her jaw slightly agape, "You just met this guy and you had unprotected sex? Seriously June, I thought I taught you better than that."

I shrug amused. This conversation is flipped around from the way it normally goes. I'm normally telling Liz how worried I am about her behavior. I think she's getting a kick out of this.

"What about Blondie from the other night? Are you going to see him again?"

"I doubt it. Maybe?"

"What was wrong with this one?"

"It's not that something is wrong with him. He was really sweet and we got along fine, but I guess I just want that crazy feeling like you want to spend every second with the person and I just struggle to find that."

We finish our coffee and talk about our schedules this week. I make my way to my first class after changing my shirt in the car and think about what Liz said; that crazy feeling like you want to spend every second with them. I want to get back to Lucas, but feel uneasy about my growing addiction to him. I also feel guilty, which isn't really fair. All of this time I've been holding on to my first love. I haven't seen him in seven years. You would think with the internet it would be easy to find him, but I can't find anything, and I mean zero, zilch, nada. I've searched property records for his dad's farm, but the title records show new ownership from the same summer I was last there.

I have to wonder how much is real between Lucas and myself, and how much has to do with his resemblance to Jake?

It's all too much. By the time I finish class and start work at the bookstore, I've decided that I need to give myself a little space from Lucas. I need to make sure what we have is about us and not about my feelings for Jake.

I'm distracted at work and my manager basically tells me to pull my head out of my ass or go home, so I shoved all thoughts aside and busied myself. On my way home, I stop at a different drugstore, find the magic pill and immediately take it.

I wake up Tuesday with a text on my phone from an unknown number that simply says, "Wish you were here." I don't text him back, but I do think about the fact that it would've been nice to wake up in his arms.

The Scene is a local paper that covers what's hot in Cleveland's scene. It has a few current topics with fairly liberal views, but mostly if you want to know what is hot in Cleveland, this is your paper. I was lucky to get an internship here. They pay me minimally, but it's giving me experience that I wouldn't get most places.

I turn my paper in and meet with the editor, make a few changes that she suggests and debate on whether or not to call Lucas. I don't have to make that decision though because when I step out of the newspaper building and walk the short distance to my car, Lucas is leaning against it, sipping on a Starbuck's cup.

"Hey." He looks nervous, almost as if he wasn't sure how I'd react to him being here. "I couldn't wait any longer."

I smile. I can't help it. Any unease about his similarities is washed away when he bends down and immediately takes my lips.

"Hey back," I say when we break apart, "Not that I'm complaining, but what are you doing here?"

"Work was slow, so they gave me the afternoon off. The guys called and want to do an impromptu practice. I know we talked about getting together today, so I was hoping you would come?"

"I'd love to come." I love music so much and watching these guys sounds like the perfect afternoon. "I'm excited," I lean into his side and ask, "Did you drive here?"

"No, it's not that far from work and I figured you wouldn't want to leave your car so I had a guy from work drop me off. Coffee?" he asks handing me his Starbuck's cup he was just drinking from.

I take the Styrofoam cup and bring it to my lips, "Mmm caramel, my favorite." The steam through the tiny hole at the top of the cup hits the cool air.

Lucas smiles at me, and it's a beautiful smile. "You want me to drive?" he asks.

"Sure," I say handing him the keys to my old Ford Taurus.

We drive for about ten minutes. In that ten minutes, I ask about Lucas's day yesterday and work today. He also tells me more about the band. For a brief moment, I think about how if any other guy stopped by my work like this it would bother me, but I am, in truth, just as eager to see him as he is to see me. I'm the only one fighting it.

We walk into the side door of a small white house and then immediately down a flight of stairs into a basement.

Rhett, Eric, and Dietz are setting up their instruments. I didn't get a chance to meet Rhett the other night, so I begin to introduce myself when Dietz yells, "June, no shit, surprised to see you here!" He barrels towards me and wraps me in a hug. I am not a-hey, let's hug even though we just met- kind of girl, so I'm awkward at best. "Loosen up kid, I don't bite. Not unless you want me too." Dietz laughs at his own joke.

"Hey everyone," I give a small wave, feeling a little intimidated by the overwhelming presence that is Dietz.

"Rhett, this is June. You would've met her after the show if you didn't have your head up your ass," Dietz explains, like he and I are best friends.

Lucas sits down behind a keyboard and motions to a large over-sized couch, "Get comfortable, June." He flashes me a huge smile. Lucas looks like a kid at a carnival who has won the ultimate prize.

"June," Rhett acknowledges my existence with a head nod.

The door opens at the top of the stairs and a rush of cold air comes down the stairs. "Eric, come help me with these bags," Bernie yells.

"I'll help," I offer and greet Bernie who has grocery bags in each hand.

"Good to see you again. Want to bring these into the kitchen? I have a few more to grab from the car."

"Got it," I say and head into the kitchen to unpack her grocery bags.

"There's a ton of food here," I tell Bernie when she comes back in from outside.

"These guys eat like you wouldn't believe. Half of this will be gone before practice is over. I'm making baked ziti to start with. Do you cook?"

"A little, I'm happy to help and I'm a quick study."

Bernie gives me a warm smile and begins telling me where to put everything and then once the pasta is in the oven securely covered with tin foil, she gets down to girl talk. "It's nice to have another girl around here who isn't hanging off every word Dietz spills from his moronic mouth. Don't get me wrong, he can sing. But half the time he's talking, I don't even think he knows what he's talking about."

"Have you known everyone long?"

"Eric and I have been together for a while, but I actually met him because I went on one very bad date with Rhett. Can we say disaster? Anyways, Eric saved me from the awful date. It was so bad, he kept calling me another girl's name throughout the date. Rhett has the nerve to act like Eric took something from him. It's so stupid."

"Sounds like it. What about Dietz? Have you known him long?"

"Yes! Practically my whole life. We went to grade school together. And yes, before you ask, he's always been this way." Bernie laughs and cracks open a beer. "Do you want one?"

"No, I'm good, thanks."

"Suit yourself," she shrugs.

"What about Lucas?" My curiosity wins out and I ask about him.

"He's the only one who is new. He's only been with the band for about six months, but he's awesome. They've really got something with him."

I agree, he really is awesome. I follow Bernie downstairs and we both take a seat on the couch watching the guys play. They all experiment with different sounds and techniques. For a music junkie like myself, this is heaven. They are really a very talented bunch of guys. By the time practice is over, I feel comfortable with everyone. Lucas was amazing at making me feel like I was a part of what was going on. Occasionally, he would stop and explain to me what he was aiming for in a song, and if I offered up suggestions, he would try it. It didn't always work, but the fact that he was open felt so good. It felt like I was part of something.

We eat, the band and Bernie and I exchange numbers before we go. I find myself yawning as I get into the passenger seat of my car with Lucas driving.

"Are we going to my place or yours, tired girl?"

"I have school in the morning, so can we go to mine?" He kisses me on my neck just below my ear and then starts the car. I realize that we didn't even talk about spending the night together, but it just felt natural. So much about this feels natural. It makes me nervous, but I don't fight it.

When we pull up into the apartment lot, I squeeze Lucas's hand. "That's Liz's car. She's home. Will you be terribly upset if we don't have sex? Not that I don't want to have sex with you because I totally do, but…"

"June, whatever you want. I'm not here just for sex, okay?" He brings my hand up to his mouth and lightly kisses it, tracing my fingers with his. This feels more intimate than a fling.

Inside the apartment, Liz has a textbook open and is sitting on the couch scratching her head looking confused. She looks up at us when we enter, but only for a second.

"Hey, what's wrong?" I ask sitting down next to Liz and shrugging out of my coat.

"I'm stuck. No matter how long I've been working this problem, I just can't get it. And I need to pass this class."

"I suck at math, or I'd be all over helping you," I tell Liz and watch as Lucas walks into my small kitchen and pours himself a cup of grape Kool-Aid from the fridge.

"I'm good with numbers. Can I take a look?" Lucas asks Liz.

"I'll take any help I can get." Liz hands her notebook with the problem to Lucas. Lucas grabs a pencil and tears a fresh piece of paper from the back of the notebook, then begins working the problem. After several minutes, he hands the paper to Liz. "Here try it this way. I wrote down what you were doing wrong and why?"

She looks at him a bit stunned as she studies the paper. "That's it! I can't believe it's that easy. Thank you."

"No problem. Do the next one, and I'll help you if you need it," he tells her.

Forty minutes pass when Liz and Lucas finally finish up. During that time, I was able to work on some homework as well.

"Well hell, I thought I was going to be at this all night. Thanks for your help. I think I'll go to Frankie's for a drink or two," Liz winks at me and several seconds later is out the door leaving Lucas and me alone.

"Thanks for helping her. Did you go to college?" I want to know more about Lucas.

"No, I dropped out of high school, but I've always been good with numbers. I used to take college textbooks out of the library and work the problems. It feels like I'm solving a riddle more than doing work. I like it."

"Really? I couldn't do that math, even if I had a million tutors. My mind is not built for it."

"Sure it is," he says and leans over me, sweeping a tiny piece of my pixie cut behind my ear and kissing my neck again. "With the right teacher, you could learn anything. I could teach you," he places another kiss on my neck, and then another on my collar bone. Oh, how wonderful Liz is for going to have a drink.

"We may need to be quick. I don't know how long she'll be gone," I say breathlessly as his hands slide under my shirt and begin to touch me, first stroking my sides and then moving over my taut nipples.

"We can do quick," he looks at me wickedly and shows me just how marvelous quick can be.

CHAPTER FIVE

The last two weeks have gone by fast. If I have free time, I spend it with Lucas. We are moving fast, and I feel uneasy, like I'm betraying my feelings for Jake. There is still so much about Lucas that reminds me of him, and I both love it and hate it. I'm questioning my addiction to Lucas. I don't know if I'm this obsessed with spending time with him because it's him, or because I want him to be Jake. Maybe it's not even fair for me to hold onto what I feel for Jake. I mean, I was just a kid. I can't help thinking, "What if?" I'm confused by my feelings. We have amazing sex. It is the best sex I've ever had, and yet something's missing.

I've thought about my mixed feelings all day. In fact, it's all I can think about. I told Liz about my conflicted feelings and she told me that I was having fun, and who cares that they look alike; at least I'm happy. She's convinced me that it's okay to be with him, but I'm starting to doubt myself.

We have dinner plans tonight, and as amazing as things have been, I know I'm not truly letting him in. I'm holding back pieces and parts of me, and maybe in turn he's doing the same. I can sometimes feel him staring at me while I'm in that almost asleep stage, and when he thinks I'm not watching, I sometimes catch him watching me. His gaze is always heavy and laced with intent. Everything is too familiar, making it not feel real.

I'm wearing my pink button down shirt again and a pair of black jeans that hug my small behind perfectly. I can see the appreciation in Lucas's eyes when I answer the door. My eyes have no problem roaming over him as well. Lucas has a wool coat on to protect him from the outside chill, but it's unbuttoned, showing off a white Henley that clings to his chest and a pair of jeans that fit him sinfully well.

"June, you look beautiful," he greets me. I can't help but smile as those beautiful eyes, that I could've sworn I was once in love with take me in.

We eat in an upscale, dimly lit tavern. The Irish owner, with his thick accent, stops by the table to make sure everything is meeting our expectations.

Lucas tells him how good everything is and thanks him for stopping by. He makes me laugh throughout the dinner and after a delicious glass of wine, I'm feeling spectacular.

"This was delicious," I gush, "Thank you. It's really been a great night."

"Do you want to go for a walk?" He asks stroking his hand over mine.

"We better take advantage of the weather while we can. No doubt it'll be snowing tomorrow the way the weather is here," I laugh. Cleveland weather is the oddest thing; one day it can be sunny and warm, and the next a blizzard, literally.

We walk hand in hand as we come to the large ornate fountain that sits in front of The Cleveland Museum of Art. The magnificent fountain is more than a fountain; it's one of the most beautiful pieces of art I've ever see. Enormous Angels embracing each other are on each side of a large caldron with water cascading out of it. To the left of the fountain, there is a lake that is there solely to highlight the statue.

"This is my favorite place," I tell Lucas.

"Mine too, right after Garfield's Monument and Lake Erie. It's peaceful here. If I'm ever stuck on lyrics, or I just need to clear my head, this is one of those spots that just makes it all work. Do you know what I mean?"

"I do," I agree. We sit silently until the sky completely darkens and the air begins to chill. We take in the beauty of the area. I sit and watch Lucas, taking in the beauty of him. He may not be Jake, but he is everything right for me. I thought I needed to end things with him, that maybe I was letting him in because of Jake and not because of who he is, but sitting here with him, I know without a doubt that I'm falling for the man in front of me. We just work.

"Maybe we should head back?" Lucas suggests.

I agree and we walk down the sidewalk illuminated by streetlights then stop at a coffee shop and grab coffees to warm us.

"Tonight's really been great. It's easy being with you," I tell Lucas.

Lucas stops walking and pulls me in close. "Every moment, the quiet ones, the funny ones, the sexy ones, is a gift. I'm the lucky one because I get to share them with you. From the moment I saw you, it's felt this way." He leans down and kisses me. My small frame fits perfectly against his large frame. I'm cocooned in warmth and surrounded by the importance of his words that, in truth, mirror my own.

Lucas' apartment building seems deserted as we walk through the halls, finally entering his dimly lit apartment. We don't waste time. I follow him straight into his bedroom where we're quickly pulling off our coats, then shoes and finally jeans. He shrugs off his shirt and I pause for a minute taking him in. The man is sexy. His beautiful V dips into his boxers and I lick my lips in appreciation.

"June give them to me," he says stalking towards me. I am prey to his predatory lips. With my black boy shorts on and my pink shirt, I climb on the bed kneeling in front of him and do exactly like he says. I lean up and give him my lips, but he keeps me at a slight distance, not giving in to his own desires. He's close. His breath is warm against my lips. One of his hands cups my ass, the other the back of my head, drawing me in close to him. My body is flush to his when I whisper a single plea, "Lucas.

"Shh, June. I'm going to take care of you. I'm going to take your lips. I'm going to lick every inch of you. I'm going to make you cum so hard that every time your pussy clenches, you'll remember it was me who was there and me who made it that way."

Fuck, his words are turning me on even more.

He sticks his tongue out, dragging it across my bottom lip. I lean in wanting his lips on mine. Instead of kissing me back with his perfect plump lips, his teeth pull my bottom lip. I whimper when his fingertips graze the bottom of my underwear tracing the outline. We are usually frenzied, but this slow pace is driving me even crazier.

I reach up and begin to undo the buttons on my shirt. I undo the first, and then the second. His eyes are heated and he finally gives into his own demand as he takes my lips, fucking my mouth with his tongue.

I'm fiddling with the buttons still, needing to feel his mouth on my breasts when he becomes impatient and grabs each side of my shirt and yanks it apart sending buttons flying. I catch his eyes and he breaks the kiss smirking on his way pushing down my bra to get to my nipples. The sassy part of me wants to give him hell for the destruction to my shirt, but then he is at my small pink nipples. He tweaks one nipple between two fingers while he thoroughly sucks and nibbles on the other. I moan and break contact, getting off the bed and then use both hands to slide his boxers down. He is so hard and prodding at my belly. The light moisture from his cock makes a tiny droplet.

"I want my lips around you," I say more brazen than I normally am. There is no way I can drop to my knees and have him in my mouth, I'm much too short for that, so I'm pleased when he sits on the edge of the bed, his legs outstretched on the ground since the box spring sits on the floor.

"Yes, June. Give me those." His eyes darken looking more like deep waters than the Caribbean shade they normally are.

I lower in front of him, my eyes locked on his.

I feel bold.

I feel alive.

I start at the bottom of his dick and draw my tongue upwards, swirling it around his head, eliciting a groan. In one fluid movement, I take him in my mouth applying suction. I move lower, my mouth taking him as deeply as I can while sliding my tongue along that beautiful vein running up his shaft.

Another groan from Lucas tells me he likes what I'm doing, so I continue on. Bringing my eyes up to meet his I find him is watching me move my head up and down him. I taste the saltiness of his pre-cum and he pulls back, knowing that if I don't stop this, it will all be over all too fast.

"June. Oh God, the way your lips feel around me."

My lips are swollen from sucking him. Lucas sees this and runs his thumb over my lip and whispers, "Beautiful." I dart my tongue out and lick his thumb to which he responds by pushing it in my mouth and sliding it against his tongue. I moan from how erotic it is.

Lucas guides me to the center of the bed, all while I continue to suck his thumb. "Roll your nipples," he orders and I happily comply. His naked body brushes against mine making me painfully aware that I still have my panties on creating an unnecessary barrier. He hovers above me, just barely and grabs two pillows from above my head. He removes his thumb as I stare at him, wild with desire.

"Lift your hips. I want these lips next," his voice is laced with a silky smoothness as he slides two pillows under my ass, and tantalizingly slowly, he peels back the black lace separating us.

Starting at my knee, his tongue moves higher and higher until finally he's licking the outside around the soft flesh. It's a tease. I want more. "Lucas, I need..." I'm breathless and can't finish my thoughts as Lucas pushes two fingers deep inside of me, at the same time sucks my clit hard into his mouth. "Oh," I moan.

"You like that, June? You like me sucking your sweet cunt? You taste like heaven," he says and continues the perfect rhythm of sucking and curling his fingers. It happens fast, so fast there's hardly a build up to it. One minute, I'm moaning and trying to get out Lucas' name; the next moment, I clench around him so fast. My stomach muscles tighten. My toes curl. I'm no longer playing with my nipples, but grasping frantically at his hair. I'm not sure if I'm pushing him into me or moving away. The pleasure is so great that I'm lost in the moment.

"Yes, Lucas. Yes!" I finally shout out. He moves his fingers and then he is sliding his tongue into me, lapping up my orgasm.

"Fucking Heaven," he says when he moves his head back. His lips glisten and his blue-green eyes sparkle, "I'm going to fuck you now, June. Would you like that? I need to take you hard. You got me so turned on. Can I fuck you hard, June?"

"Yes! Fuck me!" I pant out.

Lucas flips me over on the pillows and with one fluid stroke, he is buried deep inside of me. He slides in so deep, his thighs and balls hit my ass. With each thrust in, I push back hard against him. It's raw and primal how hard we're fucking.

I stretch forward and arch my back almost catlike. My palms are flat against the bed, gripping onto the sheets. "Fuck me, Lucas. Fuck!"

He leans forward against my back and whispers in my ear, "You like me buried deep inside of you? So deep you'll never get me out?" His words are familiar, part of me wants to stop and think about them, but the-I'm about to come for the second time tonight-part can't.

"Answer me?" he commands stilling his movements. Did he ask me a question? All I can think about is how amazing he feels and how I was almost there.

"Yes! You're so deep inside of me. It's so good. You feel so right."

He must be satisfied with my answer because his thrusts turn wild. He pounds fast and hard. Our skin slapping against each other followed by our pants and moans has a sensual melodic sound to it. He reaches around me and pinches my clit, holding it tight.

"Oh God, Lucas! I'm coming again!" I shout out as I feel every part of me begin to tighten again.

"Yes, June. Yes!" he says pounding, once, twice, three times. Then, he comes with a violent shudder. His body falls hard and heavy against mine, wrapping me tightly in his arms.

I WAKE UP ALONE IN Lucas' bed to the sound of his keyboard in the other room. The sound feels tortured. His voice has a vulnerability and pain to it that I didn't know Lucas was capable of. I wrap a sheet around me and stand silently in the doorway watching him and listening to his words that freeze me in place.

How can you not see me,
After all this time?
I wear a mask
But you should know.
I'd know you anywhere.
Waited
Wondered
If I could bleed you dry
Make it so you were only mine
Maybe then you'd know how I feel.
How can you not see me,
After all this time?
I've only been yours
Dreaming of you
Nothing's as good as the real you
Breathing you in
Nothing's as good as the feel of you.
If I could make you see
I'd hope you'd love the real me
If I could make you mine
I'd do anything to turn back time
I'd climb mountains and sail the sea

I'd do anything for us to be
How could you not see me?
After all this time
I wear a mask
And you make me bleed.
I'd do anything to turn back time
I'd wage wars and calm an ocean
I'd break tides and change the moon
I'd do anything if you were mine
I'd do anything to turn back time

He pounds vigorously on the keys. The words of his song make it painfully clear. I move to him, still clutching the sheet around me. It feels like the only thing I have to protect myself with.

"Jake?" I ask over the heavy thumping in my chest. The melancholy look on his face is more than I can take and I fear that I did something to put it there. His words make me feel like I let him down somehow, but he knew it was me this entire time. I have a flood of emotions, but the biggest feeling is that for the first time in so long I feel like I'm whole again. I move to him, even though I'm suddenly shy and afraid. My fear might be irrational, but I'm afraid this isn't real, and I need it to be real. I have a million questions, like why didn't he tell me, being the first on the list.

He turns on the stool away from the keyboard and towards me.

"June," he says my name in barely a whisper. I press my forehead to his

"I see you," I tell him responding to the words in his song, "I thought it could be you. I hoped it was, but you're older and I thought I was just imagining all the resemblances because I wanted it to be true."

A loud banging at the door silences me.

"Jake Daniels. Police."

His eyes dart to me in a panic. "June, I know you have questions. Shit, I wanted to tell you, but we don't have time." My heart is pounding hard. It feels like it's going to strum right out of my chest. "I need you to promise me something."

Another loud banging on the door, "Jake, open the door, or we will be forced to open it. We have a warrant."

"Promise me that you won't tell them how you know me. Promise you won't talk to them. As far as they're concerned, we met the other night for the first time and you thought my name was Lucas."

"Jake I don't understand?"

A loud bang on the door sounds, followed by another.

"Promise me, June!" he says frantically

"I promise," I yell. Suddenly, the apartment is charged with a small team of police officers. It's a blur of blue uniforms, and Jake is slammed to the ground. His Miranda rights are being read. He remains quiet and my eyes are locked on his.

"Do you understand each of these rights I've explained to you?" the officer finishes. An officer moves into his room and grabs a pair of jeans, "Put these on," he instructs Jake and then he's handcuffed sitting on the couch. I'm standing in the middle of the room clutching my sheet. I'm stunned, the last few minutes seem unreal. Lucas is my Jake and he's being arrested.

"Miss, can you please get dressed? We have a few questions for you." I don't want to take my eyes off of Jake, even to get dressed. He pleads with his eyes for me to do as they ask, and so I do.

An officer follows me into the room, "Miss, grab your clothes. Get dressed in the bathroom. We need to search this room for evidence and can't leave you in it."

I dress on autopilot and hurry back to the living room. Jake doesn't seem surprised by the arrival of the police, but there must be some mistake. There has to be, right?

Two officers, one wearing a visible bullet proof vest and the other in uniform, are walking Jake to the door. My heart feels like it's breaking all over again. I can't lose him, I only just found him. Jake's eyes are still fixed on me when an officer asks me, "Miss, how do you know Jake Daniels?" I think about my promise to Jake and know I have to do as promised. I need to lie.

"Who's Jake? His name is Lucas. What's going on?" I play dumb the best I can and see the slightest nod of approval from Jake.

"Miss, this man's name is Jake Daniels and he's wanted in connection with the disappearance of his father Mike Daniels."

I look shocked when I hear the officer's words. I know Jake isn't responsible for the disappearance of his dad. I know without a shadow of a doubt.

And the reason I know this with complete certainty is because I killed Mike Daniels.

CHAPTER SIX

Past

Jake Daniels fell in love with his sweet Juniper the moment he laid eyes on her. She was only fifteen and far too innocent for his seventeen-year-old self. He fought his attraction to the tiny auburn haired girl with the biggest blue eyes he ever saw, watching her from far away. He figured the summer would go by quickly enough with all the work his old man had been making him do and she would leave the summer vacation home without much thought to him. He never figured that she would take an interest in him, and even when she did and she had witnessed his dad calling him a useless piece of shit, she would realize right away that he wasn't good enough for her. Jake never thought that when he was swimming in the river by himself right before sunset that she would join him by jumping in the murky water and for once he was grateful that the current wasn't that fast. He didn't know what kind of swimmer June was and he didn't want anything to happen to her.

Sometimes he would wish the current would take him away. Maybe down the river far enough where his old man couldn't find him and beat the shit out of him. Sometimes, he wished the current would swallow him whole, but that was only after a real bad beating. Today he was grateful for calm waters.

"What are you doing?" he asked June when she swam up to him, wearing a tank top and jean shorts.

"I'm tired of waiting on you to say hi." June tread water with ease and it gave Jake comfort to know she was a strong swimmer.

"I wasn't planning on saying hi," Jake told her making sure to keep a distance.

June ignored his comment, swimming around Jake on her back while he tread water and carefully kept an eye on her. The rational part of his brain wanted to tell June to go away, but no matter how much he should tell her to go, he didn't.

"It's nice out here. Do you swim a lot at night?" June asked, doing her best to engage him in conversation.

The sun was dipping behind the trees and it was becoming increasingly dark.

"When the current's slow, but if it's fast, you can't swim in it."

"Noted. Fast current, you're not in the river. So, where are you if the current's fast?" Jake found himself answering her. It was as if they were two magnets and the pull was too great to fight.

"I'm either cleaning fish, or cleaning the barn, or doing something my old man has me doing."

"Don't you ever get any down time?" She moved from her back to tread closer to Jake, knowing that her parents would be mad if they caught her swimming right now. She also knew that when she spotted him swimming while on her walk that she couldn't miss the opportunity. She'd been on the river for two weeks with her parents and failed to get Jake's attention.

"I guess so. If the old man is drunk and my work is done, then I'm off the hook. Usually, I just work until my body gives out."

She thought about his body and how she admired it when she saw him shirtless, and since he was shirtless whenever he was working, this was quite often.

"My parents inherited this place from my Aunt Merda. She was my dad's aunt and he always tells stories of spending summers here when he was a kid. What he failed to mention is that I'm the only fifteen-year-old for miles. So, I have a lot of time on my hands."

She was hinting at spending time with him and he knew it, but his insecurities put in place by his dad made him think that maybe she wanted to hang out with him because he was her only option. Jake couldn't pass up the opportunity, though, and so he offered up, "I'm in the barn usually early and then before dusk. If you ever want to feed the chickens or see the steer, you're welcome to come by."

June's face lit up at the invitation. Even under the darkening sky, he could see the joy in her big blues eyes and right there, he decided they were the prettiest eyes he'd ever seen. They were the kind of eyes he would think about always and the kind that would get him through the hardest nights.

"Really?" June asked. "You'd show me your cows?" Heck, for that smile, he'd do anything she asked. He didn't remember the last time anyone had looked at him without barking an order, let alone with that much happiness. He felt his playful side coming out and he gently splashed water at her.

"Sure I would. Where are you from anyways?"

She moved water towards him to mimic his splash, but she really was so excited he was talking to her that she didn't want to play. She wanted to get to know Jake. She remembered meeting him a few summers ago when she visited with her parents, and even at twelve his blue-green eyes always stuck out to her.

"Ohio. I'm June," she offered up shyly.

"I know, sweet Juniper." He didn't mean to say that part out loud, but there was no taking it back once he did. Of course, he knew her name. His dad wouldn't shut up about how Bill Withers and his brat daughter June -and what kind of man names their kid June anyways- inherited the property that old Merda wouldn't sell to him. "I'm Jake. Jake Daniels."

June sucked in a breath. He called her Juniper. No one called her Juniper. She liked it. She ducked under the water and swam close to him. When she resurfaced, she was closer to him than she'd expected and hoped he couldn't tell how hard her heart was beating. "I know that too," she said shyly, her breath hitching for a moment.

Jake's breath also caught because of June's nearness and he needed to make sure she didn't notice. He splashed her again, but this time it was a big splash, and she didn't hesitate to splash him back even harder. The two splashed until Jake found himself picking up the petite girl and tossing her into the water. She laughed like she never laughed before, and in those thirty-minutes had more fun than she had the entire two weeks she'd been there.

Over the next few weeks, June would wake up early to find Jake hard at work in the barn. She wanted to help to lessen his workload. At first, he was reluctant but when he saw how much she enjoyed it, how could he deny her? He quickly learned that he couldn't deny her anything.

June enjoyed working with Jake. He was strong and knowledgeable. She sometimes felt like a kid around him, but he was always patient with teaching her something new. She hated the way his dad talked to him whenever he would come around. Occasionally, he would ask what the hell she was doing there, but she couldn't seem to be scared off from Jake. His lure was too great.

In those first weeks, it took Jake a while to open up to June. He held a deep fear that he was no good for her. Eventually, her easy nature made him open up. She was somehow able to get him to talk to her about anything and everything. He told her about his mom's early death and how his dad used to be an okay guy. He wasn't great, but okay enough, that was until she died, then he cared more about a bottle than he did about Jake. Jake told her how he was forced to drop out of school when he turned sixteen, the earliest age the state allowed, so that he could work.

Every confession Jake made only made June fall harder for him. She hated his father. Hated him for taking so much out on Jake and for not being a better man, hated him for making Jake work instead of getting to be a kid. June thought that Jake was the strongest person she'd ever met because of how well he seemed to handle everything.

Jake loved the fact that June had a fairly easy life with parents that were teachers and loved her very much. When he met June's mom and was invited for dinner, he was more nervous he thought than possible, but as soon as he saw June, she calmed him. They were easy going and approved of the young couple's budding friendship.

The Withers' were not blind to the cruel way Mike Daniels treated Jake. They saw the black eyes and bruises, but knowing their daughter, they knew that if anyone could bring happiness to that boy it would be her. Bill Withers even made a point to tell Jake he approved of their friendship, but Jake better not dream of taking it any farther with his fifteen-year-old daughter. Jake admired Mr. Withers and took things incredibly slow with June.

The first time they kissed, it was June who pushed it. It was always June who pushed things. Jake's world turned upside down when he finally felt her small perfect lips against his and as soon as the kiss was over, she asked him to kiss her again. Of course, he couldn't deny her. He didn't let it go farther than that, not that day anyway, even though she riled him up and turned him on like no other. Jake had girlfriends at school and would make out with them on walks home, occasionally getting to third base, but nothing ever felt like it did with June.

Eventually, Mike Daniels even seemed to put up with June's presence. Occasionally, he would put Jake down in front of June, but mostly he tolerated her and couldn't be mad when he found her cleaning fish or shoveling shit. He hated doing those things and having another hand to do it wasn't something that even Mike Daniels would argue.

The summer was coming to an end and every moment that Jake and June spent together was a moment they cherished with big dreams of Jake running away to Ohio and finishing school to be near June. Promises that they would somehow figure out a way to be together were made with late night goodbye kisses. It was the same for both of them. They were hopelessly in love, so much so that the Withers started to worry that it was turning into too much of a grown-up relationship for June. As much as they liked Jake, they didn't want their daughter's heart to be broken when it was time to go home; after all, she was only fifteen. That's why when Mr. Withers got a call asking him to come home early and take over an assistant coach position for the middle school's football team, he quickly agreed.

June was already out for the morning running around with Jake by the time Mr. Withers took the call. They figured they would give her this last day and get the house packed up, knowing she wouldn't take it well, but hoping they were doing the best thing.

June and Jake met early in the morning, it was the first time they moved beyond kissing and into more. Jake couldn't believe when June asked to touch him. It was something he fantasized about at night.

"Can I touch you?" June asked wanting to know this part of Jake. The outside air was warm and the trees surrounding the clearing made the two feel completely alone and untouchable.

By the end, June gave Jake an orgasm, which wasn't hard since the feel of her hands on him made it hard for him to last even a few minutes. It didn't matter that June didn't have an orgasm. The moment was perfect for her and everything she could've hoped for her first sexual experience to be like.

Jake finished washing up when he heard his dad yell for him. "Jake! Where the hell are you? We should've been out on the water by now!" Shit Jake thought, the old man didn't sound good today. He wondered if he even slept. When Jake left early this morning his old man hadn't come home yet which could mean so many things.

Jake looked over to June who was decent and breathed a sigh of relief as his dad walked through the clearing. If his dad was just minutes earlier he would have seen June. The thought sickened Jake.

Before he knew it, they were on the boat fishing with Jake's Dad. The last thing Jake wanted was to have June spend any time with him, however, June was fearless. And he knew where ever he went she would follow. That was until his Dad sent Jake into the river to retrieve a fishing rig. The water was rough and even though Jake was a strong swimmer, he struggled against the current. A scream from June had Jake rushing to get back to the boat. He couldn't believe what he was seeing. Jake reached the boat just as his dad's belt buckle was being undone.

He was consumed with rage as he lunged for his dad. Hate from deep within Jake pumped adrenaline through him as he slammed his fist into his dad's ribs.

June landed on the ground when Mike Daniels released her head in order to fight his son. Mike never thought his son had it in him and was pleased that he might get a little bit of a fight from him. It would make kicking his ass all the more fun.

Jake fought hard, but was no match for his dad. The moment Mike got his bearings, he went wild on Jake hitting him with all his force. Mike had always a big man, the drinking didn't make him fat like it did some men. Right then, his six foot three frame was towering over Jake, slamming his head against the deck of the boat. Jake could faintly hear June screaming, but one of the blows to his head created a ringing that was drowning out all other sounds. Normally, he would have passed out by now, but he had to stay conscious for June.

June couldn't take it any longer. It was killing her watching every blow that Jake took. She had to do something to stop the beating that he was taking. She looked all around the boat for anything should could use to get Mike to stop hurting Jake. An oar attached to the side of the boat caught her eye, and without much thought, she grabbed it and swung it at Mr. Daniels' head.

Blood splattered and she knew it cut his head, but he was still conscious. His fists stopped connecting with Jake and he was momentarily stunned that the tiny girl had hit him. June didn't wait as she leaned into the oar like it was a baseball bat and she struck again. Mike stood and approached when her second blow hit. The combination of the alcohol, the boat swaying in the storm and the last hit to his head was all it took to send Mike overboard. She watched for a second, stunned that she was capable of something like that and stared silently, with tears staining her cheeks as the rough river seemed to swallow him. What had she just done? She meant to save Jake, not kill his dad, but as he disappeared into the river, she knew that is exactly what she had done.

Jake brought the boat in and tied it to the dock. The two were eerily silent on the walk back to June's place. Jake hated that she was leaving, but even more than that he hated what she witnessed. A part of him broke when he watched his father grab her and then even more of him broke as he said goodbye. He vowed to be with her again. He wouldn't let anything get in his way.

Jake returned home, a place he wasn't even sure if he belonged anymore with determination to be with June again. Jake's hope diminished when he smelled the cigarette smoke on his porch and then he saw the man standing in the shadows. "Who's there?" he called out thinking that it was probably his old man, he wouldn't believe he was gone until he saw a body.

"Who I am isn't as important as why I'm here." A man almost twice the size of Jake, wearing a black cotton t-shirt, black dress pants and black shoes, stepped out of the shadows. A dragon tattoo snaked up his neck and danced around a scar that went over his face across his eye and disappeared into his dark hairline.

"Why are you here?" Jake asked trying to be brave even though he was spent from his emotional day.

The man smiled sinisterly, "I'm here to collect a debt. Your father owed me a sizable one and seeing as I watched you and your girlfriend knock him overboard, that debt falls on you."

"But it was an accident," Jake pleaded with the man.

"An accident, huh? That's why you can swim after a rig, but not after your old man? Way I saw it was you let the water take him. You didn't have the balls to kill him yourself, though. You let that sweet little girlfriend of yours do the work."

"Leave June out of it!" Jake squared his shoulders and tried to look bigger than he was.

The man laughed, "I could use her as repayment. Take care of her parents in their sleep before they go and make it look like it was you. I bet she can repay the debt real nice."

Jake felt sick. He did this. He knew he was no good for June and now all of darkness was threatening to hurt her. "What do you want?" Jake asked feeling defeated. In the last several hours, he was beaten, watched the girl he loved being attacked by his Dad, watched the current take his Dad and then had to say goodbye to June. He felt like he was shattering. Everything that mattered was suddenly gone and now this man was going to harm June, his June.

"What do you want?" he asked again clearing his head from his thoughts and willing to do anything.

"Simple. You're going to work for me. When I tell you to do something, you do it. No questions asked. If you don't, I'll turn you and your pretty little girlfriend in for murder, or worse I'll make good on my threat for June. And don't worry, I have the police in my pocket around here so if they need any convincing it was the two of you, I'll be sure to get them all the evidence they need." Jake could see it in the evil glint in the man's eyes that he was serious fueling Jake's feeling of hopelessness.

"Just leave her alone. I'll do anything, if you just leave June out of this." He would do anything to keep June safe. He knew the moment he saw June that she would be the only thing to shine in his gray world and he would be damned if he let this incident color her world dark. He would sign on with the devil himself if it meant protecting her. That, certainly was what this felt like.

The man smiled and threw his cigarette down on the ground stomping it out, "I'll be in touch, Jake."

Jake sat on the porch stairs staring after the man for hours thinking how the old adage went, better the devil you know, and that he would do anything the man made him do, to keep June safe. He wouldn't risk her. She was the best thing to ever happen to him.

CHAPTER SEVEN

Present

They say there are moments in life when time freezes. Moments when your reality is suspended because the event itself holds so much power that it freezes time. Maybe actual time doesn't stop and it's your heart that stops? Right now, at this moment, my heart has stopped. The air has left my body and I'm suspended, stuck in this moment. It's too much. One second was everything I wanted and the next took it all away.

My stomach roiled as the police officers began their search. I wanted to fall to my knees and scream, but I promised Jake I wouldn't. "Ma'am. I'd like your name and contact information in case we have any questions for you," an officer who didn't look much older than myself asked. On auto pilot, I give him my information.

"We need you to vacate the premises. We'll contact you if we need to."

Just like that I'm being dismissed. "Wait, I'm so confused. I want to talk to him. How long until he's able to have visitors?"

"It will at least be forty-eight hours. A piece of advice for you. This guy is bad news. If you're smart, you'll stay as far away from Jake Daniels as possible."

I leave Jake's apartment and walk home since he picked me up. It's like I jinxed us yesterday because it's freezing outside. The cold helps keep me from completely spiraling. I make it home even though I feel completely lost and I probably shouldn't even be walking home considering it's the middle of the night. I should've called a cab and by the time I walk into my apartment, the sun is starting to rise.

When I walk into my room I have a mission. I open my drawer and I take out the picture that Jake took of me. I clutch it in my hands and hold it against my heart. After all this time, the only man I have ever loved was in my grasp and now he is gone. I'm left with so many questions. Why are they arresting him for his father's disappearance? Why did he tell me his name was

Lucas and not tell me the truth? I would've run with him if that's what he needed. I would've done anything for him. I promised him I wouldn't tell the police, but why? None of it makes sense. I feel sick about it. I had him. I wanted it so badly to be him and I had him all along. I love the boy I fell in love with and I just fell in love with the man he became, even if I didn't know for sure, I knew. Deep down, I knew. I was just so confused by his lie, I couldn't see it.

I close my eyes and weep silently, the guilt for what I did to his dad feels raw and fresh again. It took me a long time to get past it. I became reckless and wild. I hated myself for killing someone and felt so low about myself that I gave up my virginity to the wrong kind of man as soon as an opportunity presented itself. Even now, I haven't been in a serious relationship. This is all my fault. If I had told my parents the truth then and not let them take me away maybe none of this would be happening, but Jake promised he'd find me one day and that it would all be okay. Nothing about him being arrested seven years later is okay. I hate how I feel. I'm so stinking sad. It's like the world was given to me for the briefest of seconds and then that same current that took Mr. Daniels away came in and stole Jake from me all over again.

If it comes to my freedom or his, I need to confess. I need to make it right. I can't let him take the fall for something I did.

I hear Liz wake up and I don't make a sound. I don't want to see her right now. I know my eyes are puffy and I need to sort my head out before I tell her anything. She has an early class and she probably thinks I'm still at Jake's at least I'm hoping she does. Before long, I hear the front door open and close and I'm glad that she's gone. She would ask questions, questions I don't have answers for.

I call the police station only to confirm what the officer said, that I can't visit yet. I'm a wreck. I get in my car and I drive to the band's house. No one answers the door. I call Bernie and leave a message asking her to have Dietz call me. Until I talk to Jake, I don't know what I should say, but I need to see if Dietz knows anything.

Five restless hours later, I finally get a return call from Dietz. My pulse is racing rapidly as I answer the phone.

"Dietz, thank God. I've been trying to get a hold of someone, anyone."

"What's up, buttercup? You sound panicked. Everything alright?" his easy demeanor irritates me.

"No, everything isn't alright. I was with Lucas and he was arrested."

"Shit! What the hell for?" he questions, "I told him the cops were asking about him. He said he had it covered. Let me see what I can find out."

"I don't really know what's going on. They said he's wanted for the disappearance of someone. I know that's a lie. I know him. He wouldn't do that! What did the cops ask you?" I'm frantic, but can't help it. Everything feels like it's spiraling out of control.

"They showed me a picture of Lucas and they asked me if I knew Jake Daniels. They said they thought he could be going by a different name. I told them I didn't know shit. I even told Lucas and he said it was some kind of misunderstanding and that he had it covered. Fuck."

"There were at least half a dozen cops. It was insane. I'm scared," I admit trying to stop my body from trembling.

"Shit. Let me see what I can find out. I'll call you. And June?"

"Yeah?"

"Hang tight. Lucas is a good guy. You're right, I'm sure he didn't do this. It's gotta be like he said and one big misunderstanding. It'll be okay, you'll see." Dietz does his best to reassure me, but the slight shake in his voice tells me he's scared too.

We hang up and I feel no more settled. Dietz doesn't know anything. He thinks his name is Lucas just like I did and until I talk to Jake, that's what he'll continue to believe.

Over the next day, I am frantic. There is nothing I can do. I get a call from Dietz that says basically what the cops said, forty-eight hours, and really is Jake Daniels wanted in the disappearance with Mike Daniels. Dietz is stunned. I promise to call him, even though the band is the least of my concerns.

I skip my classes. I can't concentrate on anything. I call in sick to the bookstore. Liz can tell something is wrong, but I tell her I'm sick and that everything is fine. She looks at me skeptically, but I can't tell her.

On the second day, I'm at the police station as soon as the sun is up. I ask to speak to Jake Daniels and an officer tells me that he is in with the prosecutor and it will be a few hours. I wait in a chair. On my right are two large, black men, one sporting gold teeth and an airbrushed jacket with a picture of him and his dog, and the other is dressed in black from head-to-toe and gives an evil stare to anyone who looks his way. I keep my eyes averted, because he makes me nervous. On my left is a dirty, white man with skin so dirty you'd think he had been buried alive. His stench is the most grotesque thing I've ever smelled. The man with the gold teeth eventually gets up yelling for someone to hose the man down.

After what feels like hours, a petite police officer with blonde hair pulled back into a tight bun, finally calls my name. She checks me for contraband in one room, then I follow her down a long hallway. She opens the door to a small room with blank white walls and a single table where Jake is sitting with his head down; his hands are handcuffed to a small metal loop in the table. He looks up and his eyes connect with me as I take a seat in front of him.

"Stay seated at all times. No touching the prisoner. You have five minutes," the police officer recites as if she has said it dozens of times and walks out of the room.

"Jake," a strangled plea leaves my lips, "Why didn't you tell me it was you? What's happening? Are you okay?" I long to stroke his tired face. His blue-green eyes that I love so much look sad and broken. He nods to a sign behind him that reads, "You are being monitored and may be video recorded."

"I'm so sorry, June. I never meant for you to find out. It's just when I saw you I couldn't help myself. I had to get to know the woman you've become. You've turned into such a strong beautiful woman. The kind of woman I knew you would always be."

"You're not answering any of my questions, Jake Daniels," I say his name with a sneer angry at him for not telling me the truth. "Did you mean for me not to find out like that or were you not going to tell me?" I'm angry and confused.

"I wasn't going to tell you. There is so much more going on here than you could possibly know. I've kept things from you, June, but I did it to protect you. Please believe me. You need to let me go. This has to be goodbye. Promise me you'll live a happy life; be happy my Juniper," his eyes plead with me to give in and let go. They gut me. He is gutting me.

"No, I'm not letting them arrest you for something we both know you didn't do."

"It's done June. I just met with the prosecutor. They have strong evidence against me, so I took a deal for involuntary manslaughter. If I'm lucky, I'll be out in four years. I need you to forget about me and do whatever you have to do to pretend you never met me."

"Forget you? I fell in love with you when I was fifteen and I just fell in love all over again at twenty-two. You think I can forget you? You think I can move on? I didn't move on then and I sure as hell can't now. You need to tell me what is really going on or I will go out there and tell them it was me." I spit out desperate for him to listen to me. I can't lose him again. He is all I have and means everything to me.

"June, I swear to Christ. You will not go out there. Listen to me, and listen to me very carefully. You're not responsible for this. It wasn't you and if you start opening your mouth to people about how you know me, you are going to be in danger and then everything I've done to make sure you are safe will all be for nothing, do you understand me?" he's angry. His voice is raised and slightly manic.

"What the hell do you mean, I didn't do this? We both know that's not the truth."

"It wasn't you, June," he says with so much conviction it makes me doubt everything that happened.

I glare at him. "Why go by Lucas?" I ask wanting an answer to why he told me his name was Lucas.

"I know it isn't fair, but I had to get to know you."

The door opens and the police officer says, "Time's up."

I'm frantic. This can't be it. This can't be happening.

"Goodbye, my sweet Juniper. I love you."

"No, this can't be it. I need more answers. I love you, Jake." I'm frantic and reaching for him as the police officer begins guiding me out of the room.

"This isn't goodbye, Jake," I promise as the door closes shutting him out.

"I love you!" I shout again, but the door is closed. I feel like I'm drowning and this tiny room is swallowing me whole.

I'm angry and devastated. Broken, yet wanting to attack. How can the world be so cruel to me? It gave me love twice and took it away. Each time I thought I had it, it was ripped brutally away from me. The first time it was taken was by Mike Daniels, and this time it's by Jake.

CHAPTER EIGHT

"I need to speak with the prosecutor," I tell the police officer. I know what Jake said, but there is no way that I'm letting him go to jail for a crime he didn't commit.

"Ma'am, the prosecutor is in meetings all afternoon. Let me get you her card. I'm sure that you can call and make an appointment."

I am escorted back to the lobby to where I see the same men sitting there from before. It's hard to believe that only fifteen or so minutes have passed. I feel like in that short time, my entire world has shifted.

I pull out my cellphone and call the number on the card. The secretary tells me she has an opening in a week. A week! That's crazy. I'm not waiting a week. I look up the office on my phone and see that it's across the street, on the sixteenth floor. Her picture also comes up on the internet so I know exactly who I'm looking for.

I take the elevator up, giving myself a pep talk. I'm turning myself in no matter what Jake says. I'm not letting him take the fall. I take a seat in the lobby and pretend that I'm supposed to be there. I see a door open and a pretentious looking prosecutor is sitting at a large conference desk surrounded with files and other people.

An hour passes and then another. Finally, the room clears out and the prosecutor walks out. It might be my only chance, and I'm taking it. I follow her towards the restroom and then stop her.

"Excuse me? Ms. Peterson? My Name is June Withers. I need to talk with you about Jake Daniels."

Her eyes squint on me and I can tell she doesn't like that I'm accosting her in public. "You need to make an appointment, Ms. Withers."

"Look, I tried and they said it would at least be a week. I have information about Jake that can't wait a week."

She squints her eyes at me again and I take a good look at her. She is wearing a designer dress suit. The kind that screams money. Her nails are perfectly manicured and there isn't a hair on her blonde head that is out of place. Her nose is tipped up, like she believes she is superior.

"A plea bargain has already been reached with Mr. Daniels, Ms. Withers, so I'm afraid you're wasting your time."

"You need to retract the deal; he's innocent."

"He said some girl might try to tell me she did it. Is that you? Do you think you can try and martyr yourself to make his case get thrown out? Do you know how much evidence we have against him? Ms. Withers, I don't know what you think your play is, but this is done. We gave him the best possible plea deal he could get. If you're smart, you'll shut up because the case we have against him is so strong that if you push this, he'll still be found guilty and he'll get a heck of a lot more time than the measly four years he got."

"But you don't understand," I feel small and helpless as I say this. This bitch just put me in my place and I don't know if there is anything I can do to help Jake.

"I understand perfectly. If you try and stick your nose in this case, your "friend" might get real time." The bitch air quoted me. I hate her. I hate this entire situation. Not even a moment later she walks away from me, leaving me speechless

I drive to Jake's apartment; the need to be near anything reminding me of him is overpowering. I lift the doormat and find the key Jake showed me. There is police evidence tape and the apartment is wrecked. Not that he had much here to begin with, but what is left is trashed. The only thing worth any real value in the living room is his keyboard. I move my fingers over the keys. Was that only two days ago that I heard Jake's song. It was like he was screaming at me to see that it was him all along. His words at the police station don't seem to add up. He wasn't going to ever tell me, but his song practically shouted it. Maybe I wasn't met to hear it, but he bled his love out to me in those lyrics. I feel the first tear slide down my cheek, certainly not the last.

I move to his bedroom and it's equally as trashed. His mattress is flipped and clothes are everywhere. I right the mattress on the bed and grab a dirty shirt from the floor. I slip it on and inhale deeply. I need him surrounding me. I need to make sense of this. He said it wasn't me like he almost believed it when we both know what happened. What did he mean by protecting me and what kind of danger? It was self-defense with his dad. I'm sure we could've cleared it up, but that damn prosecutor. I can't risk him going to jail even longer than he already is. My heart feels so broken and utterly lost. I thought I found the man I loved, the man I would spend the rest of my life with. Even when I thought he was Lucas, I fell in love with him. I didn't want to, but I did and now he's gone.

I curl up on his bed and bring the blankets around me. I can smell him everywhere. I can still smell us together, like the air knows we were once us, even if the rest of the world will never know that Jake and June were once in love. I push my head into his pillow and grip the sheets I was once so tangled in and that's when it happens, I lose it. I fall apart, breaking and splintering. I let out a loud scream, angry at Jake, angry at the circumstances and at the world for taking him from me. My body shudders and I break. I don't know how long I fall apart, but I sob so hard that my body eventually gives out and I sleep.

It's a restless sleep filled with memories and nightmares of the day Mike Daniels died. The water brought him under over and over again, only this time he popped back out of the water and killed Jake. Jake died in my arms, and I couldn't do anything to help him.

I wake up and hear screaming. It's loud, hurting my ears. I pause for a moment and realize it's me. I'm shaking and decide I need to pull myself together.

The sunlight from a new day filters through the curtain. Maybe I can visit him again today and get more answers? On that thought, I gather some of his things from the floor deciding I'm going to keep whatever I want. I pick up a hooded sweatshirt off the floor and find a stack of notebooks. One by one, I scan through them. Song after song fill each page. Some have a few lines written down and others have notes. Most of it is random, but then I find words that I can only hope are about me.

You were my angel
My saving grace
You gave me summer
I gave you me, but the sky grew dark around us.
It darkened everything
It took you, my love
Now all I can do is hate

Another page, more lyrics,
Beyond reproach sweet, sweet bug
Unworthy of your gaze
Battered heart and bleeding pain
Those eyes of yours take it all away
More lyrics,
My sky is darkened gray, but you knew that
Is it dark for you too?
Shadowing everything
My sky eclipsed yours and made your sunshine as dark as night
I'm the monster that they made me
Walking streets all by myself
I have no heartbeat
No soul
I make them bleed
Only you fulfill my need

I gasp reading pages after pages filled with the same heartfelt lyrics. He was in as much pain as I was being separated, and it sound like even more. What could he have gone through? I gather the notebooks in my arms. I want to savor his words and take my time with each song; each note; each written word. They are my lifeline to him, but I also want to see if I can find anything else out.

I go back to the police station and ask if I can see Jake Daniels. They tell me he is in the middle of being transported to The Mansfield Correctional Institute, and that it usually takes a few days for inmates to get settled so I should go visit him then.

How can this be so final, so fast? I leave the police station, stop and get boxes, and go back to Jake's. I'm packing up his things when I hear, "Whoa, Lucas! Man, are you here?" I come out of Jake's room and I know I look a mess. My eyes are swollen from crying and I'm listless.

"He's gone, Dietz," I cry silently. "I'm packing up his things. I just have to keep busy. He doesn't have a lot, but is there," I stutter on my words, "Is there anything you want?" A loud sob escapes my throat. I can't believe I'm doing this.

"What do you mean gone? Is he...Is he dead?" Dietz asks looking almost as lost as me.

"No, but we're not going to see him again. He took a plea deal and is serving at least four years," I explain.

"Fuck! What did he do?"

"His name isn't really Lucas. It's Jake Daniels and he plead guilty to a crime he didn't commit."

"What the hell? Why would he do that? Who is Jake? Who the hell lies like that? He's one of my best friends and what you're telling me doesn't add up." Dietz begins pacing around the living room. Before I can answer him, a short balding man walks into the apartment.

"Excuse me? What are you doing here? No one is supposed to be here."

"Who the hell are you?" Dietz asks the man.

"I'm the super, and if one of our tenants goes to prison we rent their place. So, I should ask you, who are you? The way I see it, you're trespassing." The way this man is talking makes me think he was going to rifle through Jake's belongings. Plus, how many of his tenants go to prison?

I set the box I was carrying down, "I'm June, Jake's friend. Jake's paid his rent through the end of the month, right?"

"Well, yes but..."

"Do you have a copy of his lease? I think I saw it, hang on one second." I walk into the bedroom, grab the lease from the drawer and return to the living room. Pretending that I've already thoroughly read it, I pass it to the super. "Look at that lease and tell me where it says you have the right to a tenant's apartment even if they are incarcerated? It's not there, is it?" I'm bluffing.

He stutters a little, "I...uh, no, but..."

"But nothing. I'm a journalist for The Scene. I'm sure my editor would love for me to write a piece on how slumlords try to rifle through a tenant's belongings. And don't even get me started on the security of this place."

He puts his hands up in surrender, "Now, now, don't start getting any ideas. I just didn't want anyone else snooping through his stuff. You clear what you're taking out of here and then let me know when you're done. Okay?" he ask. "I'm the first apartment on the left when you walk in through the front," he finishes leaving the apartment.

"Wow June, you just handed it to that guy," Dietz says sitting down on the sofa and running his hands through his hair. "So, what do you know?"

"I know that Jake isn't guilty, but the evidence against him was supposedly strong so he took a plea deal. The prosecutor is a real bitch. I tried to talk to her, and she basically told me Jake was lucky to get such a deal and if I pushed it, he would go to trial and end up in jail a lot longer than the 4 years he's getting. So he made a plea and they are already shipping him to The Mansfield Prison. The guard told me to give it a few days for the transfer and then I could try and visit. I can't believe this, it all feels so surreal."

"Why would he go by a different name, then?" Dietz asks still very shocked by the ordeal. Jake's words filter through my head, "Promise me you won't tell them how you know me," he'd said.

"I don't know I think he was running from something or trying to protect someone."

"Who do you think he was trying to protect? The person that really did it?"

Guilt slams through me. I hate this so much, but I promised Jake. He also said I would be in danger. I'm not even sure from whom, but I feel like he'd want me to keep all of this a secret. "I really don't know. All I know is I was falling hard for him, and he's not who I thought he was," I say and start crying again. I can't help it. I thought I'd cried out all of my tears, but maybe when you love someone like I love him, you can never cry out all of your tears. Maybe when you lose a love like that, your tears can be infinite, flowing freely until you find peace or figure out how not to feel. I know I will never be at peace with what Jake has done. I wish I was numb.

"Aww girl, come here," Dietz says pulling me into his arms. I let him hold me for a few minutes, taking any comfort I can get. I pull away and then say, "I have some boxes. I'm going to take some shirts and a few of his notebooks. Do you want anything? Maybe his keyboard?"

His eyes are soft and I can tell he doesn't feel comfortable seeing me hurt. "Why don't you take what you need, and then leave the rest to me?"

"Really? You wouldn't mind?" I ask.

"Lucas, I mean Jake would want me to. We talked last week and he told me you were the girl for him. I know you two shared something. I'll take care of it. You call me when you go see him. Let me know if you find any more out, yeah?"

"Thank you," I say nodding and go back to the bedroom to finish packing what I want. Dietz helps me with the boxes I'm keeping and tells me that he and the guys are going to store the rest of Jake's stuff.

I'M LYING IN BED STILL wearing Jake's shirt. I just finished going through his notebooks for the second time. Staring at the wall, I wondering how this all happened. I hear the door to my room open knowing that it's Liz. "Alright, spill! What's going on with you? Did you and Lucas have a fight?" Liz asks sitting down next to me on the bed. I turn from the wall to face her. My eyes are swollen from crying.

"Yeah, it's about him." I can't even say his name, it hurts so badly.

"That motherfucker. What did he do to you? I'll stab him."

"Good luck with that; he's gone," I say and wrap my arms around Liz's waist and cry some more. She strokes my head, moving the hair behind my ear with her fingers.

"Did he leave town for work or something?"

"Or something," I tell her not wanting to get into exactly what happened just yet.

"Honey, you tell me when you're ready, okay?"

"Thanks, Liz." I close my eyes and let my heart ache seep from the corners of my eyes.

"It's going to be alright. You'll see whatever this is, we'll work it out."

"I loved him," I whisper out.

Liz lets out a breath, "I was afraid of that," she sighs. "We'll get through this." I stay in her arms for a long time until I finally fall asleep.

"Morning! Rise and shine, sleepyhead," Liz bounces into my room. I feel like hell. Days of crying are worse than any hangover. My body hurts. My head hurts. My heart hurts. Everything hurts.

"Go away," I mumble.

"No, you've missed two days of classes, and I know you can't miss any more. You know what you have to do?"

"Go back to bed?"

"No! You have to get out of bed and fake it 'til you make it. You might be heartbroken and this douche might be gone, but you can't let it break you. You're strong, June. The strongest person I know. You can do this. You need to do this. If you get put on academic probation, you will never get that junior editor position offered to you. You know a strong GPA is one of their requirements. This guy just took your heart. I won't let him take your dream."

"Liz," I mumble again knowing she is right, but also knowing he was my dream and that burns.

"No, I know you want to wallow and I don't blame you, but you can't afford to. I won't let you screw up because of some jerk."

I suddenly feel very protective of Jake, "He's not a jerk."

"Have you been crying for the last few days?" she asks.

"I guess."

"No, I guess about it. He's a jerk because he's not here." I couldn't argue with that logic.

"Come on. We'll hit the gym before class. I'll have your thighs burning so bad you won't be able to think about anything other than how much you want to kill me."

"I already do," I relent and get out of bed and throw on some workout clothes deciding I'll shower after she kicks my butt.

Liz does as promised and as has me working out so hard I want to puke. She's right. It helps keep my mind off of Jake, and I make it through the day. I go to my classes, and the bookstore. She does the same to me the next day, and then the next.

Dietz calls to check in on me, but it feels forced like it's out of obligation.

On Saturday, I have an assignment for The Scene and Liz doesn't let me skip out on that either. I have to give it to her, she is one determined friend. I would give up and curl in on myself, but she won't let me.

On Sunday, I get in the car, ready to drive two hours south to the prison. I'm a ball of nerves. I'm anxious, sad, apprehensive and somewhat excited to see him. As I start the car and put it in reverse to pull out of the spot, my passenger door swings open. "Where are we going?" Liz asks.

"I'm going somewhere," I say hoping she'll get the hint and leave me. I need to do this.

"You're going to him, aren't you?"

A guilty look flashes across my face and before I can protest again Liz has her ass planted in the seat beside me. "Let's go."

It's not ten minutes into the drive before I hear, "No judging, I swear. Where are we going?"

"You won't understand. Heck, I hardly understand."

"You'll feel better having someone on your side. You can tell me."

"Where to even start," I sigh.

"How about at the beginning?" she asks. I know I need to tell someone. I can't keep this in and let it eat away at me. Besides, soon enough she'll know we're headed to a prison.

"Lucas' name is really Jake Daniels."

"Wait a minute, he's Jake? Like Jake, Jake? The one you've held on to for all of these years?"

"He is, but I didn't know it for sure until the other day. I thought they resembled each other and I was actually struggling with my feelings for him because I thought I was misplacing them or some shit. Like maybe I was into "Lucas" more because I thought he reminded me of Jake. But I fell for Lucas too. No matter what he calls himself, I would. So, here's where it gets interesting. When we were kids, I was so into him. He was the first guy that I did anything with, but it wasn't about that, you know? We had this connection that went deeper than physical. It was like he just called to me in every way.

"His dad was an asshole. He beat the shit out of him; it was bad. He made Jake drop out of high school and pretty much made him work twenty-four-seven. I wanted to spend time with him, so I helped him as much as I could. One day, when the summer was coming to an end, Mr. Daniels showed up. I didn't know it at the time, but he'd caught Jake and I fooling around."

"Oh, no," Liz looks at me wide eyed.

"Oh yes, but that's not the worst. I didn't want to miss any time with Jake so I pushed and got his dad to let me go fishing with them. On the boat, Mr. Daniels was drinking and just being mean. He kept making these comments to Jake that made me hate his dad. The water started to get choppy. There were huge signs that the weather was about to turn bad and that a storm was coming. Jake tried to warn his dad, but that just made him even angrier. Mr. Daniels lost some fishing rig in the water and he made Jake swim out after it.

I was scared for Jake. I knew he was a good swimmer, but the water was still so choppy. While he was out there, Mr. Daniels started saying stuff to me, how he saw me and Jake together and that I was a whore. He grabbed me, so I smacked him."

"Good for you," Liz is angry on my behalf. I give her a look and then continue.

"So, once I smacked him, he grabbed me by the throat and started undoing his belt buckle. I was scared shitless. Jake got there and the two started fighting. Liz, Mr. Daniels was huge. Jake didn't have a chance. He was beating Jake, so I grabbed this oar, hit him with it and he went overboard."

"Oh, my God! Thank God, you found that," Liz says.

"It was so bad. He didn't come back up and we couldn't find him. I was shaken up and Jake was badly beaten. He was able to bring the boat back in and I went to his house to wash up. He held me and told me it was all okay. He said that no one would know; that his dad was a drunk so everyone would just assume he had an accident on the water.

"When he walked me home I was still shaken up. Then we reached my place and I knew when I saw the car and the trailer packed up that we were leaving early. I remember my dad seeing us when we walked up. If Jake didn't get roughed up by his dad all the time then I think my dad would have made a bigger deal about Jake's appearance. I remember wanting to tell him what his daughter did. I killed a man. No matter what Mr. Daniels did, he didn't deserve to die."

"He would've killed you both. Don't do that. Don't take the blame for some sick old man. It wasn't your fault."

I nod and continue my story, even though I don't I agree with her. It was my fault. If I didn't push to go out there none of it would've happened, and then we didn't go after him. We should've gone after him. We shouldn't have let the current take him.

"My dad told us that he was taking this assistant coaching job and we needed to leave early. He said he'd give us a few minutes to say goodbye, and just like that we were leaving each other. I remember crying in Jake's arms. How could it all be over just like that? He told me it was okay and that he loved me. He told me he would make sure everything was okay and that he would find me. He took my number and promised to call. He told me not to stress over his dad and that everything would be okay. He said he'd protect me and make sure no one knew what happened and he assured me over and over again that I did the right thing. He even thanked me for protecting him, saying he had never had anyone do that before. I said goodbye to him that night and cried for weeks. It was the hardest thing I ever had to go through."

"And then you never heard from him again, right?" Liz asks remembering how I told her I fell in love once and hoped I'd hear from Jake, but never did.

"Right, not until that night at the bar. I thought it was him and I wanted it to be him, but then he said his name was Lucas. So the other night after an awesome date, we get back to his place and have this mind-blowing sex. I wake up to him on the keyboard and he's singing. The lyrics he was singing told me without a doubt that he was Jake. Before I could really ask him why he kept it from me, there was this loud banging on the door and it was the police."

"No!" Liz gasps.

"Yes, and they came in and arrested him for the disappearance of his dad."

"No!"

"Yes and it gets worse. I went to the police station and he tells me I can't say anything and that he's doing what's best. He says I'll be in danger if I tell anyone and that he needs to say goodbye to me. He says it wasn't me, but we both know it was. And then he tells me he already took a plea deal and is going away for four years. I tried to talk to the prosecutor and she said if this goes to trial he'll end up with a ton more jail time and that I need to stop or I'm going to seriously end up getting him more time. So here we are. We're on our way to see Jake in prison doing time for a crime he didn't commit."

Liz's face is filled with compassion, "Oh honey, what are you going to do?"

"I don't really know what I can do. I don't want to make it harder for him. I'm hoping I'll get some answers today. It's been killing me."

"Why didn't you tell me sooner?" she asks.

"Guilt I guess," I say shrugging. "I can't help but feel like this whole thing is my fault."

"Jake said you would be in danger?"

"Yeah, it doesn't make sense. Danger from who? Danger from what? See, he left me with so many unanswered questions."

We talk for a while longer and go over all the possibilities. I feel like a weight has been lifted from my shoulders by my confession. All this time, I've never told anyone what happened. My behavior changed after that summer, so much so that my parents tried to put me in therapy. I wouldn't talk to a therapist and when Jake never contacted me, I got angry. I lashed out and gave away parts of myself to men who never deserved it.

We pull up to the prison and I ask Liz to wait in the car. I need to do this alone. I'm brought to a room where other family members are sitting on one side of thick glass, and their felonious loved ones are on the other side with phones to their ears.

I wait for fifteen minutes or so, and they bring Jake in. He's wearing the standard orange jumpsuit and I can see a black eye as soon as he gets close.

He picks the phone up, "June, you shouldn't be here."

Not the warm welcome I was expecting, "You left me with too many questions not to be here."

"I told you it wasn't safe and it's still not. You need to leave and not come back."

"Jake, I can't just let you sit in here. You're innocent."

"And so are you. Everything that happened was in self defense. It's not your fault. You need to go live a happy life, but I need you to let me go. I'm going to be in here for a while. You can't wait on me."

"This isn't fair, Jake. Nothing about this feels okay. Why are you pushing me away when we only just found each other? How is this so easy for you?"

"Are you kidding? Easy for me? Look at where I am, June. Nothing about this is easy, but you know what? I was never good enough for you. You know it and I know it. I'm a selfish prick. I should've stayed away from you then and I should've stayed away from you now, but I couldn't. You're the most amazing woman I've ever met. I'm sorry I didn't tell you who I am, but there's a reason for that. It's to protect you. Trust me." He's pleading with me. His eyes are asking more than his words. They're asking me to say goodbye. I can see it.

"I can't not see you. You know you're the only man I ever loved, right? I don't care that you're here. I'll visit you as often as I can, and I'll be waiting for you when you get out."

"No, June. I won't see you again, if you come here. I don't want you to see me here."

I'm shaking my head at Jake not understanding how he can be turning me away. "Don't push me away," I plead.

He sets the phone down and gives me one last hard look. His eyes stare into mine; looking at me like it's the last time he'll ever see me; like he's taking me in and memorizing me. I'm at a loss. I don't know what I can do or say. A few tears leak out of the corners of my eyes and then he's gone.

CHAPTER NINE

6 months later

"That's the last box," I groan to Liz, setting the pile of returned mail on top and then sealing the cardboard box shut.

"I still can't believe he never responded to one of your letters. I mean if he'd opened one letter, just one, he'd know that you're about to have his baby."

I rub my stomach that's been hiding my feet for the last two months. Apparently, Plan B is only 97 percent effective in the first 24 hours. After that, it's 85 percent and then so on and so on. So, I have about a month left to go until my son or daughter is born. I finished school and I'm moving in with my mom and dad who bought a house about forty-five minutes east of Cleveland when they retired last year. It's about as rural as you can get.

They were shocked when I told them I was expecting. Even more shocked when I told them I ran into Jake Daniels, who was passing through town. I told them it was a one night stand and that we didn't exchange numbers. They couldn't believe how careless I was, but ultimately being the good parents they are, they've accepted the fact that they're going to be grandparents.

I wish Jake would respond to one of my letters. He won't see me either. It makes me angry. If he would get his head out of ass and talk to me, maybe I would understand. I stopped going out there when I started showing. His words from our last face to face sent chills through me. What if I am in danger? I can't put our baby in harm's way. So I've been writing him in hopes that this month will be the month he finally decides to respond. It's wearing on me, though.

I start to lift the box and get the death glare from Liz, "Oh no, you don't. I've already seen you carry way too much today and that box is heavy. If you try and lift that one your back is going to be killing you."

"Fine. It's all you," I say throwing my hands up in surrender. Liz helps me pack the last box into my car filling it to the brim and snagging a blanket in the corner of the door when she slams it closed. She has to open it and close it again before walking to her car so she can follow me to my parent's house. I don't know what I would've done without Liz. She's gone with me to every doctor's appointment and stood by me while I cried over the loss of Jake.

By the time we make it to Mom and Dad's house, I have to pee so badly. I swear this baby dances on my bladder. We pull up to their house and I take nothing in, but the single thought racing through my mind; pee.

"Hi, Mom!" I waddle past her as fast as I can. "Love you, but I gotta go," I say racing to the bathroom.

I finish and Liz is already handing my dad boxes. "Hi Daddy!" I say grabbing a box from him. He leans down to kiss me and asks, "How's my baby girl doing?"

"I'm okay, Dad," I stifle a yawn.

"You're exhausted, why don't you lay down for a bit," Mom offers throwing her arm around my shoulder.

"There's so much to do. I'll help for a bit and then lay down."

"She's been like this all day, not wanting to stop for anything," Liz says tattling on me.

"I can't help it. I need to feel useful," I say walking back to the bedroom mom told me I'd be staying in. I open the door and gasp. Tears fill my eyes as I look around the room. A window air conditioner unit hums, blowing cool air into the room. My parents hate forced air. Even in the hot, humid summers they refuse to use air, settling for fans and natural breezes from the Lake. A full-size bed with my favorite quilt, the one my Grandma spent three years making while I was a little girl, is on one side of the room. Next to that is a beautiful white crib with yellow and green giraffes on the bumper. I'm sure if I run my fingers over it, it would be the softest material I've ever felt. Across from that next to my bed is a changing table stocked with diapers and neutral clothes. In the corner by the window is a gliding rocking chair with a matching footrest.

"You guys," I say wiping my eye, "this is amazing. Thank you."

"Your dad put the crib together and even helped me shop," Mom says hanging up some clothes in the closet.

"It's perfect. I love it." As soon as I say that the baby kicks me hard enough that you can see it's foot or elbow- I'm not sure which since I can't keep track of Olympic gymnast-jutting out the side of my stomach. "Dad, feel right here." I grab Dad's hand and press it against my stomach.

"That's incredible," Dad says as the baby does somersaults in my belly.

"I want to feel." Mom pushes Dad's hand aside and looks at dad and says, "Our baby's having a baby."

"Your baby needs to rest," Liz says, besides being the best friend in the world Liz has taken to being a tad overprotective.

"Okay, okay. You win. This baby officially just kicked my butt. I think he or she just stuck their foot right into my spine." I yawn and then with a glance at the soft bed say, "I really do love the room, guys."

"Rest. We'll bring everything in and then I'll wake you before I go," Liz orders. Liz is taking her dream job in New York City and getting on a flight tomorrow.

I do as I'm ordered and lay down in my new bedroom, with a hand on my belly to calm my tumultuous baby, despite the fact that everyone is moving boxes in and out of my room, I fall asleep.

"Hey honey, it's time," Liz's soothing voice wakes me.

The bed dips next to me as Liz takes a seat. "I wish I didn't have to go yet," she sighs.

I sit up on the bed and smile at my best friend, who I first thought of as superficial and have learned what a great heart she has. "I'm really going to miss you," my voice cracks as I try to not choke on the emotion strangling me.

"None of that. I'll be back when the baby's born. It's only a couple hours flight. I'll be back so often you won't even know I'm gone."

"Liz, thank you so much for everything. If it wasn't for you, I don't know how I would've gotten through these last few months," I swipe a tear from under my eye.

"Nonsense, you're the strongest person I know. You're brave and strong and you have the best pregnant ass ever. All I did was make you work out at an unhealthy level," she laughs trying to lighten the mood. Liz has had me at the gym all throughout my pregnancy and I can't argue with the fact that despite having a bowling ball for a belly, my buns have never looked so good.

I stand up and walk Liz out. My mom and dad hug her and thank her for taking such good care of me and moments later I'm waving goodbye to Liz as her car pulls away.

Over the next several weeks, I settle into a routine with Mom and Dad. They let me sleep in and are understanding of their pregnant over-emotional daughter. I sometimes find myself crying for no other reason than I'm lonely.

Looking out at the lake, I silently let tears fall, oblivious to anything going on around me. Warm hands close around my shoulders. "Oh, June, What's the matter?" Mom cradles me close.

"It's nothing, just hormones I guess." I don't want her to know about the gaping hole in my chest that I'm ignoring.

"I can't imagine being pregnant without the father. Dad was so sensitive to my every need. He'd rub my back and my feet, and he never got mad when I blew up at him." I stifle a sob because she's right it's so hard. "Oh, honey, no. I didn't mean to upset you further. You're going to be just fine, and it's okay to get a little misty-eyed."

I hug Mom tight and do my best to reign in my emotions.

"How about we go have some sundaes? Ice cream always makes everything better."

"You're right on that one, Mom." I follow her into the house and wipe my tears. I attempt to grab bowls, but like everything else lately, I can't seem to do it. Lately it feels like everything is hard to do. I get tired often and the weekly trips to the doctor tell me that the baby is going to be big. My doctor is slightly worried because of my small frame, but she tells me I'm in good hands and that they will be prepared for anything.

On a Tuesday, one week before my due date, I wake with stabbing pains. I call out for my parents and they rush to the bedroom. My parents are frenzied because their house is a good thirty five minutes from the hospital.

"Everything's going to be fine," I try to reassure my Dad as he loads my overnight bag into the car. We're not even out of the driveway when I hear Mom calling Liz.

"Liz is on her way," Mom tells me like that is what was on my mind.

"Oh, God." The pain is so fierce I grip the handle on the door. I can't wait for us to get to the hospital.

"I'll start timing them," Mom rubs my back trying to calm me.

We make it to the hospital in record time. I'm assuming Dad broke all kinds of laws to get us here so quickly.

They settle me into a room, put a band around my belly to keep track of the baby's heart beat and monitor my contractions. They are at a steady four minutes apart for far too long. I'm exhausted. I wish I could say that I had some profound thoughts during labor, but really all I'm thinking about is that I hope everything's alright. I just want my baby to be healthy. I want to do a good job. I'm exhausted and have been in labor for at least twelve hours when Liz makes it here.

"I caught the first flight I could. How are you?"

"How the fuck do you think I am?" I shout as another contraction takes over.

"They wanted to hold off on an epidural until her labor has moved further along," Mom explains to Liz.

"Screw that! Everything I read said to get it as soon as possible. I don't care what they say, my girl needs an epi stat!" Liz says leaving the room in search of a doctor. It isn't much longer when the anesthesiologist comes by and has me bend forward so he can stick a needle in my back. The epidural medicine gives me chills that make me shake so hard my head hurts from the constant rattle of my teeth. Labor moves along, but the medicine finally kicks in relieving some of my pain. Liz takes turns with my parents being as supportive as she can.

The doctor checks my cervix and decides after a full twenty-four hours of contractions, it's finally time to push.

"I got you. You can do this!" Liz holds my hand tightly.

"I can't. Oh fuck, it hurts!" I scream. I've been pushing for so long I have no concept of time. Alarms sound and I panic.

"The baby is in distress. She's getting stuck. I don't want anything to happen to either of you. We have to do a C-section," Dr Anderson explains as she starts barking orders for the nursing staff to rush me to an emergency Cesarean Section. My heart plummets and I'm so afraid. My daughter is all I have left. Please, God, don't let anything happen to her. I pray over and over again that my baby will be alright.

An hour later and with much better drugs, Lily Marie Withers is born. She weighs a whopping ten pounds four ounces. My mom and dad both cry when they see her, "She's perfect," Mom says rushing into my room with a huge pink balloons.

"She looks just like you did when you were a baby," Dad coos holding her close. He tickles his beard on her face and she scrunches up her face like it tickles. "She's dark like you," he smiles in between soft baby kisses.

I know that can't be true, though, because everything about her, including her full head of dark hair and her perfectly shaped lips, reminds me of Jake. I can't help but let a few tears leak out of the corners of my eyes. I wish he could share this moment with us. I'm both exhausted and overwhelmed with emotion. Becoming a mom is a moment like no other. One moment you think you have a full life and that your heart understands love. I know that I love Jake, Liz, and my family, but the moment my eyes latched onto the sleepy, half-open eyes of my baby girl, my heart grew. I have so much love now. It's like there were sleeping parts of my heart that weren't fully awake until my eyes met hers.

Liz catches on to my tears and kisses my forehead and then whispers into my ear, "She's perfect, honey."

Mom, Dad, and Liz fuss over the baby and me. I'm tired the first few days and the three of them take turns helping me with Lily. One of them is right next to me, to grab her from her plastic hospital bassinet and hand her to me when she needs feedings. They help with changings and Liz even goes so far as to convince the nurses to let her help bathe her too.

On the third night in the hospital, I wake to find Liz in the darkened room sitting in the small rocking chair that each room has, patting Lily on her bottom and softly whispers to her, "Your mommy and I have no brothers and sisters, so I'm going to be Aunty Liz, okay? I work in a big city called New York and when you're older I'll take you shopping and teach you about boys. Your Mommy and I love you so much, but she has been missing your daddy for a long time, so it's up to me and you to bring smiles to her, okay? I bet you can handle that, can't you? Oh yes, you can," her voice changes as she coos in baby talk. A lump forms in my throat when I think about how long I've been holding on to the hurt. It's not up to Liz or my baby to make me happy. Somehow, I'm going to find a way to move on from Jake. Looking at Liz and my baby, I decide right at this moment that I will not let any of my heartache with Jake taint our beautiful daughter's life.

I'm in the hospital for five days. The recuperation for the C-section isn't fun, but I'm really grateful that Liz made me work out so much. I think being in such great shape has helped. None of that really matters though because Lily is the most perfect baby and she makes up for all of the pain.

LILY IS ONLY A MONTH old and is already wearing three-month clothes. She has the cutest baby fat I've ever seen. Her eyes are the same blue-green as her dad's and I'm sure that they're going to stay that color. I often find myself thinking of him when Lily is sleeping and I'm alone with my thoughts. It's the only time I'll allow my mind to go there. I sometimes get angry at him. He had the opportunity to talk to me. He could've filled me in on what was happening and who he was.

After talking with Liz, she helped me see that to let go of Jake completely I need to write one last letter. I take out my stationery and write the last words I will give to Jake Daniels.

Dear Jake,

I'm not sure if you will see this or if you will return it like you have all of the others. I've tried to tell you in so many letters that I was pregnant. I wanted to let you know you have a daughter. I named her Lily Marie. She was a huge baby, so big they had to cut her out of me. The scar is healing nicely, though. I don't even know what to say at this point. It's not like you've been responsive.

I'm so mad at you. We could have figured something out. We could have talked with the prosecutor together. We could have come clean all those years ago. It wasn't our fault. For a long time, I thought it was, but Liz has helped me see that it wasn't. Your dad was sick and he would've killed us both. I don't understand the choices you've made.

I'm a mom now and I need to do what's best. I need to let you go. You obviously don't love me the way I love you, or you would have responded to one letter.

I do want you to know Lily one day. She looks so much like you and when she's hungry she gets this dazed look. It's the cutest thing ever. Anyways, here is a picture of her.

I love you and always will. I guess when you said goodbye I should've listened to you. I get that it's done. I need to write this to say it to you, even though I'm sure it will come back to me.

Goodbye Jake

I'll always love you, June

I fold up the letter and include a recent picture of Lily. A single tear falls on to the page and I know I have to let that be the last tear Jake gets. I have to move forward; for Lily.

A month later, I check the mail, like I do every day and I see the same white envelope marked return to sender and nod my head, accepting the fact that Jake may never know he has a daughter.

CHAPTER TEN

6 years later

"Lily! Hurry up, or I'm going to be late," I shout up the stairs while slipping on a flat. I get no response from Lily so I slip on the other shoe and run up the stairs. Lily is sitting in the middle of her floor, half of her dresser is spilling out and she's wearing her favorite purple shirt with a huge green monster on it and her underwear. "Lily, why aren't you dressed? It's time to go."

"I can't find any bottoms to wear," she whines.

"What was wrong with the jean skirt you had on all day with that shirt?"

"It's not the look I'm going for." I roll my eyes at my daughter who gets her fashion sense from her Aunt Liz.

"The skirt looked great. I want you to put it back on. We need to leave."

"But Mom," I glare at Lily to let her know I don't appreciate her mini diva behavior Liz is only here for business today and has limited time.

"No buts. We're running late. If we don't hurry, Aunt Liz will be waiting for us at the restaurant." I begin shoving her clothes back into her drawers and grab the skirt off the floor that was good enough to wear all day so it's good enough to wear now. She sticks her hand out for me to hand her the skirt. I hand it to her and then take a minute and regard myself in her mirror. My hair looks good today. I just had it done and its long auburn waves look incredibly shiny. I no longer sport the semi-punk look or pixie cut I did in college. I'm wearing a flower print tunic with black skinny jeans and my favorite pair of flats. Seconds later, she is dressed and I hand Lily her favorite pair of pink high top Chuck Taylors that I fished from under her bed.

We race down the stairs and I grab my purse and keys off the entryway table and hurry into my black SUV. I didn't buy it new, but it's been a godsend in the winter and it's mostly reliable. Lily secures herself into her booster seat and we make the twenty-minute drive to one of the only restaurants in downtown that was smart enough to secure a place right on the Lake.

"Aunty Liz!" Lily shouts as she makes a sprint for Liz who is already seated by the window. Her phone is in hand as she looks up and smiles huge. Liz has only gotten more beautiful with time. Her blonde hair is pinned in a tight bun and she's wearing a navy blue suit dress with matching pumps.

"Lily!" She exclaims opening her arms wide for a hug. "I missed you so much, let me look at you," she says pulling away and giving a once over on Lily's outfit. "I love the purple monster shirt."

"I missed you soooo much more. Mommy says you have a meeting and it has to be a quick lunch today."

"I do, but I had to make sure I made time for my favorite girl."

I give Liz a huge grin and take a seat across from her. The waitress comes over and takes our order as Lily fills Liz in on all the kids in her class; who she sits with at lunch and which boys she likes to chase on the playground.

"Only six and she's already chasing boys," Liz laughs watching the iPad consume Lily's attention.

I roll my eyes. "So, how is everything? Are you dating?" I ask taking a sip of my iced tea. Liz is habitually single. She's only changed her habits because of her busy schedule. I wish she'd find someone, but every time I try to really talk to her about it she shuts me down.

"Ah, you know a little of this, a little of that," she sighs. "What about you? How did that date go with Alister last weekend?"

Alister is an investment banker that Liz set me up with. Last night was our third date, if you count the second date as the time we met up for coffee on our lunch breaks.

"It was," I pause and think about what I want to say next, "nice?"

"That man is hot is what he is," she sighs, "So what's wrong with this one?"

"Nothing. I promised I'd give him a chance, but I just don't feel that spark."

"June, you can't keep," she pauses to make sure Lily is completely engrossed in her game and paying zero attention to us, "comparing everyone to your first love."

I blanch, "That's not what I'm doing. He's hot alright, it's just he has these habits. Like when he orders, he orders for himself and then is all like oh, did you want something? He's hot, but it's like he knows it and so he expects everything to be easy for him. I want a man who will work for it."

"Honey, no offense," she whispers and then gets close to my ear to be sure Lily doesn't hear, "Maybe you should take the hot for what it is. How long has it been since you got laid?"

I roll my eyes because we both know it's been over a year, "Fair enough, Liz. I need to at least like him."

Lily looks up from the iPad, "Who are you guys talking about? Alice? Total noob. He was all, so you like Dora? I'm all like Dora was so three years ago," Lily scrunches up her nose in disgust.

I laugh at Lily's nickname for him.

"He met Lily?" Liz asks aghast.

"Not intentionally, believe me. I thought it was my coming to pick Lily up for their sleepover, but Alister was early and Mom was late."

"Oh God!" Liz says.

"I know. Then, my mom met him too."

"Oh."

"Yeah, oh." Liz knows my number one rules is that I don't introduce men to Lily unless it's serious and this thing with Alister is not serious. Sure, I let him kiss me, but that's about it.

Liz checks the time on her watch, "I hate to do this pumpkin, but Aunt Liz has to go."

Lily sets down the iPad and looks up at Liz with her big beautiful blue-green eyes, "Do you have to? Already?"

Liz, with a look that says I do, but I really wish I didn't, nods her head.

"But we just got here," Lily whines.

"I told you Lily, Aunt Liz only has a small amount of time today." I look at my daughter sympathetically.

Liz pays the bill because she never lets me pay and we hug goodbye.

I watch in my rear-view mirror making sure Lily buckles herself in her booster when my phone rings. I dig it out of my purse, spotting the tie dye case that Lily said I had to have and answer it smiling when I see it says Daryn. Daryn is Grace's dad, Lily's best friend.

"Hey, Daryn!" I answer with a smile.

"Hey, June. Grace has been at me all day and I need her to have company so I can get some work done around here. Can Lily come over? Save me?" he asks hopefully.

"I can take them, if you have a lot of work?"

"No, I just need to cut the grass and trim my hedges before Mr. Applegate calls the city because I can't keep my lawn neat. Besides, I promised Grace that if you said yes, I'd take the girls to see that new Pixar movie."

"Hang on. Let me ask if she's up for it," I look back at Lily smiling, "You want to go to Grace's?"

"Yes!" she squeals.

"That's affirmative. I'm just leaving downtown now. I can be there in twenty."

"You're a lifesaver, June," he says disconnecting.

I make the drive, thinking that if it wasn't for people like Daryn, Liz, or my parents that this whole single parent thing would've been a lot tougher. I lived with my parents for the first two years of Lily's life, until I saved and finally landed a great job with the newspaper. I know newspapers are not the most current form of in the know, but we print online as well as the good old fashioned black and white and I cover politics which, considering all of the scandals Cleveland has had, keeps me very busy.

I pull up in front of Daryn and Grace's bungalow-style house and Daryn is outside working on his hedges. It's warm out. Daryn is already sweating, based on the fact that his tight black undershirt tank top has dark spots. Daryn is an attractive man with his dark hair, tanned skin, and chiseled chest. We have a lot in common. He lost his wife four years ago to breast cancer and has been going at it alone the best he can. Maybe that's one of the reasons our girls have bonded so well.

Grace is doing cartwheels in the grass and runs up to the car as soon as Lily's car door opens.

"Hi, Lil!" Grace jumps up and down, her blonde curls bouncing as she does.

"Grace," Lily squeals just as excited, "I can't wait to tell you about this fashion game that my Aunt Liz had on her iPad."

The two girls run into the house with barely a backwards glance from Lily. I laugh and shake my head.

"No 'bye Mom or anything," I mumble and Daryn laughs. it shocks me a little. I give him a good hard look. I'm not sure I've seen him really laugh. He's always had this look of loss hiding beneath the surface. For the first time, it looks like it's gone. I flash him a huge grin.

"What?" he asks.

"Your laugh. It sounds good on you," I smile and get back into my car, "Call me when you want me to pick her up."

"I can drop her after the movie." The look on his face changes, like he forgot he wasn't supposed to be happy. I immediately regret bringing attention to it because somewhere deep in the buried recesses of my heart I remember how that feels.

I take advantage of my afternoon and clean my closet out, then when that's finished, I clean my hardwoods. It's nice for once not to have to work twice as hard keeping Lily off them while they dry. I take a call from Lily begging me to let her stay the night, so I talk with Daryn and give him the okay and let him know that I'll pick both girls up for soccer practice in the morning.

I pour a glass of white wine and slip into a steaming hot bubbling oasis, better known as my awesome bath that I never have time for. The water feels good. I feel good. I think about Daryn and that if I was going to seriously date someone it would be someone like him. He's an amazing dad and he's hot, okay more like drop dead sexy, but his pain is still so raw. If things were different, I would ask him out. I think about my date with Alister and decide that if he asks me out again, I'm going to politely decline. He isn't for me. I haven't had anything close to that spark I had with Jake, and I sure as shit don't have that with Alister.

I try not to think of Jake. It hurts too much. The slightest comparison to Alister has my chest feeling funny. Even if Daryn is ready, am I? Will I ever be? Jake never contacted me, not once. A year ago I looked him up on the State's inmate search only to find that he was released a year previous to that. He could have googled me, I come right up. My phone number is listed too, so it's not like I'd be hard to find.

I sink under the bubbles letting the hot water clear my thoughts. I promised myself long ago to not let him have more of my heart. He doesn't deserve it.

I finish the bath and wrap my over-sized, terrycloth robe around me then head to the kitchen to pour myself another glass of wine. I sit in the small window seat and look around. My floors look good. I'm proud of how they turned out. My house isn't the biggest, but I've worked hard to make my home nice. Mom and Dad splurged and bought me new over-sized off-white sofas for Christmas three years ago; they're perfect for having friends over. I swear every time Liz comes to visit we end up finding some brilliant piece of furniture for dirt cheap. She does corporate investments, but you would think she was an interior designer. With her keen eye for decorating and my obsession with Sensibly Chic on HGTV, the place has turned out to be my own personal paradise. I've worked hard to give Lily a perfect place to call home.

My cell rings in the living room. I set my glass of wine down, that I've barely touched and hurry to retrieve it. I smile when I see Liz's name flash, "My plane is delayed, please tell me you can get a sitter?" she asks like my answer holds a cure for world hunger.

"She's gone for the night. Staying at Grace's."

"She's the one with the hotty dad, right?" she asks.

I giggle, "Yep, Daryn,"

"You have to come meet me. I have four hours to kill and don't really want to do it sitting in an airport bar."

"Alright, I'll pick you up and maybe we can go to that Mexican restaurant you love."

"We have a few hours and you're kid-free. We're going downtown and not for Mexican as much as I love guac. Wear something cute and going out worthy. No exceptions," and with that she hangs up.

Not wanting Liz to spend more time in the airport than necessary, I race up the stairs and throw on a red blouse and black high-waisted shorts. To dress it up, I throw on my black strappy 3-inch sandals. I grab my make-up bag, deciding to fix my make-up at as many red lights as I can, and throw it into my over-sized purse and race out the door.

"Thank God, you're here. I just checked and this storm in New York has just added another two hours to my delay. We could drive there in the amount of time it's going to take to get a plane in the air," she bounces into the seat and looks over my outfit, gives me a smile of approval once she sees my hot, fuck me heels, as she would call them.

"I'm not driving to New York!" I look at her sternly making sure she knows that's off limits.

She guffaws at me, "As if I would ask you to take me to New York," she says on a smile.

"How did your meeting go?" I ask.

"It went really good. If things go as planned I'm going to make a shit-ton of money," she gleams.

"You already make a shit-ton of money."

"This is a completely different caliber."

"Well then, let's hope everything goes as planned."

"Amen!" she says dramatically.

I find a parking spot on the street, which is usually virtually unheard of. Feels like luck is on my side. Liz and I walk arm in arm like we used to in college. We turn down the street that's closed off to cars. Huge strands of lights hang over the street and crowds of people bar hop from one bar to the next. We walk the short street and stop at a high-end bar. It's dark inside, even though the sun is still shining bright outside. We take a seat at the bar and immediately a man sends a drink over to Liz and me.

She smiles at him and I shake my head. "Not even here for five seconds before the vultures start circling."

Liz and I laugh, and have a great time. A few guys come over to talk with us and the shameless flirting is fun. I limit myself to just the one drink since I'm driving and had a glass of wine earlier. Before I know it, hours have passed and I tell Liz we need to get her back.

"You don't have to drive me. It's the opposite direction. I'll grab an Uber ride since I know you have to get up early," she says.

"Okay, then walk with me to my car and we'll have Uber pick you up there."

We leave the restaurant, no doubt with a bar full of eyes following Liz's behind as we go and make the short walk to my car, only when we get to the spot where my car once sat it's gone.

"It was here, right?" I screech at Liz. I'm already panicking and look to Liz to confirm. "Yeah, honey it was."

"Oh, my God! I think my car was stolen."

"Shit," Liz hisses, "I think you're right."

"Freaking Cleveland, with your clean streets acting like it's safe for me to park my car. No, some asshole is always lurking around here to rip you off. I see it every day at work. I should've known better." I'm shouting at the street as I pull out my cell phone and dial 911.

"911. What's your emergency?" a shrill female voice on the other end asks.

"I'm at Euclid and E 12th St., and my car is gone!"

"Well, are you in a tow-away zone?" she asks.

"No, I'm not in a tow-away zone. Listen, I'm telling you I parked my car here and it's not here anymore. It's gone. Someone stole it!" I'm a bit hysterical, but someone stole my car!

"Okay, ma'am. An officer is on the way."

She takes down my name and contact information and I hang up with her. "Police are on their way. Fucking Shit! I can't believe this happened. What am I going to do?" I semi-yell at Liz.

"Oh honey, come here." She pulls me in for a hug.

"What am I going to do, Liz? I need my car."

"It's going to be alright. You have insurance, right?" she asks me soothingly.

I nod against her shoulder.

"So what we're going to do is; we're going to give the police a report. Hope they catch the fuckwad who took your car and then you're going to call your insurance. It's going to be okay," she soothes me until a squad car shows up.

Two police officers pull up, double parking and step out of their car. The officer who exits the driver side is a tall intimidating black man and the officer in the passenger seat is an average looking guy with blonde hair sticking out of the rim of his hat.

"June?" he questions like he knows me. I stare at the officer trying to figure out if I know him. "It's Ed. Ed Harrington. I sat behind you in English Lit at Cleveland State."

I think when I had English Lit, and remember that I was in the beginning stages of pregnancy. I was always running out to pee and, "You took notes for me when I was running to the bathroom every ten minutes!"

He chuckles, "That was me. Went a different route, though. So what happened here?"

"My car was stolen. It was parked right here," I say pointing to the spot a new car has since parked in.

The police officer who was driving is harder with his posture and gets right to business, "Ma'am, my name is Officer Reynolds. We've put out an APB on your vehicle which means the local police will be looking for it. Often times, your car will turn up in a day or two. I suggest you go home and we'll call you if we have any news."

Ed hands me his card and writes the case number on it. "Call me if you have any questions or if there is anything I can do for you," he seems sincere. "It was nice seeing you again June, even if was under these circumstances."

I shake my head at the ordeal as the police car drives away.

"I'm getting an Uber car for both of us," Liz tells me and a minute or two later a car pulls up to take me home. I hug Liz goodbye and she makes me promise to call her tomorrow or if I hear anything.

I call Daryn on my way home. It's almost eleven so I know it's late and he's probably asleep. "Hello," his voice sounds gruff and tired when he answers, "June?" he asks. "Is everything okay?"

"Hey, Daryn, sorry to call so late. I was out with Liz and we were downtown. My car was stolen."

"Shit, June. are you alright?" his sleepy voice laced with concern.

"No," I answer and then change that, "Yes. I'm fine. I feel a bit shook up that someone would steal from me, but physically I'm fine. We weren't even in a dodgy part of town. We went to East Fourth Street. That's like the "It" place. I can't understand how someone steals a car right where everything is going on."

"June, that's terrible. Where are you now?"

"I'm on my way home in an Uber."

"Shit. Is there anything I can do?"

"Can you take the girls to their game in the morning, while I call insurance and get a rental? I hate to ask because I know you've had them all day."

"Of course, I can. I can't believe this happened to you."

"Yeah, you and me both. How were they today?" I ask knowing those two can get chatty.

"I was glad to have Lily. You should see my yard. I finally think my home-owner's association won't have anything to gripe about."

I let out a light chuckle. I can't help it; he's funny when he's all sleepy. "Thanks, Daryn. Sorry for waking you," I sigh.

"No problem, June. Call me if you need anything." We disconnect and it's another ten minutes until the car pulls into my drive I lock up the house and quickly go to bed.

I wake up to my cell phone blaring. A quick glance to the clock tells me it's seven a.m.. I sleepily answer my phone wondering who the heck would be calling me at seven on a Sunday.

"Hello?" I answer.

"June, Ed Harrington. I didn't wake you, did I?"

I grumble and then lie, "No."

"Found your car. They caught a couple of seventeen-year-olds using it to run drugs. When they caught on that they we're being followed they crashed it up pretty good. Took off on foot, but our guys caught 'em."

Shit, fuckity, shit. "How bad is the damage?"

"It's not good. Listen June, normally we have cars involved in stuff like this taken to impound, but seeing as I know you and I don't want you to have to go through more hurdles than you need to, I'm having them tow it to a buddy of mine's shop. It's on 55th and Euclid. Same side of the street as the Agora. You can't miss it."

I grab a pen and paper and jot down the name of the shop. "Thanks for helping me out Ed. I really appreciate it. Are they open on Sundays?"

"Technically, they're not open today, but my buddy said him and a couple of the guys came in to work on this hot-rod."

"You think I could stop there today to see the damage and get a few things out of the trunk?"

"Sure, I don't see why not."

"Alright, thanks again for your help Ed."

I disconnect and head downstairs to start a pot of coffee; I think I'm going to need it.

BY ELEVEN, I AM PULLING up in front of a large garage with two identical tow trucks that say Stout's and a phone number. This is the place. I rub my temples. After several hours of phone calls with insurance agents and then my parents, my head is killing me. My rental was delivered an hour ago and here I am.

I swing my purse high on my shoulder and walk through a large gray metal door, even though there's a closed sign in the window. The air smells like oil and gasoline. There is a reception desk that is empty and a small vinyl couch with outdated magazines covering a small coffee table.

"Hello," I call out.

"Sorry lady, we're closed," A man with a salt and pepper beard and a backward baseball cap says sticking his head in through an open door to the garage bays.

"Oh, I know," I'm suddenly nervous. "My car was stolen last night and Ed Harrington had it towed here for me. I was hoping I could see the damage and grab a few things from the trunk."

"Ed's friend, right?" he says looking me up and down, smiling. I wouldn't go so far as to say Ed and I were friends, but if they're helping me out more because they think that, who am I to argue? "Name's Stout. This is my place. Car's back here. Did you bring the keys?" he asks.

I reach into my purse and pull the key off of the ring and hand it to him.

"Lead mechanic is looking at it now, but he won't get a full idea of the damage until tomorrow. You can get a look and grab whatever you need from it now if you want."

"Thanks," I say and follow him through the open door into the bay.

Several men are working on a red car that looks like it would be in Fast and Furious. I walk over to my car and my heart sinks. As I approach, I can already see the glass is shattered in the back window. I walk around the driver's side, and despite a long scratch in the black paint, it doesn't look that bad. I round the front, where the bent hood is propped open and a man is bent over it, his eyes staring down. My front windshield is also cracked as well as a huge indent on the front passenger side. "Shit," I hiss taking it all in. The mechanic under the hood freezes and very slowly raises his head towards me. He stands. I take him in, as the air leaves my lungs in a huge whoosh.

He's tall.

Taller.

Tattoos cover his arms. Broad shoulders. Muscular like he frequents a gym. His hair is trimmed short close to his head.

His eyes.

Piercing.

Blue-green.

Watching me.

Just like my daughter's.

Just like his daughter's.

CHAPTER ELEVEN

I remember a moment like this. One where it felt like the entire universe paused and shifted right under my feet. A moment where a truth changed everything. At this moment, I am altered.

Jake Daniels is standing in front of me.

"No, I can't believe it," I say with a fierceness I didn't know I was capable of.

"Listen, I know there's some damage, but don't worry we'll get it fixed," Stout says in an easy going voice.

My body is locked tight ignoring Stout, my eyes are locked hard on Jake.

"Juniper," Jake's voice is soft as he sets down the wrench in his hand and takes a careful step towards me. Careful like he is afraid I'll bolt, like he sees something in my eyes that he isn't quite sure of. It's an emotion he has never seen before on me; straight incomprehensible fury.

"Don't you dare 'Juniper' me. You lost that right you son of a bitch!" I hiss and watch Jake freeze him in his step. "You Goddamn motherfucking..." I don't finish. The anger I feel towards him overwhelms me. I lunge for him and smack him as hard as I can. He's taller than me by a lot and I have to reach to hit him. I claw and scratch. Kick and punch. I'm so angry.

"Twenty-five minutes from us. You're twenty-five minutes." I'm hysterical.

Jake lets me get hits in on him, then says, "Enough." His voice is darker and deeper than I remember. He scoops me up and throws me over his shoulder as if I weigh nothing.

"Boss, need a few," he says like I'm not pounding on his back and screaming.

"Put me down, Jake Daniels!"

"Feisty one huh, Jake," Stout chuckles then says, "take all the time you need."

Jake walks us up a set of metal stairs and through a door. My world is flipped upside down when he rights me and deposits me on the edge of a desk, then wraps his arms tightly around me, including my arms so that I can't move.

"Calm down, June," he says.

I breathe in and out, deep breaths, trying to calm myself. I won't look at Jake. I can't. I'm afraid that if I do, I'll get drawn right back into him. My eyes are trained on a certification award on the wall behind the desk. My body is rigid. I try not to think about the fact that I am in Jake's arms and his beautiful masculine scent is surrounding me. Instead, I focus on my behavior and try to get it under control. I've thought about how I would be if I saw him again, but no way did those thoughts include me going batshit crazy.

I focus on my anger. He pretended to be someone he wasn't. He left us, without an explanation and broke my heart. He has a daughter that he doesn't even know about because he wouldn't read any letters and now he's out of jail working relatively close to us and he hasn't even tried to look me up.

Oh, God. Lily. What am I going to do? How can I let him know about her now? He could leave her feeling the way I do. Get her to fall in love with him and then disappear. Is that fair to her? Could she forgive me if she knew? I suck in a lungful of air and demand, "Let me go."

"You going to hit me again, if I release you?"

I glare at him and my breath catches in my throat seeing as I'm eye to eye with him again. I don't want to look, but I can't help it. "I won't hit you. Let me go," I demand.

He releases my arms but doesn't retreat, "Someone stole your car. What kind of shit are you in, June?" he asks directly with little emotion in his voice.

I glare even harder at him.

"Answer me, June," he growls. Although this is a beefier version of the Jake I knew, something about his tone makes me question that I know him at all. He's harder, prison must have made him that way. For a second, my anger resolves, thinking about him behind bars for four years.

"That's the first real thing you're going to ask me? No 'hey June'? How have you been? Or 'Hey, I've been trying to find you'? Or even better, 'I lied because...'?'No, you think I'm in some shit? I was out with Liz last night on East Fourth Street and my car was stolen. That's it. They found it and the cop knew me, so he called in a favor and had it brought here. Now, nice seeing you Jake," I say with a sneer, "but I think it's time we end this reunion."

"No," he says sternly.

"What does that mean 'no'?"

"It means," he grits out, "I've stayed away from you for your own good for a long time, and now you walk in here and your car has been stolen and you attack me? It's been a long time since I let anyone get a hit on me and to have a blow come from you, June, what the fuck?"

I suddenly, feel bad for hitting him. He got enough of that from his dad. How could I be that person? How can I put my hands on the man whose had my heart since I was a girl? My guilt takes over for my anger and all I want to do is retreat and figure out how I feel. This isn't me. This isn't the woman I want to be. I hate that I just hit him.

"It was a shock seeing you. I shouldn't have hit you." It's not an apology, however my eyes hold nothing but remorse.

"No, you shouldn't have," he says breathing hard. "You got insurance on your car?"

I nod my head and feel my body relax, even though my heart's still beating wildly. My head is a whirlwind. I feel my anger recede and replaced by confusion. I stare hard at him and then my chin quivers and my eyes flood with tears. I don't want them to spill out. I hate that I still carry this pain inside of me.

"Good. You're a priority. I'll get your car fixed right away."

Is that it? Is he just going to fix my car and walk away again? God, this hurts. My chest feels tight and those tears seep out of the corner of my eyes. I don't think I meant anything to him. How can he be so casual? It burns deeply in my soul.

"Shit, baby. Don't cry for me. I don't get your tears. I'm going to fix your car. When I get off work tonight we'll talk. Yeah?

He wants to talk about car repairs? My world is falling apart and being flipped on its axis and that's where we are? "I'll cry for me, then." I look away, wanting to curl up and pretend the last twenty-four hours hadn't brought me here.

He grips my chin between his fingers and redirects my eyes to his and wraps his arms around me again; this time in comfort, not to restrain me. He must feel bad for me. This has to be sympathy for the poor, broken woman in front of him. I want to harbor my anger so badly. At least anger is something I can grasp. This helplessness with him in front of me is more than I can handle.

I know I should fight against his embrace. I should push him away, but the way he has always provided me with comfort comes so naturally that my body betrays me by curling into him. The soft fabric of his shirt and the smell of oil and sweat surround me.

I let a few more tears leak out and whisper, "Why?" I hate the sound of it coming out of my lips. I hate that I sound desperate and needy, but I'm angry because he left me for six long years with no answers.

He sucks in a breath and says, "Meet me tonight?" Lily's been gone for the last day and I'm not so sure I can get a sitter. He must sense see the conflict on my face. "I know you don't owe me your time, but let me explain things to you. I owe you that. I can come to you. Meet you at your house?"

"No, that's not going to work for me."

"You got a man at home?" he questions.

"I don't owe you that either." I push away from his embrace, stand up and walk towards the door. "I have to get out of here. This is too much."

"I get seeing me again is a shock. I'll give you a day to get used to the idea and then we're talking," he says as I walk out of the office. I begin to descend the metal stairs when I hear, "June?"

I look back to see what he has to say.

"Don't hate me" It's a plea, one he doesn't have to make. I'm angrier than ever, but I could never hate Jake Daniels.

CHAPTER TWELVE

"Liz, I swear to God. You better call me back the second you get this." I leave the second message in fifteen minutes on Liz's voicemail. Daryn is dropping Lily off in fifteen minutes and I was hoping to get my head on straight before she got home. I need advice and I need it pronto.

I don't hear from Liz and before I know it, my door is thrown open and a hyper Lily bounces in.

"Hey, Mom! Whose car is that in the driveway?" she asks.

"Hi, I didn't say anything to her," Daryn says from the doorway.

"Say anything to me about what?" Lily asks.

"Oh, I had some car troubles and this one is a rental." That seems to placate her and she runs off.

"I left Grace in the car. Did you get everything taken care of?" Daryn asks.

"I did, thanks again."

"Don't mean to pry, but are you okay? It looks like you've been crying." Drats. If Daryn can pick up on that, then so can Lily.

"Yeah, I'm totally fine," I lie. "Thanks again."

Daryn gives me a smile that says he doesn't believe me, but that he respects my space and waves goodbye. "Okay, call me if you need anything, June."

I fix myself up in the bathroom mirror while Lily plays in her room and start an early dinner, trying to keep my mind off of Jake.

After an hour and a half of watching Sofia the First and the two of us curled up on the couch with bellies full of beef stroganoff, my phone finally rings.

Liz's name flashes across the screen, "Finally," I answer.

"Is everything okay? Is it Lily?" she asks.

"Hold on," I say looking at Lily who is so engrossed in the TV, she doesn't pay much mind to me getting up. I walk in the kitchen and pour a glass of white wine and walk out my backdoor to sit in one of the large, over-sized patio chairs.

"No everything isn't okay," I tell Liz.

"Why what happened? Lily?"

"Lily is fine. You'll never guess who I saw today,"

"Who?" she asks concerned.

"I went to this shop that my car was towed to, and Jake was under the hood of my car."

"Jake? As in Jake?" she asks and I can hear the panic in her voice.

"Yes, as in Jake," I whisper even though Lily is in the house.

"Oh, my God. What happened?" she asks.

"I freaked; I went nutso. I started hitting him and screaming at him, and then he threw me over his shoulder brought me in the other room until I calmed down and then basically said he wants to talk and that he'll give me until tomorrow. I don't know what got into me. I can't believe I hit him. I can't believe he's been here. I'm a wreck, Liz."

"Holy shit," she says releasing a breath.

"Yeah, holy shit. What am I going to do?"

We talk for over an hour, going over what he said to me and if I want to tell him about Lily. I know I should, but I want to protect her. Liz thinks I should do it right away, but I feel more cautious like I need to hear his story first and then decide. We finish debating how I should handle this with a final plea from Liz, "June, it's been a long time and I know you've never truly gotten over him. Hear him out, if no other reason than to give yourself some peace. You deserve that."

I chew on that all night until I finally fall asleep. I wake up and get Lily ready for school, drop her off and call off work. I tell them that my car was stolen and that I need the day off. My boss is completely understanding and we discuss doing a piece on car theft in Cleveland. I pace around my house, cleaning things twice, then three times. I'm antsy and I can't help it. At ten o'clock my phone rings and I don't hesitate answering it.

"June," Jake's voice washes over me from the other end of the phone line.

I didn't give him my number so I'm surprised to hear my name roll from his lips. I'm also surprised to find I'm not holding on to the same hostility. I guess Liz's talk really helped. "How did you get my number?" I ask.

"The police department gave us all of your contact info."

Well, I guess that makes sense. I pause waiting to hear what he has to say, "I need to meet you, June."

"I took the day off. Can we meet during the day?" I ask.

"What time were you thinking?" he asks.

"The earlier the better. Can you get out of work?" I ask pacing my living room, anxious to finally get some answers.

"How's one?"

"That can work. Meet me at the Lake?"

"Hmm, that's closer to me, I can do twelve-thirty then," he says and I get a ball of butterflies in my stomach as butterflies swirl around in my stomach. This sounds so much like the Jake I remember.

"Sounds good," I say and pause not sure what to say next.

"Okay, see you then," he says and disconnects, letting me off of the hook for my loss of words.

I struggle with what to wear and ultimately decide on jean shorts and a t-shirt. I don't want him to think I'm dressing up for him, even though I can't help but spend an extra ten minutes on my make-up. I text Liz and let her know that I'm meeting him and promise to fill her in on all of the details as soon as it's done.

I make it to the Lake before Jake. I do this on purpose, hoping my nerves will calm down by the time he gets here.

There's no wind today. Everything feels still. Even the Lake is flat today. They call it glass because it's so calm you can actually see perfect reflections. The only ripples in the water come from the occasional boat passing through, but even then, the break walls stop most of the momentum. I stand on the small bridge, the freshly stained wood sticks to the bottom of my shoes. As I watch where the river and lake meet, I notice the tremble in my hands. I try to calm myself and focus on the water. I take in the scent of fresh water and fish filling the air.

There's no current today, at least if there is I can't see it. I wonder how our lives would have turned out if there had been no current all of those years ago and if Mike Daniels had never gotten swept away.

I see him pull up in a newer black truck. When he steps out my breath hitches. He looks like the Jake from my past, but he's different too. He's even more beautiful than the Jake I remember. He's filled out so much and I imagine him working out in a prison yard. I hate that thought. He looks around seeking me out and once he spots me his walk is quick.

"June," he greets me. I war between wanting to hit him and wanting to run to his arms, so instead I stay put and wait for his lead.

"You remember this place, huh?" he asks.

"I remember everything, Jake. Or shall I call you Lucas?" I sneer.

"Jake's just fine, June. Walk with me. I'll do my best to explain."

My feet are frozen in place and I suddenly feel like this is a bad idea. After all this time, does it even matter what his explanation is? What if whatever he is going to tell me hurts more; or even worse than that, what if I want to forgive him? I'm not sure I'm ready to forgive Jake Daniels, but on the flip side I owe this to Lily.

Sensing my hesitation Jake takes a tentative step back, "Please?" he asks.

I nod and walk towards the beach. It's empty. I figured it would be since school started last month.

I take my flip flops off and leave them in the sand feeling the warm grains beneath my toes.

"Alright," he lets out a deep breath cutting straight to the chase, "You remember that day on the boat?"

"Of course I do," I remember everything about that night. I stop giving him attitude. It's not going to get us anywhere and now that he started talking I really want to hear what he has to say.

"Well, when I got home after dropping you off at your parent's summer house, a man by the name of Eli Doyle was waiting for me. He saw everything that happened on the boat. My dad owed this guy a lot of money from the tables, so he was pissed. He told me he would hunt you down and he would make me suffer watching what he planned on doing to you if I didn't start working for him. I'd heard of this guy, June and he was no good; worse than my dad ever was. So, at first it was easy stuff, I'd pick up money for him when he told me to and then it turned into bigger things, like taking a bat to someone when they didn't pay. It got bad. I hated doing the shit he made me do. The only good thing at that time of my life was Mrs. Jones, one of the librarians. She noticed that I was always taking out books on music, so she offered to teach me some things. I took to it like a natural. I swear if I didn't have that, I'm not sure what I would have done. I hated my life, and June I gotta tell you, there were times I felt like ending it."

I suck in a deep breath. I can't imagine Jake beating people for money and I can't imagine him being so low that he'd want to kill himself. My mind is going a million different directions. "Jake," I say softly tilting my head towards him feeling compassion above all other feelings.

"I never went through with it, obviously. Like I said, Mrs. Jones was there. Anyways, this went on for a few years. There was this one night where Eli showed up. At this point, I was living in a small one-bedroom apartment he rented out to me. He took ownership of my dad's farm. Guess my dad bet him and already gave him the deed. So, Eli handed me a gun one night and wanted me to kill Jim Anston for not paying up. Only, I grew up with Jim. We weren't best friends or anything, but he wasn't a dick. I couldn't do it. I packed my bags and took off, just praying that after enough time I could find you and that he would forget about me. God, I was stupid to think I could out run that fucker.

"I hitchhiked and made it as far as Virginia when I completely ran out of money. I met a guy. He gave me a job at his shop working on cars. Guess all the years working on farm equipment paid off because I was a natural. I saved up some money and got a car. Even got my keyboard for a steal. Once, I had enough money saved, I made my way up to Cleveland. I found a job, a place to stay. Met the guys in the band and life seemed good."

"You know that night wasn't the first night I saw you."

"No?" I ask confused and completely entranced by the story. I realize I'm softening towards him and I'm not sure how I feel about that.

"No, it wasn't. The first time I saw you was at the Art Museum. You were sitting by the fountain. Your head was thrown back in a laugh at a few squirrels chasing each other around the fountain. I couldn't believe it was you. You looked so beautiful and so happy. I'd go there almost every day in hopes that I'd see you. I stumbled across your name in The Scene and I read everything you wrote. Still do.

"I don't know what I was waiting for. I guess I was afraid that once I said hi to you that it might change your happiness. I was already going by Lucas, in case Eli was looking for me. I felt like if anyone knew my real name, it would put you in danger. Then, when you didn't know me at the bar, I told you my name was Lucas. I liked that guy. He never beat anyone for money. Never had anyone calling him a loser his whole life, and certainly didn't have someone threatening to kill his girlfriend. It felt good being with you, but after a while I knew it was wrong. The guilt was eating away at me. One day, Dietz has this guy show up looking for me, only Dietz was confused because he asked for Jake. Dietz said he didn't know a Jake and then the guy said maybe I got the name wrong and the guy shows Dietz my picture. Dietz got weird vibes and didn't tell him anything, but once he told me what happened, I was paranoid. I wanted to hold on to everything with you. That time together with me as Lucas felt like a gift and I didn't want to waste a second of it.

"So the day before our last day together, Eli finds me in the parking lot outside of the shop. He laid it out for me. Said he had some deal set up inside the penitentiary here and he wanted me to run numbers for him like old times. I told him to go to hell and he said I was already there because he told the police that he saw me throw my dad overboard. He told me he had friends on the payroll, and I knew this was true from when I was working for him. Hell, half of the force down there paid me on the regular. He said there was an APB out for my arrest and that he told them where to find me. They didn't even have a body, and they wanted me all because Eli said so. Eli said, I was to take the plea deal they were going to offer and he would leave you out of it. Said if I didn't do it, his friends would set it up so that you took the hit instead of me. Said they would make sure you didn't get a deal. The entire thing was a set up because he needed a guy on the inside.

"He promised he'd leave you out of it, but anytime I gave him slack about doing what he wanted he'd tell me how he had eyes on you. You'd think being in prison is straightforward. You serve your time and keep your head down then get out, but I'm telling you, Eli had me doing shit in there; and then there was this other player that I had to watch out for. He hated Eli and knew what I was doing. So one day, he had a bunch of skins hold me down, sliced me up good. I was in the infirmary for a month. I got out of the infirmary and focused on getting bigger. I wasn't going to take anymore from them or anyone else in there. The guys came at me again, and I did shit, June. Bad shit, but I survived.

"Strange thing, I was in my third year, and I stopped hearing from Eli. The guys on the inside who needed to place bets were getting antsy and the guys Eli needed to collect from stayed very clear of me, thinking I was going to beat them. I kept thinking I would hear something, then one day I did. Turns out he was in for murder down south. They had him in some maximum prison. He wasn't even in six months before his ass got shanked, and then just like that it was over. I finished doing my time and got out. Was lucky enough Stout didn't mind hiring felons."

My cheeks are wet and I don't even realize that I'm crying silently until he finishes his story. My heart wants to soften towards him, but I'm still unsure how I feel. I stop walking and face the Lake. The water has a chill to it. I reach down, grab a rock and skip it along the flat water. One skip, two, three, then four. I close my eyes and let his story wash through me. He was trying to protect me, but he lied. He could have told me. We could have run.

I ache from hearing everything he went through, but that doesn't explain where he's been, "So, that was two years ago. Why didn't you look me up? Or better yet Jake, why couldn't you open one of the forty-seven letters I sent you? During the time you were Lucas, why couldn't you have told me the truth?"

"I played you that song, and you knew. I was going to tell you everything that night. I couldn't take it anymore, but then the police came. I was going away. My fate was sealed. I didn't want to taint you with my dark any more than I already had. You deserved happiness. Then when I got out, what could I offer you? I'm a felon who's done some seriously fucked up shit. You don't think I wanted to? It wasn't right, though."

"That's such bullshit." The words leave my lips, but hold more disbelief than anger, "I deserved answers. I deserved to decide for myself what wasn't right. I would've left with you. I would've done anything for you. I would've waited."

"I know you would've, and I didn't want that for you. A life running; always looking over your shoulder. That's not what I wanted."

"And what about what I wanted?" I say feeling the burn in the back of my throat.

He doesn't have an answer for me. I watch as he leans down, finds a stone in the sand and throws it against the water. It skips, once, twice, three times all the way to six leaving ripples in its wake.

"You were always better at that than me," I tell him.

He squeezes my shoulder and I want to move away from his touch, but I'm frozen in place. The sand squishing around my feet is the only thing that grounds me.

I turn my head and see a fake half smile on Jake's face. His eyes shine in the sunlight, the green flakes practically glow. Just like Lily.

"Jake, there's something you should know," I begin to say and at the same time he says, "Shit," looking at his watch and then "I have to get back to work."

Now isn't the time for me to tell him about Lily. I'll talk with Liz tonight and decide what to do.

We turn and head back towards the bridge. I slip on my flip flops and stop when Jake grabs my hand on the bridge. His hands are callused. They feel the same, but different. "It was clear to me yesterday how much pain I left you with. Need you to know I'm sorry," and then he drops my hand and walks away.

CHAPTER THIRTEEN

"So, do you think that was it? His way of explaining things to me and saying goodbye?" I ask Liz.

"It doesn't really matter, does it?" she asks.

"No, it doesn't. I have to tell him about Lily. I decided to talk to Lily first."

"When do you think you'll do that?"

"Tonight after Daryn picks up Grace," I sigh.

"I think that's a good idea. Hey, listen my two o'clock is here. I have to go. Call me if you need anything, or if anything else happens."

"Alright. Love you, girl," I say hanging up the phone.

I busy myself for the next hour, then make the five-minute drive to the school. I got lucky with my job. They let me out by two-thirty every day so I can get Lily and Grace from school. In exchange, I work half a day for two Saturdays a month. Daryn or my parents take Lily on the Saturdays that I have to work.

"Hey, girls!" I call out as I pull up in front of the designated pick up and drop off zone.

"Hi, Mom!" Lily says kissing me on the cheek and sitting in the booster seat.

"Hi, June!" Grace says excitedly.

"How was school, girls?" I ask while looking in my rearview mirror to make sure that both girls are buckled in.

"We had an assembly today, and these people came with yo-yo's and did tricks. I want a yo-yo, Mom. Can I have one? Please?"

"Oh, me too, me too," Grace adds.

"Fine, I'll pick you girls up some yo-yo's next time I stop at Target."

"No, mom they can't be any yo-yo's. They have to be Ed's yo-yo's. They move on their own. I have a paper in my bag for you to read. They're just eight dollars. Can I have one, Mom?"

"I don't know, honey, Eight dollars is a lot for a yo-yo."

"That's the cheap one. They have a silver deluxe yo-yo that's twenty-two," Grace informs me.

I shake my head. Twenty-two dollars for a yo-yo seems crazy. "I'll think about it, girls." I get moans from the back seat and I shoot Lily a look that says don't whine.

We pull into the driveway and the girls barrel out of the car and immediately grab a bucket of sidewalk chalk that is against the side of the house. "I think I can draw Mickey Mouse," Grace says. I smile at the girls, grab their backpacks and unlock the front door. Once inside, I make the girls a snack and set it aside so when they come in it's ready for them. I spend the next hour going through work emails, and trying to make sense of things since I missed work today.

By five-thirty, Daryn picks up Grace and Lily and I sit down for supper. I made homemade macaroni and cheese, and grilled chicken. The mac is her favorite; the chicken, not so much.

"Mom, I love your mac n' cheese. It's so cheesy," Lily smiles at me and digs in, barely touching her chicken.

"I need to talk with you about something.

Lily looks up at me, between bites, taken aback by the seriousness of my tone.

"It's about your father.

She takes a drink of her milk and then looks at me with big eyes, "My dad? We never talk about him. I didn't think I had one."

Gosh, that hurts.

"You know how when we talked about where babies came from and I explained that when two people love each other, if they love each other a whole bunch their love can make a baby?"

She nods, wanting me to continue.

"Well, I know I never talk about your daddy, but we loved each other so much that you were born. Only your daddy had to leave before he ever got a chance to find out about you."

"I know this part already, but Mom, are you finally going to tell me where he went?"

"Yeah, honey, some people said your daddy did something bad and he got in trouble for it, but I can promise you with everything I am that I know for a fact your daddy was innocent."

"Did something happen to him? Is that why you're telling me?"

"No, honey, I'm telling you because I saw him recently and I'm going to tell him about you. I wanted you to be prepared; and if you have any questions, I wanted you to be able to ask me."

"I'm going to meet my daddy?" she cries excitedly.

"Yeah my Lilypad, you are; but like I said he doesn't know about you, so it might come as a shock to him."

"What's he like? What's he look like? Will he like me? What if he doesn't want me?"

"Of course, he'll love you and if he doesn't want to be a part of your life then that would be his loss. You are the best thing in the world, and he would be lucky to know you."

She thinks on this for a few moments and I'm second guessing my choice to tell her before him. What if he doesn't want her? What if…

"But what if?" she asks mirroring my thoughts.

I cut her off knowing I can't let Lily go there. "I'll talk to him very soon, but if for some reason he doesn't want to be a daddy, that in no way reflects on you. You are so special. You look like him. Did I ever tell you that? All those green flecks in your eyes come from him."

"They do?"

"Yeah honey, and your brown hair too."

"Really?"

"Yeah baby. I don't want you to worry about a thing. Everything's going to be okay," I tell her, willing myself to believe it.

I RETURN TO WORK AND find myself busier than ever. A day off in the news will do that to you. Things are always happening, and we're always on our A game. It's nearly noon and I feel like I've hardly left my desk, when Wendy Reynolds one of our chief investigator's makes her way to my desk, I barely notice her. I'm too immersed in research.

"So, I heard about your car," she says startling me by sitting down on the edge of my desk.

"Yeah, it happened right in the heart of downtown, can you believe it? My friend and I were having a drink on East Fourth Street, and I came out and it was gone."

"That's crazy," she says grabbing one of my pens and clicking it a few times. I want to grit my teeth because Wendy is all kinds of annoying, but I need to play nice, even when she drives me crazy.

"I was thinking we should do a story about it. Can you find out how many car thefts there have been in Cleveland this year? We might be able to write a cool piece about needing more police presence and how one of our own was a victim. Would you be up for it?" she asks.

"Of course. Sounds great," I smile brightly even though I am inwardly cringing. My workload is overflowing from taking the day off.

I work through lunch, eating a granola bar I threw in my purse last week before one of Lily's games. The day flies by and before I know it I'm walking into the parking garage. I plug in my phone and see that I have a missed call and voicemail. My heart beats fast as I listen to the message. I'm anxious. I want it to be him. I don't want it to be him.

"Hi, Ms. Withers. This is Stouty. We took a look at your car and your claims adjuster from the insurance company was just here. It looks like it's going to be a few weeks, but your insurance is going to cover everything. Please give us a call if you have any questions."

I release a breath I didn't know I was holding. It wasn't him. My phone rings with another unidentified number and I answer it again in hopes that it's him.

I sync the car's Bluetooth and answer the call. "Hello," I greet.

"Hi, is this June?" a man's voice asks and I'm certain that it's not Jake's. Again I feel let down for a second

"Yes, who's this?"

"Hey, June. It's Ed."

"Hi, Ed. Are you calling about my case?"

"No, um actually, I was wondering if maybe you wanted to go out sometime?"

Well, this is unexpected.

"Thanks, Ed. You're a really nice guy,"

"But, you're seeing someone, aren't you?"

"No that's not it, but my life just got a little complicated, and I'm not really sure I want to add anything else to it right now."

"That's fair, but I gotta tell you June, I always regretted not asking you out. So I might not give up that easy."

I laugh and I don't mean to, it just comes out. "You do know I was pregnant all those years ago, right?"

"You were?"

"Yeah, why do you think I had to pee all the time?"

"Small bladder?"

I laugh again and then say, "Well thanks for the offer, Ed." We disconnect and I'm flattered, but right now is not the time at all for me to date someone new. I head home and field more questions from Lily about her dad and by the time we fall asleep I think Lily has asked me all of the questions she possibly can.

On Wednesday, I'm equally as busy at work. I've worked through lunch again discovering that car thefts, in general, are on the rise in the city, but are on the decline in the outskirts. We have come up with a map and have found hot spots. I actually called Ed and have been able to get some very good insight from him.

It's just after one when my cell phone rings with another unknown number. I answer this time not even thinking about who it is.

"Hello," I say walking into the break room where it tends to be quieter than my cubicle.

"June," his voice washes over me, "I want to talk. What time are you done working?" Jake asks, not bothering with hello.

"Hi to you too," I reply, my heart beating faster than normal with the sound of his voice.

"June," he says scolding me for not answering his question.

"Fine, I'm usually home by three-thirty."

"Alright, I'll talk to you then," he says and disconnects. Shit, why did he sound so abrupt?

I leave work and pick the girls up. Lily and Grace are their normal chatty selves as we round the corner to our house. They laugh and giggle about something that happened in gym class. They're infectious with their good mood and even I have to smile as Grace re-enacts Mrs. Montgomery's chasing around Ryan Dermount. That boy is fast.

What I see as I pull in front of the house has my gut twisting. Parked in front is the unmistakable black truck belonging to Jake. Shit. He said talk, not what time would I be home. One look at Lily and he'll know before I say anything that she is his.

"Girls, I need to talk to someone. I'm going to pull into the garage and I want you to stay in the house.

"Is it him?" Lily asks.

"Baby, stay in the house." I avoid her scowl. I know she's anxious.

I don't look at Jake. Instead, I hit the garage switch, pull my car in, which I never do, and unlock the door to the house, all while praying that the tint on the rental is enough to hide the girls. I dig out my phone and call Daryn asking him to get the girls. He's concerned and I quickly tell him I have a minor crisis and I'll explain later. He grumbles a bit and tells me that he can be here in fifteen.

I turn on some cartoons for the girls and walk outside to Jake's idling truck. He turns it off and gets out. His larger than life frame is still new and slightly intimidating to me. He smiles and motions to the house, "Can we go inside to talk?" he asks.

I shake my head no, "Jake, I thought you were going to call me. You really shouldn't have just shown up here. We do need to talk, but not here."

"Is it because you got a kid?" he asks throwing me for a complete loop. I don't know what to say to him. My look of 'how the hell did you know that' prompts him to explain.

"I saw some soccer balls in the back of your SUV. Plus the sidewalk chalk all over your driveway is a pretty big clue."

My heart feels heavy in my chest and I feel a swell of panic. My hands visibly shake and I try to clasp them together so that Jake won't notice. I don't even know why I'm panicking. It's not like I did anything wrong.

"June?" Jake's voice is laced with concern for me. I put my hand up to tell him I'm okay when I hear another car approach and and car door open and close.

"Who are you?" Daryn asks as he approaches. His tall stature matches Jake's. Next to these brooding males, I feel small.

I meet Daryn's concerned gaze. "It's okay, Daryn. He's a friend."

"Who are you?" Jake asks mirroring Daryn, his body is locked like he's ready for anything. I'm still shaken, but know that I need to defuse the situation.

"Hey Daryn, can I talk to you for a second?" I lead him towards the house and leave Jake without giving him an explanation. Jake showed up here unannounced, so I really don't think I need to give him one.

"Once I'm out of earshot from Jake, I pull Daryn to the side. "What's going on, June?" Daryn asks.

"That's Lily's dad," I whisper, "and I just became reacquainted with him. When I found out I was pregnant with Lily, I tried to contact him. I sent him letters and he never responded. I have to tell him about Lily and I don't want her here when I do. I don't know how he's going to react."

"Holy shit," Darryn runs his hand through his hair and a look of disbelief flashes across his face.

"Yeah, I'm sorry to call you here in such a rush, but do you think I can go for a ride with him and you can get the girls out of here? I just need to make sure that this doesn't fall back on Lily in a bad way."

"Do you think this guy will hurt either of you? 'Cause I gotta tell you, I'm really not comfortable with this, June." His eyes dart from me to Jake.

"I've known him since I was fifteen. It will be okay." I want to ease Daryn's fears.

"Then, where the hell has he been all these years?"

I look over my shoulder at Jake nervously, "Can I explain later?"

"Alright June, I'll bring them to my place."

"Thank you, and thank you for getting here so fast. If he saw her before I told him, I'm not sure how that would go down."

"Call me, okay?" he says looking at me skeptically like he's unsure how this will all play out then walks into the house.

I turn and walk quickly over to Jake. He is leaning against his truck with one boot propped up against the tire. He's wearing jeans with a small tear in the knee and a black t-shirt that hugs his well-built chest. His eyes are trained on me. "Is that guy your boyfriend?" he asks once I reach him.

"No, he's not. Listen, I want to grab something from the house, and then can you take me somewhere?"

"Yeah," he says, gives me a chin lift and then continues to stare at me as I walk away, even with my back to him, I can feel his eyes boring into me.

I walk in as Daryn is helping the girls with a snack. "I just need to grab something from upstairs," I say and quickly run up the stairs and into my closet. I move a bunch of thick wool sweaters from the top shelf and grab the stack of letters that are bound with a rubber band. I give Lily a kiss telling her I'll have news soon and fly out the door.

"What's that?" Jake asks as I make my approach, the old letters clutched tightly to my chest.

I reach past him, open the door to his truck, set the letters down and use the handle to hoist myself up, "You should know what these are," I close the door and watch as he rounds the truck and gets in.

The cab feels small and suffocating once I'm closed in the small area with Jake. He starts the truck and pulls away from the curb. "Where to June?"

"Anywhere. I want to tell you about my daughter."

"A daughter," he mumbles under his breath like he's getting used to that idea. "Was that guy the dad?"

"No, Jake." I gulp knowing there is no time like the present. I roll down the window a little hoping the fresh air will make this easier. A warm breeze hits me, and I take a deep breath preparing myself for what is about to come.

"These are the letters I wrote you that you never responded to. I want to read you one."

"June, I know I caused you pain. I'm so sorry. We don't need to rehash those letters."

"You need to hear it, Jake," I say sternly annoyed that he is trying to brush aside what I have to tell him, even now. I pull the rubber band off of the stack and grab a random letter since they pretty much all say the same thing.

"Dear Jake,

I don't know what's going on. I don't know why you won't read any of my letters or what happened. I tried to make things right, but that stupid prosecutor wouldn't hear anything I had to say and now I know I have to look out for someone else. It breaks my heart that you don't know. I'll probably get this letter back too. I don't even know why I'm trying. That's not true. I want you to know what you have waiting for you.

I went to the doctor's today. I'm twenty-two weeks along and they did another ultrasound, since the last time this little peanut wouldn't uncross her legs. And do you know what? She finally showed us the goods. That's right, I said she. We're having a baby girl. I decided to name her Lily. I know if you..."

Jake quickly pulls into the Walmart parking lot that we were about to pass and throws the truck into park.

He's breathing hard and gripping the steering wheel tight. His head moves forward against the steering wheel like he's trying to contain his anger. "Fuck," he hisses making me flinch.

I take a deep breath continuing the letter, knowing I need him to hear every word of at least one of them.

"I know if you knew about her you would want her to have your Mom's name. It's the only thing I can think to give her.

"Heck, maybe you wouldn't want her either since I'm beginning to feel like you never wanted me. What was this? Was it all a joke? I wish to God you would just answer one of these letters. Please. We need you. Even if you're in there. I'm scared to death of doing this without you, but I swear to God I'm going to love this little girl enough for the both of us.

Dammit, Jake! Open a letter.

Here's her ultrasound.

I love you and am so pissed at you I can barely breathe. If you would just answer a freaking letter.

June"

I rub my thumb over the black and white image of Lily.

"Jake, Lily is your daughter," I announce wanting to make sure everything sinks in.

"Fuck," he hisses a second time hitting the steering wheel over again.

I'm crying silently, overwhelmed with the emotion of this.

"You gave her my mother's name," he finally whispers.

I nod, "She has your eyes."

He's silent for a moment and then says, "I didn't know. I thought I was protecting you. Shit."

"You weren't protecting me. You abandoned me."

"Eli could've killed you, or put you behind bars and then who would she have had?" he yells.

"You. She would've had you."

"If you're asking me to be sorry that I did what I had to do to protect my family, I won't do it."

"Then, what about the two years you've been out?" I ask angrily because he referred to us as his family.

"I didn't know," he says desperately.

"Yes, because you couldn't open one letter," I shove the letters at him. "If you didn't want me, you should've just opened a letter and responded. At least, you would've known about Lily. And I get it if you don't want her too. I've done fine for the last six years without you and we'll be okay." I know he has his reasons for staying away, but it hurts still. All of it feels so raw, and I want him to hurt for how much I've hurt. I want him to hurt for the hole he's left in Lily's life. She deserved to know that she has a father.

Jake inhales and the entire atmosphere in the cab changes. I don't know how I know it, but I know that whatever is going to come out of his mouth is going to change everything.

"I wanted you. I wanted you so badly that it killed me every time I'd see a letter and knew that if I opened it and read your words, I'd break and put you in danger. I knew I couldn't have you, but I wanted you. God, if you only knew how much I love you. Loved you then and I love you now. Whether you want me or not, I'm not going anywhere. It's been you and only you every day since I was seventeen. You've always been the only one for me, so don't for one second think that I don't want you.

"I should've come for you when I got out. As much as I wanted you, I wanted you to have a good life. I didn't know that all these years later, I'd still be a part of yours. I wanted you to be happy. Fuck, June. I don't give a shit about any of that anymore. I want you and I want her and I don't give a fuck about anything other than that," he pants hard staring at me, waiting for me to give him something. Anything.

My heart feels so much; the beating is a rapid drum. It's on overload. I prayed to hear these words, but at the same time, they scare the shit out of me. They make my heart beat so wildly, letting in a barrage of feelings.

"You want me?" I ask my chin wobbling.

"Jesus, June. With every breath. Every single breath I take, I want you."

Jake leans over me. He's so close, his fresh soap fills my nose. He unlocks my seatbelt and in a swift move scoops a hand under me and cradles me in his lap.

He strokes the side of my head, then places a kiss at my temple. I curl into him, wrapping my arms around his chest. I don't want to be angry. I don't want to hurt. He wants me and he wants Lily. How can I be truly angry at him for wanting to protect me? I take a deep breath. I can let our stolen years fester and burn, or I can breathe them in and then let them go. It was unfair the way the world dealt our cards, but they were dealt and now I need to play my hand. I lift my face towards his and place a light kiss along his jaw, hoping that what he's saying is true and that he wants me as much as I've always wanted him.

"In all these years, I've never stopped loving you," I admit and kiss his neck leaving myself completely vulnerable.

He breathes out a low rumbly breath, "Thank Christ," he captures my chin in his hand and then in the most melodic rumbly voice demands, "Give me your lips."

I press my mouth to his and it's like coming home. Our lips collide and then part for our tongues. It feels like everything that's been broken is put back together. His mouth moves ever so slowly, his tongue is making sweet love to me. He nips and sucks. His hands cradle the sides of my face and his lips finally pull away from mine. His eyes dart back and forth searching my eyes.

"I can't believe this is real. God, I love you. Always have. Never stopped. Never," he whispers and then kisses me again. This time, it's hard and demanding. His lips practically bruise me and when his tongue enters my mouth it's on a thrust and instead of feeling like he's making love to my mouth, it's a hard fuck.

Pounding.

Earth shattering.

Breathtaking.

Every second of missed time together and all of the anger and passion between us is put into this kiss. I grasp his shoulders holding on for the ride, feeling every bit of emotion that he pours into it. His hands tug at the sides of my hair and with as much fierceness I claw at his chest.

Our chests press together and I feel his heart beating in rhythm with my own.

Thump. Thump. A strong beat in perfect unison.

Thump. Thump. Every part of me feels alive and like I am finally whole again.

A door slams next to ours and I remember we're in a Walmart parking lot. Jake releases the kiss and presses his forehead to mine. We stay like this, staring into the depths of each other's eyes, as our breathing returns to normal. This is a feeling unlike anything I've ever experienced. It's grounding, yet euphoric, a peaceful happiness that I never knew existed.

He pulls away from me and lets out a deep breath, "So, about this guy at your house?"

"He's Lily's best friend's dad. He lost his wife to cancer and he's a single dad. We help each other out. I pick the girls up from school and he watches Lily for me when I work Saturdays. He's bringing the girls to his place."

His face looks disturbed and he shakes his head, "You've been going at this by yourself for so long."

"I've had my Mom and Dad, Liz and Daryn. We've done alright."

"Still, she's what six? I can't believe it. All this time, I thought I was keeping the darkness away from you," he shakes his head like he can't believe the mistakes he made, "I fucked up."

"Shh," I kiss his lips, silencing him. We won't get anywhere beating each other up.

He breaks the kiss and sets me back down in my seat then buckles me in and starts the truck. The stores pass by in a blur of neon signs.

"Where are we going?" I ask, a nervous uncertainty curling around me.

"Back to your house. I've never needed anything like I need to be inside of you right now."

I sigh because I need that too. I'm overwhelmed with emotion, but I know I have to have him and I don't want to wait. There's too much between us to take our time. We've both been craving us for far too long. I stare at him as he drives. The anticipation of having him again overwhelms me, but on the other hand, I'm completely shocked that this is where we are, driving to my place to have sex. No, that's not right. Sex is too casual a word for what we're about to do.

Minutes later, we pull into the driveway and I notice right away that Daryn's car is gone. Jake is out of the truck, opening my door and pulling me into my house in what feels like seconds. I don't waste time showing him around. We are on a mission. I lead him up the stairs and towards my room, but he freezes mid-step in the hallway. I stop knowing what has caught his attention. All along the hallway are pictures of Lily. Some are of the two of us, but most of them are of her.

There are black and whites starting at birth. Her chubby peach skin sitting next to a pumpkin on Halloween. Me with my head thrown back swinging her in a circle. Moments capturing our life together. Moments without him, and I feel the loss like I do every time I walk down this hallway.

"She's beautiful, June," he says tracing his finger over the 8x10 portrait of Lily on her fourth birthday. I wrap my arms around his waist and stay with him as he follows her short life from picture to picture. Once he reaches the end of the hall, I take his callused hand and lead him to my room.

Anguish mixed with love covers his face. I can tell he's at war with the emotions waging inside of him. I suppose this is why I was panicking about him knowing. I didn't want this to hurt him, because even though he had no clue about Lily, I knew this moment would tear him in two.

"Jake," I say shutting us in my room and leading him to the bed. He sits automatically, staring past me, blankly at nothing in a state of shock. It's one thing to hear you have a daughter, it's another to see her.

I stand in front of Jake needing to take this loss away from him. And maybe I can't do that. But maybe I can fill his heart with something new. Without any reservations, I begin unbuttoning my shirt. I slip out of it and let it fall to the ground. His eyes darken, but he is still inside of himself. I reach behind my waist and unzip my skirt, letting that pool on the floor. I'm wearing a black lace demi-cup bra, matching black lace underwear and my conservative heels.

He takes in a deep breath and I know I have him back. "Touch me," I say needing his hands on me and igniting something fierce within him.

I'm no longer in charge and leading this. His hands are on my waist and pulling me to him. He bends and kisses my stomach, his tongue traces a pattern. My hands grip his back. I want nothing more than to feel his skin. I need to feel his body against mine. I need the constant reminder that this is real and not a dream. His skin against mine is one of the things grounding me to this moment. I cherish his touch.

Slowly, his mouth moves along my navel making goosebumps rise over my skin. His thumbs brush tentatively over my small cesarean scar. His eyes meet mine and I give him a gentle nod letting him know that everything was okay, that I'm okay. He resumes his kisses. His rough hands move against my skin, upwards until he reaches the outline of my bra. Jake's thumb traces the outline of the material and his warm breath blows against the lace. He bites at my already hardened nipple through the black barrier making my insides pulse at the need I have for him.

"Take off your shirt," I plead knowing his hands on my skin are no longer enough. I need to feel all of him against me. Jake doesn't hesitate; he lifts his arms and pulls his t-shirt free from his body, and holy shit. I knew Jake was bigger than before, but I had no idea. Each muscle on his chest is formed in deep ridges. Tattoos cover his entire chest and my breath hitches when I see a small sprite nestled against Juniper berries right over his heart. Her fairy wings are realistic almost like feathers and the small blue berries are a unique contrast. "Jake," I sigh, feeling my chin wobble. The sudden onslaught of emotions from seeing me so clearly branded on his chest seeps out as a single tear trickles down my cheek.

" None of that, my Juniper. Don't cry. See it. See that you've always been with me."

A strangled sob leaves my throat and instead of letting the pain of all of our years apart destroy this moment, Jake claims my mouth with his. His lips press softly against mine, but then the warm wetness from his tongue quickly makes my mouth part and he is inside of me. It's a hard, menacing kiss, meant to take my mind from everything and anything except for this moment.

I barely register my bra being unclasped and falling at my feet until his firm chest brushes against my taut nipples.

He breaks from the kiss only to flip me around so that I am on the bed and he is over me. My heels dig into the mattress as I take his weight on top of me, pressing me into the white down comforter. I grip at his back and suck at the salty skin on his neck. I feel his thick length against my core and shift my hips to feel the friction. He moves off of me and I sigh, not wanting him to be any further away than necessary. I let out a low whimper and am met with a smirk as his fingertips graze against my sides and then up and down my thighs until finally they hook the edge of my lace panties and pull them down.

I reach for his button on his jeans wanting to feel his silky skin just as much as I want him to touch me. As soon as I undo the button, I slide my hand inside, moaning as I grip his length in my palm. He's so hard. His thick shaft strains against the material.

Jake lets out a low feral growl and I'm rewarded when his fingers slide up through my slick slit, circling my clit and then a long hard finger slides deep inside of me.

I moan and arch my back.

Jake's mouth takes in my small pert breast and sucks and bites at my nipple. This is good, but not enough.

I need more.

I release his hard length and focus my attention at ridding him of his jeans. He lifts his hips and with his free hand helps me undress him. His body is nothing like I remember. It's so much bigger, more colorful and more riddled with scars. I want to examine every change in him, but then the slightest move of his fingers inside of me has me forgetting everything, but the pure bliss he is creating.

"Jake baby, I need you," I whimper.

He removes his fingers from me, sits up and grabs his wallet from his jeans and fishes out a foil packet. I pang of hurt courses through my chest at the thought that he would have condoms so accessible. I push the thought aside and watch with rapt attention as he sheathes himself.

When I was fifteen, I thought he was the most beautiful boy I'd ever seen. When I was twenty-two, he was sexy and sensual. Now at twenty-eight, he is the most beautifully intoxicating man I've ever laid eyes on.

My pussy clenches at the realization that he is going to be inside of me. I let my legs fall open inviting him in in. Jake wastes no time moving on top of me. His body, slick with a fine sheen of sweat, slides over me. I yearn to lick the moisture from his chest, as his cock prods at my opening. He uses his hand and slaps it against my clit making me cry out. Damn. Wherever Jake has been, he's a different kind of lover.

"Fuck," I hiss.

And then he's pushing inside of me. It's fast and hard as he buries himself deep. I hook my heel around his leg drawing him in even more.

"Dammit, June. I've thought about this. Dreamt about it. But never did I think it could be this good. You're so fucking tight. So fucking good."

He pulls out almost all the way leaving just the tip at the opening. I need him. I try to move my hips up, but he only backs away.

Using his hand, he pulls himself in and then out again. It's not enough, it's a torture.

"Jake, please," I beg relentlessly.

He enters me slowly, filling me to the hilt and stills again. I can feel him throbbing and pulsing inside my needy walls.

"You're mine. I won't let you go again. Mine. You hear me, June?"

"Please," I say again nodding my head.

He abruptly pulls out and slams in again. His force is a fucking meant to claim every single inch of me. I lift my leg and circle my heel around his shoulder. The black pump slaps against his hard muscle as he fucks me, deep and hard.

I cry out. "So good, baby!" I'm panting and grasping, holding on for dear life as Jake fucks every inch of me.

My entire body is lit up. Every nerve ending is a glorious spark of need and fire and then it all pulses together, "Fuck, baby I'm coming." I squeeze my leg around him, let my head fall back and my eyes roll as waves of pleasure crash through me.

He gives me a minute to have mine, then his greedy pace is on again.

Fast.

Deep.

Insatiable.

I'm breathing hard. Our bodies are slick with sweat. He pulls out of me and flips me to my stomach, raises my hips, then pounds into me from behind making me scream. It's euphoric. If sex was a drug, then his thrusts are a shot straight to my soul because with each deep thrust, I get higher and higher. Every single time he moves, it's a rush. His balls slap against my clit, making the thrumming need inside of me beat harder and harder.

"Oh my," I moan.

"Yes, baby. Come again. Need to feel you clench. You're so fucking drenched," he whispers into my ear and then bites down on my shoulder.

Jake grips my hair in a tight fist. His other hand grasps my hip as he rides me and guides me back and forth matching each thrust.

I begin to scream and call out incoherent pleas of pleasure.

And then I feel my orgasm happening again. His pace quickens and I know he's close. He releases my hair and presses hard on my clit and then slapping it with each deep thrust.

"Holy fuck!" I scream as my walls climax against him. He pounds me like this, once, twice, three times, and finally stills letting out a melodic groan. His pleasure, the most thrilling, guttural noise I've ever heard.

CHAPTER FOURTEEN

"That was incredible," I gasp noting the red numbers on the bedside table flashing six o'clock. After round one, we had round two. Now looking at the clock, I know we need to get out of bed. "I need to get Lily."

"I want to meet her right away. Is that okay? Can you bring our daughter back here, so that I can finally meet her?" Jake asks getting up from the bed and throwing on his jeans.

"I'm so glad you said that. She's so anxious." I move about my room quickly getting dressed, then tame my long auburn sexed-up hair.

Jake sits on the edge of the bed watching me as I get ready.

"Daryn's a couple of blocks from here, so I should be back pretty quick."

He runs a hand through his short hair. "Are you nervous?"

"Nervous doesn't even begin to cover how I'm feeling."

Without thinking, I walk to him and give him my lips, as if my body remembers what he wants. "I'll be back soon."

I hop in the car and make the short drive to Daryn's. Daryn walks outside and meets me by my car before I even get a chance to step out.

"Everything okay?" he asks.

"Yeah, I think it's going to be alright."

"That was pretty intense."

"You're telling me."

"And that guy? How did he take the news?" Daryn asks, his voice laced with concern.

"To say he was surprised is an understatement, but he's anxious to meet her. How did the girls do?"

"Lily was a little wound up, but they talked me into buying them some new app on the iPad and they've been engrossed in it ever since. Listen, are you sure everything's okay? That guy seemed a bit wound up."

"I've known Jake since I was fifteen. We have a lot of history and a lot we need to work out. When he showed up unannounced, I'm sure it was to work some of that out, but then you were there, and he had no idea who you were."

"Alright, June, just be careful. I'm worried about you. You let me know if you need anything. Yeah?" he asks turning towards the house, "I'll grab Lily."

Lily races out of the house, her dark hair bounces off her shoulders. "Hey, Mom. Can I meet him now?" she asks as soon as she sees me. I smile, both excited and nervous for her.

"Yeah, baby. Let's go meet your daddy." I smile at her and then meet Daryn's eyes, "Thank you," I mouth to Daryn. He gives me a lift of his chin, and closes the door to his house behind him.

I open the car door for Lily and gesture for her to get in. "He's really excited to meet you," I tell her, looking at her in the rearview mirror and watching satisfied when her seatbelt clicks in place.

"He is?" she asks unsure about the situation, then she breathes on the glass window and draws a heart with her finger. "What if he doesn't like me? What if I don't like him? What's he like? Is he nice?"

"Relax, honey, he already loves you."

"How do you know?"

"Because you're you and he's him. As soon as he learned about you, he loved you."

When we pull up in front of the house, I don't know why, but I'm relieved that Jake's truck's still here. A part of me thought he would disappear again, and that the entire afternoon was a figment of my imagination?

I release a breath I didn't realize I'm holding, and lead Lily into the house to meet Jake.

He's sitting on the couch, one leg kicked out further than the other as we walk through the kitchen and into the living room. Jake immediately stands, brushing his nervous palms against his jeans.

I give him a reassuring smile and walk with my hand on Lily's shoulder, guiding her and calming her as she takes in her dad for the first time. Jake is tall, broad, muscular and tattooed. I would imagine to a child he could look intimidating.

"Hello?" the soft word leaves Lily's mouth. She's shy and curious at the same time. Jake is no longer standing and staring at her. He moves so quickly to her that I barely notice the tear running down his cheek.

"You're beautiful," he says falling to his knees and wrapping her small frame in his arms.

"So are you," she cries. In that moment, when my daughter falls in love with her father, I realize how much she was missing out on all of these years.

I don't realize I'm crying and how impactful the moment is, until Jake looks up at me from the embrace with our daughter and whispers, "Thank you."

I move to the pair and suddenly I'm pressed against them. Jake pulls me in so that Lily's and his heads are pressed against my stomach. I cling to them, like they're my lifeline because they are.

"I'm sorry, I haven't been here. I missed so much. You're so big, Lily," he pulls back appraising her. I attempt to move away and give them space, but Jake grabs my hand imploring me with his eyes to stay. "You look so much like my Mom. Her name was Lily too. Did your Momma tell you that?"

"I do?" Lily questions, "Can I meet her?"

"No honey, my mom is in heaven singing with the angels, but she would've loved you."

"Oh," Lily says a tad disappointed. She pauses, thinks for a minute, and says, "My grandma's really nice."

"I know she is. I haven't seen her in a long time, but she was always good people."

"You met her?" she asks as the three of us move to the couch. Lily, still hugging onto her dad and me holding his hand.

"Yeah, the summer your mom and I met."

"Where did you meet?" Lily asks.

"We were at Grandma and Grandpa's summer home," I explain to Lily.

"Your folks still own that place?" Jake asks.

"Yeah, I haven't been there since that summer, though." Lily whines loudly, "Mom never lets me go with Grandma and Grandpa. They invite us every year and then they invite me, but she always says, 'Noooo.'"

"I'm sure there's a good reason your Mom hasn't wanted to go there."

'Maybe," she says taking a breath, "and maybe she'll want to go now that you're back? You're back, right? You and Mom are going to be together right? Like a real family?"

Wow, there are so many questions and assumptions pouring out of Lily.

"Lilypad, Jake and I just found each other again. How about we have some dinner and start with tonight, okay?" I can't help it. Even though Jake and I emptied our hearts out to each other, I don't trust him yet and deep down, I'm not sure if I ever will.

"Lily, how about you see what coupons we have for pizza?"

She gets up from the couch, but not before glancing back at Jake, as if she too thinks he might disappear.

"You doing okay?" I ask him.

He nods, "I don't know what I did to deserve that moment, but thank you so much for giving it to me. You've done so well with her. She's perfect."

"Mom, I found Guido's and Mama Catina's. I want Guido's. Can we have Guido's?"

"Sure, honey."

"Dad, can I call you dad? Ever had Guido's? It's the best," Lily's habit of talking to cope with her anxiousness is coming through full force.

"First, I'd be honored if you called me Dad. You know, I only ever dreamt about babies with your mom so you're a dream come true," Jake says grabbing the coupons from Lily's hands. Her eyes light up big and I see the way she's looking at Jake. It might be the same way I looked at him when I saw him all those years ago like the sun could rise and set with Jake Daniels and I'd be a happy girl because he exists. "Second, if my girl likes Guido's then we should have Guido's." Jake fishes his cell phone out of his pocket and calls Guido's ordering way too much food.

While we wait for dinner to arrive, we sit on the white, oversized couch with Lily tucked in between us. She has a photo album out and is going through each picture, animatedly telling Jake about each one. "This is when Grace and I played in the sprinkler so long our skin got all wrinkly and Mom had to shut it off. Oh, and this one here, we're at Chuck E. Cheese's. I got so many tickets."

The doorbell rings and breaks up our trip down memory lane. "I'll get it," I say getting up and grabbing my purse, but Jake is faster than me. Before I know it, he's opening the door and handing the delivery guy a wad of cash.

I give him a look that says, 'I could have gotten it', but he shakes his head at me.

We take seats at the dining room table and eat our pizza, because... 'hello, white couches', while Jake and Lily carry on a conversation.

"What's your favorite color?" he asks in between bites.

"Green. Yours?"

"Green," he smiles, "Favorite food?"

"Easy. Guido's," she says taking a bite of her pizza and grinning at him. The sauce coats her teeth with tiny red specks. After she chews she asks, "Favorite sport?"

"Easy, MMA."

"What's that?" she asks.

"It's like boxing, but without gloves." He holds up a fist.

I think about what it was like the first night I met Jake when he was pretending to be Lucas. We sat on Garfield's Monument looking out over the city and asked similar questions. Both of us were intoxicated, but in many ways, it was a rapid-fire get to know you. I wonder what it would've been like if Jake just told me it was him. We could've run. Made a life together. I know he says he was running from bad things and it was all to protect me, but it hurts that he didn't trust me enough to let me in. We could've had Lily somewhere else and Jake could've spent the first six years of her life with him. Instead, he was in jail and I was alone.

I finish my pizza and bring my plate to the sink; it clinks as I set it down. I look out my back window as I wash it and all I see is darkness. The darkness is a cloak, shielding me and letting me wallow in my train of thoughts. This isn't fair to Jake. He thought he was protecting me. I have to, at least, give that to him. He wanted to keep us safe and truly we were. One thing that gets me so angry is that this Eli guy who used Jake is dead and didn't have to pay for what he did to Jake. I mean, I guess he paid for something he did to someone, it just feels like everything that happened was for nothing.

"Alright, honey. It's bath time," I call out to Lily. She groans as I climb the stairs and pour pink bubbles into the tub and start the water. Once the tub is filled high enough, I shut off the water. Lily and Jake are still talking, when Jake notices me and tells Lily, "Time for your bath. I'll be here when you're done."

She searches his eyes as if she is making sure he's telling the truth. It's not just me who's going to have a hard time trusting Jake. I watch as she smiles and kisses him on the cheek, then makes her way towards me, practically stripping on her way to the tub.

"Mom, did you see his tattoos?" she ask me once she's finally in the water. I laugh, "Yes Lily, I saw them. Let's wash your hair. It's getting late and you have school in the morning."

"Do I have to go?" she whines.

"Of course, you do. I have work tomorrow and I'm sure Jake does too."

I begin lathering her hair when I spot Jake's shadow in the hallway. I'm betting he doesn't want to miss a moment with her. I know I wouldn't.

"Will I see him again? Is this it? Will I get to have a real Daddy?" she asks in small worried voice.

I know Jake heard this and there's nothing I can do. I want to protect him but I need to protect her. "Yeah, baby. I think we will see him again," I say as I dump a cup of water over her head to rinse her hair.

I dry her off and wrap her towel around her. When we walk into the hallway, Jake isn't there. We move to her room and I hand her clothes to dress for bed.

"Do you want me to send him up to tuck you in?"

Her eyes light up, "Really?" she asks.

"Sure," I say kissing her on her head. I walk down the stairs to find Jake in the kitchen washing the last couple of plates. "She's about ready for bed, do you want to tuck her in?"

"Really?" he asks hopefully.

"Yeah, she'd like that. She likes you, but she's nervous that it's not going to last. See that it does, okay?" I say this to him as a warning. Don't you break my little girl's heart. You've broken mine and I know the pain. I bore it, but I won't let her. He gets it and I know he wants to say something to me, but time is of the essence when there is a six-year-old getting ready for bed. He walks upstairs and I hold my breath. This entire thing is scary to me in so many ways.

Five minutes pass and then ten. I wonder what's happening. What could they be saying? My curiosity gets the best of me and I walk quietly up the stairs, not wanting to disturb them. It only takes me a few minutes until I hear Jake. He's singing to our daughter. I freeze, the last time I heard that beautiful, melodious voice was when Jake poured his heart out to me in that song, letting me know who he really was.

He gets to the chorus of the song and with my eyes closed, I instantly recall the past.

"Step by Step. Oh, Baby. I'm gonna get to you, girl. Step One: We can have lot's of fun. Step Two."

"Stop, June, I get it, I get it. New Kids on the Block is your thing," Jake teases, throwing his hands up in the air. I'm not a good singer. I know this, I also don't care. If I want to sing, to hell with everyone's ears.

"Okay, Jake. No more NKOTB, but you have to sing for me."

"I'm not singing for you."

"Fine, Step Two: There's so much we can do."

His hand slaps over my mouth. "Alright, alright. You win. Just please, June, no more."

I laugh and giggled hysterically. Once I am under control I say, "Okay Jake, sing to me."

"It's a country song. Not like that New Kids junk."

"That's alright. I'd love anything you sing," I say hoping Jake can sing. I've overheard him humming to himself sometimes and all I wanted was to hear his voice. Somehow, I know it's going to be perfect. I climbed on top of a hay barrel, the course straw scratched at my legs. He watches me with amusement. "You ready?"

I nod vigorously.

Then he opens his mouth and the most beautiful lyrics come out. I think some guy named Tim McGraw sings it.

"Johnny's daddy was taking him fishin'
When he was eight years old
A little girl came through the front gate holdin' a fishing pole
His dad looked down and smiled, said we can't leave her behind
Son, I know you don't want her to go, but someday you'll change your mind

And Johnny said "Take Jimmy Johnson, take Tommy Thompson, take my best friend Bo
Take anybody that you want as long as she don't go
Take any boy in the world
Daddy, please don't take the girl"

The words continue on about a boy who doesn't think he wants this young girl around him, but as they grow up, she becomes his everything. By the end of the song, tears stream down my face, because this man would do anything for his girl. I love that Jake sings this to me.

"Was it that bad?" he laughs when he sees the tears on my face. He's trying to make light of the situation. He doesn't like attention, but he just floored me.

"Bad! Are you kidding me? That was the most beautiful thing I've ever heard," I laugh as I wipe my tears. "You know now, you're going to have to sing to me all the time."

"No way, June! That was a one-time thing," he says shyly.

"Jake! Where the hell are you, you little shit?" Mike Daniels calls walking into the barn and ruining our moment.

Just like in my memory, by the time Jake finishes I'm crying, but Lily claps her hands and says, "Daddy, that was so good, but what happened?"

"What do you mean?"

"Did he get the girl?"

"I'd like to believe he did. Their love was so powerful he got the girl."

"Can you sing it again?"

Jake chuckles, "You have school in the morning, but I promise I'll sing to you at night as often as I can."

Lily moans a whiny, tired protest, "I don't want today to end."

"Oh, Lily. There will be more. I love you so much, and now that I know about you, I will always be here. I promise I'm not going anywhere. Okay?"

"Okay, Daddy."

"Night, pretty girl," Jake says, and I imagine him kissing her on the forehead.

"Night Daddy," she whispers sleepily.

I brush my tears away and smile up at Jake as he closes Lily's bedroom door. In a quiet voice, I say, "It's warm out tonight. Want to sit on the back patio?"

He nods and we walk down the stairs and out the back door without saying another word. The sky is dark but lit up by the many stars. The air has that wet soil smell to it, letting you know that Fall is on the horizon. I feel a chill and goose bumps raise over my skin.

"Sit with me," Jake says motioning to a small glider meant for two. I do and he pulls me close to him, rubbing my arm as he notices my chill.

"You know the song you just sang to Lily, I'm pretty sure she dies."

"Not in my version. In my version, he gets the girl and his kid."

I reach up and kiss his cheek, thinking that I like his version better.

"She's so amazing. I can't believe I missed that?" he says after several long minutes of silence. I don't know what to say because truthfully, I can't believe he missed that either. We started the day with so many wild feelings needing to get out, but now? Now, it feels like we are both on emotional overload. Maybe today was too much, too soon?

"She's so much like you. She's so perfect." He strokes the side of my arm.

"She is pretty great, isn't she?"

"You did so good with her. I can tell you're both nervous about where I think I'll fit in your life. So, I'm laying my intentions out there."

I pull away from him a little so I'm eye to eye with him, staring at those blue-greens I've loved since I was fifteen. I need to hear what he has to say. What if he isn't interested in this instant family? What if he breaks our hearts all over again?

He clears his throat, "I plan on dating you like I always wished I could. I plan on being at every soccer game Lily has, every school function, and any other kid thing she needs. I'm going to be the man I should've always been for you, and when the time is right I'm moving in here, or we're getting a place with the three of us, whatever you want. I don't plan on waiting a long time for that. I want this family. I want Lily more than my breath, and God help me June, I don't just want you, but I fucking need you. You're the piece that's always been missing. You're my current; the only thing that's kept me moving all these years. I hate what's happened to us, but I promise you June, just like I promised Lily, I'm not going anywhere."

CHAPTER FIFTEEN

True to his word, Jake is over the next night for dinner and the next, and the one after that. I haven't had him stay the night. I want to give Lily security and no matter what Jake has proclaimed I feel like he needs to prove that he's here to stay. Maybe it's not fair and maybe it's just a result of constantly being ripped apart.

Jake has talked with Daryn a few times and I think, besides the fact that Jake very obviously staked his claim in front of Daryn, that the two are getting along. It's important to me that they do since Grace and Lily are so close. I think Jake doesn't like that Daryn and I have come to rely on each other, but once I explained about Daryn's wife, Jake seemed to calm down.

I finish securing the back of my diamond stud earring. They were a gift from Liz the first time she secured a multi-million dollar deal. I hardly wear them, but I figure tonight being the first official date that Jake and I have is as good as a reason as any. Lily is staying overnight at Grace's, so we have the entire night.

I splurged for tonight and bought a red dress that cinches at the waist. It's fitted, but not overly tight. I can't wait to see Jake's reaction. Even more so, I can't wait to see his reaction on the tiny red thong and matching bra underneath. I check the bedside clock. It's five minutes past six; Jake is late, which isn't usually like him. I slip on my heels and walk downstairs and open the front door nervously peeking out for him.

His back is to me and he's waving to a few guys who are pulling away in an older black sedan. My face lights up with a huge smile. My SUV is in the driveway and his truck is parked behind it.

"My car!" I squeal, "I thought it wasn't going to be done for a while!" I rush to Jake and he grabs me in his arms, lifting me up with one hand on my ass and the other around my back.

"The dress looks good, Sprite," he nuzzles his head into my neck.

"Put me down," I laugh and playfully slap Jake's chest.

"I thought, you'd like your SUV back," he smiles shyly.

"I thought it wasn't going to be ready for another week?"

"I might've pulled some extra hours that last few nights to get it done."

"Thank you," I squeeze Jake's hand, and finally take in the sight of him. He's wearing well-fitted jeans and a black button-up shirt that's rolled to his elbows showing off his inked arms. He looks amazing, but he's so much different than he used to be. Years in prison have given him a harder exterior.

Suddenly, I'm nervous. Here is this man that I've known since I was a kid, but we are so different now. Sure, we proclaimed our feelings for one another, he's made his intentions clear and we had sex, but what if we are too different?

"What's going through that mind of yours, June?"

"What do you mean?" I look up at him, trying to hide the guilty look on my face. The look that is questioning everything.

"You know exactly what I mean, Juniper." He's close to my ear and his voice is husky.

I shiver, "I was just thinking how nice you look, and how much bigger you are now."

"Yeah, well working out in the prison yard, lifting a ton of weight, for anyone who might want to fuck with you to see is one way to make guys think twice."

I gulp. I hate when he talks about prison. I get that it wasn't my fault, but I can't help but feel responsible. I change the subject, "Let me grab my purse from inside and lock up, then we can go. Okay?"

I grab my bag and lock the house up. When I walk out towards the car Jake is standing next to the open passenger door of his truck. In his hand is a single red rose.

"I wanted to come to your door before and bring you a flower like a proper date, but you beat me out here." He hands me the rose and I blush.

"Thank you," he extends his hand and helps me into the cab of his truck. "So, where are we going?"

"I made us reservations at that new Chef Symon restaurant."

"No, way! You got us in there? I heard you had to make reservations well in advance."

"We did a custom car for him and he told me if I ever wanted to come in and see him to give him a call."

"That's awesome. I got to help with a piece we did on him. It was pretty cool. He is such a laid back, local guy. Even though he's a big shot on TV, he still puts so much effort into our city. I love that he's still opening restaurants here and hasn't moved his family. I got to meet his wife, she's so nice and genuine."

Jake smiles and listens to me talk about work. It reminds me of how he used to be. When we were young, he would encourage me to talk for hours and it was easy with him. I realize it still is. Maybe my fears about him being different are unfounded?

The restaurant is classy with white linens, low music, and dim lighting. White tea light candles flicker on the table and the waiter brings us menus.

"Would you like me to order for you, June?"

"How do you know that you know what I'll want?"

"I know you. Just because time has passed doesn't mean I don't know you. I remember everything about you. The thing is June, when all I had was time on my hands, thinking and savoring every single thing I know about you is what got me through. So, I know what you want."

Damn, that felt heavy and I'm not ready for heavy. "Okay, what do you think I'll want?"

He smiles, "That's easy. You'd like the steak, because you always love a good steak, but then there is the clam bake and you love seafood way more than steak. In fact, I bet reading everything in the clambake has your mouth salivating."

I slam the menu shut and grin at Jake.

"I'm right, aren't I?"

"Yes," I laugh nudging him with my foot. "Okay smarty, let me try you." I reopen the menu and look over all of the entrees. Double damn, I was hoping that bacon was in something. That would have made this easier. "Ugh, it's a toss-up for you. You were never as cut and dry as me. You either want the halibut, or the strip steak."

"I'm in the mood for steak tonight," he smiles and his eyes twinkle in the candlelight.

The waiter comes and Jake places our orders, ordering me a glass of Riesling and beer for himself.

We make small talk and Jake grabs my hand holding it across the table. All too quickly, our salads come.

"What's Lily's full name?" he asks in between bites.

"Lily Marie Withers." He looks disappointed and I don't get it. "Hey," I put the palm of my hand against his face. "What is it?"

"One day I swear it, you're both taking my name."

Oh, that. "My parents know that you're her dad, but I told them we had a one night stand and that you were just passing through town. I couldn't give her your last name." I hope he understands.

"I get it. Even then, you wanted to protect me against your parents. It makes sense, but still I wish my daughter had my name."

I nod because I understand that too. "I gave her your name the best way I could."

"Yes, you did. Thank you for that. My mom would've loved it. How did you know it?"

"You're not the only one who's spent countless hours filling the silence with memories. I remember everything there is about you."

Our dinners come and we devour it. Everything is delicious and this restaurant is every bit worthy of its hefty price tag. On the drive back to my place, I ask him about his work. He tells me stories about the guys he works with and I laugh when he tells me about the way they joke on each other.

"What did they think when I went all crazy on you?"

"As soon as you left Stouty was like, whatever you did, you need to fix that. He said any woman willing to beat my ass like that must love me, 'cause only a woman in love can hold onto that much hate. He didn't have to say it, though. I knew as soon as I saw you that you loved me," he chuckles, "The rest of the guys teased me about getting my ass handed to me by a tiny woman."

"Damn straight," I laugh as we pull into the driveway.

Inside, Jake kisses my shoulder. "I know I said it earlier, but you look incredible." He lights a few candles I have in the living room. I watch silently as he moves to the stereo and slips in a CD.

Soft music strums through my living room. I don't recognize it. No one's singing, it's just a nice slow, steady beat.

"Dance with me, June." He doesn't give me a chance to respond, but reaches out his hand and grabs mine. In the living room, we sway back and forth. I stare up at him, my heart beating wildly. Thump, thump. I'm so in love. Thump, thump. It's never gone anywhere. Thump, thump. He's going to kiss me.

Those lips meet mine, soft and tender. Then he pulls away. "Before the other night, singing to Lily, I hadn't sung in so long. Hadn't even wanted to write any lyrics."

The song ends, a new one begins and I sway with Jake to a new beat.

"Never did I want to let you go.
You sang to me
My muse
Never did I want to say goodbye
You came for me
My muse
Never did I mean to hurt you, June
I'm begging you, please
My muse
Open your heart
Let me back in
I'm begging you, please
My muse

The music continues and Jake looks at me shyly. "That's all I have for now. Still working it all out."

"Jake," I pull his head down to meet my lips. I'm so overwhelmed with his words. I'm already letting him in. I love him. I just need to work on trusting that he's here to stay.

He kisses me sweetly again and a moment later he turns me around and unzips my dress. I reach up and move it off my shoulders so that it falls to the ground.

Jake sucks in an audible breath, "Jesus." In the lightest possible way, he starts at my neck leaving barely there kisses. His lips are so soft and gentle that it gives me goosebumps along my skin. He is tortuously slow kissing between my shoulder blades, my lower back, down the backs of my thighs and behind my knees. He's careful where he touches. It all feels so gentle, so deliberate.

He moves to the front of me and lifts each of my feet, grabbing my calves gently in each hand, so that he can completely free me of my dress that's pooled on the ground. He walks behind me and mirrors his movements, kissing up my legs, my hip bones, and all over my stomach. The pads of his thumbs trace the outline of my panties. As his kisses move higher, they brush the outline of my bra. He kisses the tops of my breasts, but never moves the fabric to kiss below it.

"These new, Juniper?"

I smile and nod, "Yeah, for you."

A sound close to a growl comes from deep within him. "Beautiful," he says,, and lowers me to the ground. Normally I am a rush of grabby hands on him, but something about the way he is kissing me and taking his time tells me he needs it like this.

I watch with hooded eyes as Jake unbuttons his shirt and then shrugs it off. His rippled abs make my mouth water. His shoes and jeans go next, followed by his boxer briefs. I want to rid myself of my bra and underwear, but this is his show, so I watch with anticipation.

"I'm going to go slow. I want tonight to just be me and you, June. A man and a woman. None of our baggage in the way, not us trying to reconnect in some frantic way. Tonight's about a man taking his woman out, and then bringing her home, so he can worship her. We've never had this; just us, Jake and June. Something has always hung over us."

I get what he is saying. Seven years ago, we were June and Lucas. When we had sex the other day, we were a frenzied mess of hurt and regrets. Now, it's just us. I'm suddenly slightly nervous. I want everything to be perfect. A soft look from Jake and a kiss to my collar bone has me forgetting any nervousness. "It's just you and me baby."

More languid kisses against my skin, and finally his hands release my bra, and then my thong. His skin against my own ignites little sparks all over my body. It's not so much that I'm turned on, (which I am) but that I'm completely tuned in. Every single time his lips hit me, I wiggle and squirm. I want him. No, that's not completely right.

I need him.

I whimper and am rewarded with Jake's lips against my own. His fingers run between my breasts, over my stomach, slide down my clit and very gently inside of me.

"Already so wet for me, Juniper."

I can't help but reach out and stroke his hard length. "Already so hard for me, Jake," I mirror his words.

"Always," he leans over me, sliding his body up and down mine and then sliding himself against my clit. He links our fingers above my head and stares deeply into my eyes as he slowly slides into me. We make the most deliciously beautiful, painfully slow love of our lives.

Jake is right. Slow can be so good. Every moment between us is savored. Every kiss, stroke, and thrust feels like it binds us and mends a little bit of what's been broken.

Afterward, Jake carries me up to my bed and holds me close to him, his leg thrown over mine, my head buried in the crook of his neck. I fall asleep like this; completely in love and for the first time in so long, completely happy. There is no longer that piece of me that's missing. There is no longer an emptiness. I am full.

CHAPTER SIXTEEN

I wake to the ringing of my house phone and very sleepily sit up in bed, my silk sheets slide off my body. My house is quiet with the exception of Jake's inhaling and exhaling. I can hear the answering machine kick on and wonder who could be calling me. As much as I want to snuggle in Jake's arms, I need to check the machine, start coffee and get ready to get Lily.

I start to get out of bed when an arm hooks me around the waist and pulls me backward. "Where are you going?" Jake's sleepy voice grumbles behind me.

I giggle, "I have to get up. We slept late and I need coffee."

"Mmm, but I need you." he's instantly on top of me, and before I can give coffee a second thought, he's inside of me.

After one of the best wake-up orgasms of my life I get up and begin rushing around picking up blankets that fell to the floor.

"What are you doing?" Jake laughs at me as I quickly throw on a robe and make the bed around him.

"We don't have that much time until we have to get Lily. I need coffee and the house picked up and I need to get dressed."

"Settle down. You're cute when you're all frazzled. Get dressed, I'll start coffee and pick up Lily."

I nod, liking the sound of that plan, and rush to my ensuite bathroom. I brush my teeth, noticing how my face has a pink blush to it, a look that says I just got lucky. With lightning speed I run a brush through my tangles. I throw on a pair of jeans, a black blouse with cap sleeves, and a pair of sandals.

The glorious smell of coffee hits me as I descend the stairs. The living room is picked up, and there is no evidence of last night. I smile at Jake pouring two cups of coffee, easily moving around my kitchen. He's wearing the same jeans from last night and a black tank top that he had under his dress shirt. He looks delectable in my kitchen.

"Mmm, coffee," I reach around Jake and grab my cup. "You always made the best coffee."

"Still do." He takes a sip of his coffee.

I sip mine and smile agreeing completely. "Once we grab Lily, what do you want to do today?"

"What if we take her to the Lake? I know it's too cold for the water, but maybe she'll like the sand?"

"She loves it there. I've been bringing her there for forever. She'd love to go."

Jake gives me an unreadable smile. I can't tell if he's smiling because he's happy I've been bringing her, or if it's something else. I shrug off his unusual smile, and hit the red flashing light on the answering machine.

"Hey, June. It's Alister. I've been out of..." Shit, Alister the investment banker. I attempt to hit the button to shut off my answering machine, but Jake stops my hand. "Listen, I've been out of town for work, and I broke my phone so I have zero contacts. I'm hoping my girl is still in bed. I'm going to stop and bring you pastries from Bella's. I know how much you love those."

Shit. Shit. Shit. "Jake, it's nothing. We've been on a few dates, but I'm most definitely not his girl. I'll call him and make sure he knows."

He gives me a look, "You be sure to do that, June." Before I get a chance to do that, my doorbell rings. Shit, I didn't do anything wrong. Why am I acting like I've been caught with my hand in the candy jar? I move to answer the door, but Jake is on it before I get a chance. He throws the door open and standing there with a white box, no doubt filled with the best pastries in the world, is Alister, the investment banker. Alister is dressed impeccably. His hair is immaculately styled with a ton of product, keeping his blonde curls perfectly in place. Alister is well built, spending his mornings running and then a vigorous weight lifting regiment at the gym, all before seven am. I know this because Alister wouldn't shut up about himself. He's wearing a polo shirt and jeans. He's attractive, just not for me.

"Is June here?" He asks nervously.

"Yup," is Jake's one-word answer. He's fills the entire doorway and I have to forcefully move past Jake to say anything to Alister.

"Hey Alister," I say stepping outside, but it's only for a moment because Jake throws his arm around my waist and very obviously stakes his claim in front of Alister. I glare at Jake because this possessive bullshit isn't cool. "Give me a minute, will you? I'll be right in."

"Nope."

What the heck is that? I glare at him again.

"June, what's going on? Who is this guy?" Alister asks. I look at Jake again pleading with him to give me a moment of privacy, so that I can let Alister down easy. He doesn't budge.

"I'm Lily's dad and June's man. We're together. She's mine."

"I thought you were single?" Alister asks looking at me like I'm some two-timing whore.

"I'm sorry Alister, I was. This is new and we're giving it a shot." I grit my teeth feeling very annoyed that this conversation is having to happen in front of Jake.

"Maybe next time you should give the guy you're dating a little heads up?" Alister retorts with way too much attitude.

"Maybe, if you were smart you'd watch your tone?" Jake puffs his chest out and flares his nose.

Alister looks at me and then looks at Jake, "You know what, screw this. It's not worth it. He drops the pastry box and turns to walk away. Jake picks up the box, grabs a raspberry pastry, and I know this because it's my favorite, and shouts at the back of the retreating Alister, "Thanks for breakfast, but don't come back."

I aim my biggest death glare at Jake and storm past him into the house. I am pissed. I get it, he was asserting himself and staking his claim like I'm some prize, but that was not okay.

"You're an ass," I say hitting Jake on his arm. "You had no right to do that. I hadn't spoken to him in over a week. I figured he felt the same way I did, but I had the right to tell him that. Not you. That was so uncool, Jake. Now move your truck, so I can go pick up Lily."

"June, that guy needed to know. You want me to feel bad for that? I don't. No man is going to come to my woman's house bringing breakfast and not be told how it is. I told him how it was. It's done. Now, let's get in the truck and go get our girl."

Who the hell is this guy? One minute he is singing to me and making the sweetest love to me and the next he is this guy who thinks he can talk for me.

He walks outside to his truck and I follow him. "I'm not going with you. Move your truck, so I can go and get Lily."

"We're going to get *our* daughter and have a good day."

"No, I'm going to get Lily, and you're going to leave."

He shakes his head at me and walks towards his truck. "I'll be back in fifteen."

"Where are you going?" I snap.

He doesn't answer. He pulls his truck out of the spot and rolls his window down, "I'm getting Lily. Get over your pissed off mood, will you? It's a great day out today." He drives away leaving me stunned. I could race to Daryn's, but I think that will just cause a scene. I'm pissed off beyond all measure. I can't stand the way he acted.

I first send a text to Alister, **I'm sorry about that. I truly am. I didn't even think you were interested, since I didn't hear from you. I would've been with Jake anyways, but I'm sorry that just went down like that.**

I don't get a response from him, and I don't expect too. I hate that Jake just acted that way. I drink a few sips of my coffee, and try to be objective. How would I have felt if a woman was trying to claim him in front of me? I would let Jake talk to them. I'd be jealous. I'd hate it, but I wouldn't react the same way, I'm sure of it.

I give a quick call to Daryn to let him know Jake is picking up Lily and pace around my living room. His truck pulls up, the distinct sound of his diesel engine loud and clear.

Lily bounds into the house. "Hi Mom. I spilled juice on my shirt. I'm going up to change, and then Dad says we're going to the beach for a picnic. I'm so happy."

She races up the stairs and I meet Jake's eyes. "I'd like you to go."

"Not gonna happen. I told my girls I'm taking them to the beach and that's what I'm doing," he says casually, opening the fridge and grabbing items for "our picnic".

"You had Lily in your car without a booster, do you know how dangerous that is!" I accuse. I know I'm picking a fight, but I'm still so ticked.

"You must have missed the booster in the backseat last night. I bought one the other day." He grabs fresh fruit from the table and begins collecting a pile. "Do you have a picnic basket?" I don't answer and continue to stare at Jake.

"Hey Lily, can you grab the picnic basket?" Jake hollers up the stairs at Lily.

"Sure thing, Dad," she calls back.

I breathe out a deep breath, feeling like our picnic is happening no matter what I say. I look at Jake, needing distance. "I'll be in the truck." I grab my purse and walk outside to the truck, but not before catching a smug smirk on his face. Oh, how he's infuriating me today.

Jake walks out of the house, with Lily' hand in one hand and a picnic basket in the other. He loads her into her seat, and walks around the truck and sets the picnic basket down next to her. I watch in fascination as he opens my garage, gets Lily's sand toys and then proceeds to lock up the house. We're so new and he's already moving around like he lives here.

I'm silent in the car, which is okay since Lily talks Jake's ear off telling him everything she and Grace did last night.

When we pull up to the Lake, it's fairly empty. The sky is blue and the water is calm. We're lucky to get a day as nice as this. It will probably be one of our last nice days before winter. Jake unloads everything from the truck and I help Lily down. She runs ahead of us stopping on the bridge to the beach. It's one of her favorite spots too.

"Dad, look at the seagulls" Lily bounces excitedly.

"That's awesome, Lil," he smiles warmly, pointing to the bird just inches from her.

I want to let them have this moment and I know I need to stop being a bitch. I grab the basket from Jake and walk away, giving them this time.

I spread out a blanket on the sand and kick off my sandals reveling in the warmth from the silky sand. Jake and Lily take their shoes off at the end of the small bridge, and begin racing towards me. Jake's legs are so long that I can tell it's a real challenge for him to make it look like she has a shot. He gives up trying and swoops her up in the air and onto his shoulders. They pass me and continue to run down the beach. She laughs loudly and I watch her hands grip around his head.

I want to be mad at him, but watching him with Lily erases some of my anger.

So much has happened since Jake and I were here last. We're finding our way back to each other. As angry as I am, I want to enjoy the day.

I open the basket and begin setting things out, so that when they're ready, we're all set. I put grapes and strawberries on a plate, popping a few of the ripe grapes in my mouth. I smile, in spite of myself, when I get to the bottom of the basket and see the white box from the bakery filled with my favorite pastries. I don't know why he put those in there, but I can't help but crack a tiny smile.

Watching Jake and Lily, I bask in their playfulness. I thought I was happy all these years, but looking at the two of them, I can really see everything I've been missing.

We had such an amazing night last night. I know I love Jake, but I can't help but feel like if he had made different decisions, like trusting me with the truth, then things would've been so different. We could've had years like this with us together. There would be no investment bankers for us to fight about. There would only be Jake and June, like it was supposed to be.

"Heads up!" Jake yells as a Frisbee comes zooming at me.

"Come on, Mom. Let's play," Lily giggles running around. I get up and throw the Frisbee hard towards Jake. It soars and he catches it, then throws it to Lily. She tries to catch, but misses. He stands behind her and teaches her how to throw it to me. I dive for it, wanting my little girl to have a decent throw and surprisingly, I catch it.

"Good catch!" Lily says.

"Yeah, nice catch," Jake offers me his hand to help me up from the sand. I dust myself off smiling, "Thanks. Why don't we take a break from playing and get something to eat. There are these great pastries from Bella's." I wink at Jake letting him know I'm calling a truce and the three of us sit down and enjoy our pastries and fruit.

I watch Jake and Lily for hours. We're at the beach way longer than I could've thought possible and by four o'clock, I call out, "Hey, you two. We need to wrap this up. We have to have dinner. Lily has school tomorrow."

"How about I treat my girls to dinner?" Jake plops down on the blanket next to me.

"What do you say, Lily? You want to go out to eat, or do you want to just head home?" I give my girl the option.

"Can we go to Friday's?" she asks excitedly.

"I don't see why not," Jake helps me pick up the containers and gets rid of our trash.

We make our way back to the truck stopping for a moment on the bridge. Lily stands in front of us and Jake puts his arm around me and we are all quiet. I think we all needed today and to be here. For Jake and me, this place signifies so much, but now having Lily here with us, it feels like it cements us together.

After a nice dinner, Lily falls asleep on the way home. Jake carries her to her room and meets me in the kitchen. I'm pouring myself a glass of wine. "Beer?" I ask and he nods. I open the fridge and hand him a bottle and watch as his thumb effortlessly flicks the top off.

"Want to sit outside?" I ask.

Jake shakes his head, "First, I need something."

"What's that?"

Jake leans forward and presses his lips to mine. I immediately open and feel all the sweetness his kisses have to offer. He pulls away, "I get why you were mad. You gotta see it from where I stand. I needed to make it clear. I get I could've let you do that, but my point might not have been made. I don't want any man thinking he has even a shot with you, June. You and anyone else is not a possibility. I messed this up and I won't let anything come in the way again. You held out your lips from me," he accuses.

"I did not. Okay, I kind of did, but I wasn't mad about the Alister thing. I mean I was, but then watching you with Lily, I couldn't hold onto it. I guess I just was thinking about how much time we've missed."

The look on Jake's face changes. I think I see defeat. I don't want that, but I want to be honest about how I'm feeling. I put my head against his chest and wrap my arms around him. He holds me tight, takes a few more swigs from his beer, and sets it down on the counter.

"I love you, June."

"I love you too," I hug him tighter.

"Better pass on sitting outside. I have work in the morning."

I look him over trying to read what's behind his eyes. "Are we okay?"

He takes another swig from his bottle of beer and kisses me on top of my head, "Yeah," and is out the door.

I finish my glass of wine and get ready for bed. I lay down, but sleep eludes me. My mind is a constant swirl of wondering if we truly can ever be fixed.

CHAPTER SEVENTEEN

Over the next two weeks, I talk with Jake daily, but I don't see him as often as I would like. Some days, it's my schedule; others it's Lily's soccer schedule getting in the way. I feel like Jake is suddenly more guarded and that's why we haven't seen him as much. Truthfully, it's scaring me.

Tonight, we're having dinner at my parent's house. Last weekend, I spent the day at their house filling them in on Jake being back. I didn't tell them he was in jail. I lied to them when Lily was born, and I can't see coming clean now.

Jake's been here for the last hour hanging out with Lily downstairs, while I get ready. Normally when I'm at Mom and Dad's I wear whatever, but I want it to be special tonight. I even baked, which is a huge feat for me. I finish running the straight iron through my hair and decide that I'm happy with my appearance. I have on a floral print dress that cinches at the waist but is flowy enough that it's appropriate for dinner. My make-up is subtle, done in soft hues of pink with a peach lip gloss. With my auburn hair and big blue eyes, sometimes subtle is just enough.

I finish my look off with a spritz of my favorite perfume and walk down the stairs. Jake is sitting on the couch wearing jeans and a dark blue Henley. Tucked tight into his side is Lily and he's reading one of our favorite stories to her, Llama Llama Mad at Momma. She's giggling at Jake's change in voice and I laugh breaking their moment.

"Mom, you look so pretty," Lily looks up from the book.

"Thanks, baby."

Jake leaves the book in Lily's hand, stands and walks to me whispering low in my ear, "You're going to kill me at your parents wearing that dress. All night long I'm going to be thinking about getting you out of it."

I blush.

"What did he say, Mom?" Lily asks and I give Jake a look that says your words just melted me so you better answer this one.

He laughs, "Darling, that one was for your mommy's ears only."

She huffs, "Secrets. Secrets are no fun. Secrets. Secrets hurt someone."

I give him another look that says, she told you and then, "Are you about ready?" I ask.

"Waiting on you, June."

"Alright, so I might've spent some extra time on my hair."

"It looks good." He hands me my purse and opens the front door. "We're taking the truck."

"I can drive," I suggest.

"Nah, June. Not going to your Mom and Dad's for the first time having you drive."

The drive to my parent's house is filled with chatter from Lily until I give her my phone so that she can play games. When I reach in the back seat to hand her my phone, I notice a bouquet of flowers on the floor, behind his seat.

"Um, nice flowers?" I ask confused because he didn't give them to me.

"They're for your Mom." I smile at Jake and hold his hand. That's the sweetest thing.

"She'll love them."

I direct Jake to Mom and Dad's until we finally pull into their driveway. "Your parents live so close to the Lake,"

"Yeah, I lived here for the first few years of Lily's life. She's grown up on Lake Erie. It's one of the reasons why I brought her to our spot all the time. Once we moved from Mom and Dad's, I wanted her to have that still."

Lily undoes her buckle and is house bound running for her Poppa at full speed. He barely has the front door open when she throws her arms around his waist. "Hey Poppa," her voice carries.

I give Jake's hand a squeeze. "Are you ready for this?"

"Yeah, June. Are you?"

His question is a curious one to me. I don't quite understand it. Sure, I took a long time getting ready and we are a little late, but I want my parents to get to know him.

"Of course, why wouldn't I?"

He gives me another odd look and gets out of the truck, grabbing the flowers for Mom.

"Hey Dad!" I greet him giving him a hug.

"Mr. Withers," Jake offers his hand to Dad.

Dad looks him up and down sizing him up, "Call me Bill. Mom's in the kitchen. Come on in." We walk into the living room and Mom rushes out. Her dark hair is pinned up in a bun and she has a flower print apron over a gray shirt and black slacks.

"Grandma!" Lily shrieks leaving her Poppa's side and heading straight for Mom.

"Hey, pretty girl. I missed you. Why don't you check out what I just pulled out of the oven?"

"Cookies?" she asks excitedly following her nose to the delicious sugary scent coming from the kitchen.

"For my little Lil, but of course," she laughs.

"Mrs. Withers, these are for you," Jake hands Mom her flowers and the red, yellow and purple petals make her smile.

"Thank you, Jake. It's been a long time. You sure have grown since we saw you last." She leans in and gives him a hug. "I'll just go put these in water."

Lily runs back in with a giant gooey cookie. "Dad, you have to try these!"

"Well, that didn't take long," Dad mumbles under his breath. I shoot him a look that says, Dad we talked about this. To say my dad is less accepting of my relationship with Jake is a bit of an understatement. Mom seems to understand, but Dad not so much. When I told him, he kept saying things like what kind of man knocks a girl up, and then never talks to her? He promised when we accepted dinner invitations that he would keep his opinions to himself. Jake doesn't seem to notice and if he does, he doesn't say anything.

Lily breaks off a piece of her cookie and hands it to Jake, "That's delicious," he says with a cheeky grin.

"Would you like something to drink Dad, Jake, Lil?" I ask.

"Beer," Dad says and Jake nods silently telling me he'd like one too.

"Dad, I want to show you my faerie garden that Grandma and I made." Lily grabs Jake's hand and is leading him through the kitchen and then out the back door to the garden she and Mom made.

I grab Dad a beer and as soon as Jake and Lily are out of earshot I whirl on Dad, "Dad, you promised."

"He's here, right? I haven't said anything. I was just surprised Lily is already calling him Dad."

"Why wouldn't she?"

"'Cause donating sperm doesn't make a man a father."

"He's stepping up. It's not his fault that he didn't know about Lily. We're happy, Dad. I want you to please try and be open-minded."

"Stop giving our girl a hard time, and help me set the table," Mom orders.

I grab a beer for Jake and walk outside not wanting to hear what Mom is saying to Dad. She can scold her husband on her own terms and by the way she says, "Bill," as I walk out the door I imagine that is precisely what she is doing.

Outside, the sun is shining and a cool, gentle breeze comes off the Lake giving me chills. I spot Lily holding Jake's hand and leading him through the fairy garden.

I approach them, taking in my big man with our small Lily. He really is beautiful. Jake smiles at me as I approach and hand him his beer.

"Thanks," he places his hand on the small of my back.

"Shh," Lily holds her finger up to her lips, "I think they're about to eat supper." Next to few large mums is a piece of driftwood. Sitting on the wood next to a piece of celery is a small ceramic fairy with red hair.

"She looks like you," Jake laughs.

I playfully smack his arm, "She does not."

"She does!" Lily says. Realizing how loud she is, she clamps her hand over her mouth and then ushers us out of the garden.

"Dinner's ready," Mom calls out to us.

We head back into the house and take our seats at the table. Dad is at the head, where he always sits and Mom is to his left. Lily sits to Dad's right, and Jake sits next to her. I sit across from him and next to Mom.

"Everything looks delicious." Jake praises Mom on the prime rib, baked potatoes and fresh vegetable medley set before us.

"Thank you, but Bill cooked the meat. He's the beef guy around here," Mom says setting her hand on top of Dad's.

"Sounds like my kind of guy," Jake tilts his beer towards Dad, but is not rewarded with a tilt back.

"Mom, can you cut my meat?"

"I got it," Jake grabs Lily's plate and begins cutting her meat into tiny, Lily-sized bites.

"So Jake, what is it that you do?" Mom asks.

"I work at an auto shop in the city. We work on all kinds of cars. We get to do some pretty cool custom jobs."

"You make good money?" Dad asks.

"Dad," I snap not thinking that it was an appropriate question.

"What, June? He's obviously stepping up since Lily's calling him Dad. I want to know if he'll be able to finally support you."

"Dad," I grit out.

"No, it's okay June," Jake assures me. "I do well enough that I won't have a problem supporting my family. As soon I can, I plan on moving in with them and paying the bills."

"You're moving in?" Lily asks.

"Soon as your momma will have me."

Jake brought this up about moving in when he laid everything out for me, but we haven't broached the subject since. It's uncomfortable that he's laying it out in front of Mom, Dad and Lily. I wish he would've talked with me first.

"Well? That was fast. Were you going to tell us? Or just move this guy into your house and accept him as Lil's Dad."

"Poppa, but he is *my* Dad," Lil scolds coming to Jake's defense. "I even have his Momma's name. Did you know that's where Lily came from? He says I have her eyes too."

Dad has the good grace to back down, knowing that it's not cool to broach the subject in front of Lily.

"I bet Jake's Mom would've loved that you have her name, sweetie." Mom winks at Lily and continues to eat.

"Have you lived here long?" Mom asks Jake innocently.

"I've been here a couple of years. When June walked into the shop, I couldn't believe it. I'd wanted to see her for forever, but didn't know what to say. I still can't wrap my head around the fact that we have Lily. It's like fate wanted me to know. That moment when June walked in, changed my life, and every day I wake up grateful."

Mom smiles, satisfied with that response. Under the table, I get a squeeze of my leg between Jake's legs. He's finding a way to give me support.

"Where'd you take off to six years ago?" Dad asks.

"Dad!"

"It's alright. Bill, why don't we wait until after this delicious dinner you and your wife made and then I'd be happy to answer any and all of your questions. I get it. Me sitting here at your table after you had to take care of my girls when I wasn't here is shocking. Having a little girl, I'm sure I would be outraged too. I gotta tell you Bill, every decision I've ever made has been to protect June, and I'm here now and not going anywhere. I love these girls, have loved June since we were kids. Do I wish things were different? Sure, of course. I missed out on so much with Lily, but I'm here now, Bill and I'm not going anywhere."

Jake's declaration has my heart beating so hard. No matter how many times he tells me the same thing, sometimes I still can't believe it.

I mouth I love you to Jake. Mom changes the subject completely by asking Lily about soccer and school.

As dinner wears on, I'm afraid of the impending conversation between Jake and Dad. I never asked Jake not to tell Dad about prison, but I did tell Jake that I told Dad when I got pregnant that it was a one night stand and Jake left town. I think this entire situation is hard for Dad, and I'm not sure how he would take it if he found out that Jake was in prison. Maybe Jake's answer to Dad was enough to placate Dad? I have to get us out of here before that comes out. As soon as we finish dinner, I wave myself with my hand like I'm burning up.

"Oh, honey. What's wrong?" Mom asks me.

"I'm not sure. I'm suddenly not feeling good."

Jake is at my side in seconds. He feels my head, and squints his eyes at me, "You don't have a fever or anything. Do you want to sit down for a while? I can help your Mom with the dishes."

I sit on the couch and hold me head against my hand, "No, my head suddenly hurts. I think maybe we should call it a night, Mom. I'm sorry I just don't know what came over me," I lie. The truth is I'm putting on my best award winning role, so that we don't have to talk about where Jake has been.

Jake looks at me with concern and then says, "Maybe I should get her home. I'm sorry we have to call it an early night. I hope we can do this again soon."

Mom and Dad kiss Lily and me goodbye. Jake hugs Mom and shakes Dad's hand. In minutes we're packed up and in Jake's truck on our way home.

"You okay?" Jake asks me as helps me down from his truck. He's working hard at taking care of me and I instantly feel bad.

"Sure, I'm fine." He eyes me suspiciously. I have a feeling that I didn't fool him one bit. We walk into the house with Lily half asleep in Jake's arms.

"I'm going to get Lily ready for bed, why don't you lay down?" Jake suggests.

I kick off my shoes and sit down on the couch and watch Jake carry Lily up the stairs.

Thirty minutes later, Jake plops down next to me on the couch. "That girl can talk. She was practically asleep when I brought her up and as soon as I laid her down it was non-stop."

I laugh because I know exactly what he means.

"So, what was that really about?" Jake asks after several minutes of us just laying together on the couch.

"What do you mean?" I look anywhere, but at Jake.

"I mean, I don't buy that you don't feel good. Why did you want to leave?"

"Shit. I didn't want Dad to question you anymore about where you've been. I'm not sure how he's going to take it."

Jake studies me for a moment and then he sighs, "I'm not going anywhere. Don't you think it's time we tell your folks the truth? I'd hate for them to find out any other way."

My heart beats fast, "I'm not sure how Dad will react. Maybe we can wait a while?"

"You act like I should be ashamed that I was in prison. I'm not. I did what I had to do to protect you and I'd do it again."

Every time Jake says that, it grates on my last nerve. I hate it. He could've been upfront with me as Lucas. He could've made the time to tell me. We could have figured it out. "I'm not ashamed!"

"Bullshit. You just faked being sick so your Dad wouldn't find out. You're a grown woman. Act like it. It's time for us to own up to everything that's happened."

"That's not fair, Jake."

"What's not fair? The fact that you said you forgive me, but I feel it hanging around my neck like a fucking noose. Or that you can tell me you love me, but you can't seem to let any of the anger or pain go? None of that feels fair, June."

He stands from the couch and I'm shell shocked. "I'm going to go home. Give us both some space before I say something I'll regret. See you, June," he says and walks out the door.

CHAPTER EIGHTEEN

What the hell is wrong with me? Is Jake right? Maybe he is. I don't know if I can forgive him. As much as I love him and as much as I've missed him, I haven't truly let the past go. How can I when I had to raise Lily by myself for six years. Being Lucas was the most selfish thing he could've done and I'm angry with him, despite me saying otherwise.

I'm so conflicted by my feelings. How would I have felt if he was in danger? Would I have done anything including shutting him out to protect him?

Questions plague me as I stare vacantly at the door that Jake walked out. My chest hurts. I'm not treating him fairly. I need to figure myself out, so that I'm not doing this to him. I should've gone after Jake. I should pick up the phone and call him, but I don't.

He's right. He did so much for us, and here I am throwing it in his face every chance I get. I need to decide if I can truly let go of the past and move on with our future.

Monday comes and goes and I don't hear from Jake except for a text telling me he has to work late and to give his love to Lily. I don't respond because I'm a chicken. I feel guilty for how I've behaved.

On Tuesday, after a conversation with my boss about how we haven't been that busy lately and that we better take the slow while we can get it, I decide that I'm going to take Lily out of school for a few days and get out of here. Luckily, it's a short week because Friday is a teacher workday.

Although, I haven't been back since I was a girl, I feel like if I'm going to truly forgive all the bad with Jake I need to go back to where it all started. I need to face it, then maybe I can finally start to heal.

I pick up the phone to call Jake, but get his voicemail. "Hey, it's me. You're right. I haven't been fair. I feel like I need to get my head on straight. Please don't give up on me while I do. I decided to take Lily to the summer house for the weekend. She's never been there and hopefully a little bit of time away from all of this will help me get some perspective. I love you, Jake."

I disconnect hoping that he will stick this out with me, while I decide if I can forgive him. Even more unfairness, I know. God, I'm being selfish.

I leave work, pack our bags, and pick Lily up from school just before lunch. I call Daryn on the way to let him know that I'm leaving for a few days and apologize profusely, hoping he can get someone to help out with Grace in my absence. I feel like an ass about it, but I just have to get out of here.

"Mom? What are you doing here?" Lily asks when Mrs. Weinstein delivers her to the office. I have to smile at my daughter, she picked out her outfit this morning. Her yellow and pink striped leggings along with her bat t-shirt screams I want Halloween to be here already.

"We're going to go to the summer house for a few days, just the two of us. What do you say?"

"What do I say?" She throws her hands up, "What do I say? Eeps, I can't wait to see where you and Daddy met. Where's Dad? He's coming, right?"

A pang of guilt stabs me in my chest. Is it wrong for me to bring Lily there without Jake? I wish he was coming with us, but I also know that I need to figure out my headspace.

"This trip is going to be just the two of us, but you can call Dad while we're gone. It's kind of last minute, so I'm sure he has to work."

I grab Lily's hand and lead her to the SUV. "We're going to leave straight from here."

"But Grace and I have practice," she whines.

"Honey, I'm sure it will be fine if we miss one practice. We won't be gone that long and I know how much you've always wanted to go." For some reason, it feels like without Jake I have to convince her.

"Did you bring the iPad?" Of course, that will solve everything.

"I did, and I downloaded a movie on it for you."

She smiles at me and we make our trek south. It's a good nine hours, so my spontaneous "let's get my head on straight" drive will hopefully bring me some clarity.

Miles and miles of road pass by and I'm no clearer on what I'm doing than when I left this morning. A glance in my rear-view mirror tells me Lily's sleeping. I check the time, it's getting late. I'm surprised Jake hasn't called me. It makes me wonder if I've pushed him too far, but if he can give up on us already, is he worth it? I need a man who can be patient with me and won't go away again. I guess that's what my entire problem is; fear. I'm so afraid that he will break my heart all over again by leaving me. Deep down, I want him to come after me.

I pass an exit sign for a correctional institute for men. In the distance, I can see high gray cement walls surrounded by what I assume is barbed wire. There is a watch tower and although it's far away I imagine a man armed with a gun watching the yard. Jake was behind those walls, not those per-se, but he spent four years locked behind cement for a crime he didn't commit; for something I did. He protected me and since learning about Lily all he has done is be here with us. He's loved me, given me unparalleled passion, and endured hell for me. Looking at the concrete walls makes me realize that my fears of him leaving me are just that, fears. I refuse to allow fear to dictate our future.

I pick up my phone and dial Jake again. It rings, once, twice and then, "June?"

"Hey, it's me."

"I've been trying to reach you for hours, I left my phone at work last night and then was busy today at work. I just got a chance to check it. It's been going straight to voicemail for hours. Where are you?" Jake's voice is laced with concern.

"Ugh, I should've thought about that. Mountains break-up service. I'm on my way to the summer house. Didn't you get my message?" Just as I ask, my voice cuts out a little.

"Juniper," his voice is soft, "I heard your message. What are you doing? You didn't need to go there without me. I thought I'd give you space, but I don't want states between us. Where's your head at?"

"I feel terrible for how I've treated you. You're right, it's not fair," my phone starts to break up again. "Jake?"

"Be there," his voice cuts in and then out again until finally my screen flashes no service.

Well, that's just great.

A few hours later and my GPS has me pulling down a dark, dirt road. It looks different than I remember, but that may just be because I've never driven here before. I was only a kid when I was here last

"Wake up, sweetie. We're here?" I rouse Lily from sleep while putting the SUV in park. My headlights flash on the house and I can see the porch swing Mom told me about and the wind chime she picked up at a flea market gently swaying in the breeze. The air is warm and almost sticky. I open the door and my interior light goes on overhead.

Lily sits up, "This is it? We're finally here?"

"We sure are."

She opens her door, hops down from the SUV and stretches her tiny body.

"Well, let's go!" Lily grabs my hand and rushes me towards the house. I notice the small cobblestone path that I scraped my knee on when I was nine. This place has stayed the same in so many ways. The door to the front of the house is a bright red now, but other than that, it looks so much like how I remember it. Potted plants sit on the porch next to the front door and through the window I can see the darkened back of the flower print curtains.

The motion detector over the door flicks on and off and I shake my head because Mom is always griping at Dad to fix it. Maybe I can be of some use and fix that while I'm here. Who am I kidding?

It hasn't been that long since Mom and Dad were last here and a quick call earlier to Dad confirmed that the key is right where it's always been, inside the secret compartment on the planter.

Lily grins at me when she sees the secret hiding spot. "That's so cool, it's like spy gear for the old people."

I mock gasp, "Old people?"

"Grandma and Grandpa are old," I laugh at her bluntness.

"Alright, kiddo are you ready to see the house?" I open the door and flick on the light illuminating the room. It's clean and homey, and despite being vacant, it still has the fresh linen scent I remember so well. The living room has two large, brown chaises made of suede or some other soft, inviting material. An overfilled built-in bookshelf separates the large chaises. There's no TV only a large cabinet that houses board games on the top half and Dad's not so secret stash of booze on the bottom. The floor is bamboo and an outdoor/indoor rug sits on top of the majority of it.

I wasn't sure how I would feel coming here, but I know now that I had nothing to worry about. I feel completely comfortable, and admonish myself for waiting so long.

I look at Lily and see that she is anxious to explore. "Go ahead, look around. You can't hurt anything."

"Yes!" She takes off running up the stairs to the bedrooms. I move to the kitchen which, even though it could use an update, has a unique country charm with its warm wood and butcher block counter tops. I open a cupboard looking for a tea kettle. It's exactly where it should be. While I wait for my tea, I unload the SUV, unplug my phone from the car charger and call Jake.

It doesn't even ring but goes straight to voicemail. "It's Jake. Leave a message." his voice is clipped as I wait for the beep.

"Hi, just wanted to let you know that we got in safe. I love you," I disconnect not sure of exactly what I want to say.

Lily and I spend the next couple of hours playing board games and hanging out. Even though it's well past midnight, she can't sleep since she slept so much in the car.

There's pasta and sauce in the pantry so I make us an extremely late dinner and once we are stuffed and all Monopolyed out, I tuck her into the twin size bed that I once called my own.

I open the room that my parents usually occupy and smile. This is one room that has changed. The walls are a bright yellow where they once were lavender. The over-sized bed has a white quilt with yellow daisies stitched along the sides of it and large over-sized yellow pillows sit against the opulent, cherry headboard. Although, the bed and matching dresser are antiques, Mom has spruced them up to make this room look like summertime.

I shimmy out of my jeans and face-plant onto the bed. I want sleep to take me. But no, I'm not that lucky. I toss and turn and end up on my back, staring out the window into the night sky. I know deep down, I've always prayed that I would have Jake back and that he would get to be a Dad to Lily. I never expected this deep rooted fear of him leaving to hold me hostage. I want to be fair to him. I need to learn to let everything go. Tomorrow, I will face the river and hopefully by doing that I will be able to put the past behind me, so that I can move forward with Jake without anything hanging over our heads.

CHAPTER NINETEEN

My eyes flutter open. Early dawn light shines through an open window cascading a yellow glow on the edge of the bed. I draw a breath and breathe in the most familiar comfortable scent in the world; Jake. A warm large hand strokes across my belly. I press my body backward and feel the hardness of Jake.

"Morning, beautiful," Jake's raspy voice is like music to my ears.

I turn and face him. Those blue-greens that I fell in love with at fifteen stare back at me. "You're really here?"

"I left once I got off the phone with you, yesterday. I was trying to give you space, not push you away, but I decided that was stupid." His demeanor is relaxed and he grins after saying stupid.

"Stupid?" I question.

"Oh, yes," he says playfully and then nips at my ear. "We had enough space to last us a lifetime. If something's eating at you, we work through it together. If you need a minute, you do it in another room, not another state, and most of all we talk our stuff out. You're it for me, June. You've been it for me for as long as I can remember, and whatever it is, I'll be here for you. If you're scared that I'll disappear, then I'll stick so close to your side you gotta peel me off."

My lip trembles because this is what I needed all along, his reassurances.

"If you need time to tell your folks about our past, then we wait as long as you need. I won't pressure you, but I want you to know I'm not ashamed. I'd do anything for you. I'd do anything for us. My only regret is not telling you I was Jake sooner. I hate that look on your face when you found out who I was. It's seared into my brain, but I needed that time with you. I get that you have fears, June. I'm afraid too."

"What are you afraid of?" My throat is tight holding off tears. I see vulnerability in my big strong Jake.

"I'm afraid that I'll be like him. Afraid that it's not over, and that something bad is still going to happen. Afraid that I won't be a good dad. Afraid mostly that you don't love me the same way I love you, and that you'll decide this isn't worth it. God, June. I know we're going to have a long road, but you don't leave. We're in this together, yeah?"

That tear I was holding back falls and then another. "Yeah, Jake. I'm sorry I left. I just felt like I needed…"

"Shh," he puts his finger over my lip.

"I know why you left. You don't have to be sorry."

"I need you to know," I say moving his finger away. "There's never been anyone who could even come close to holding a candle to you. You're it for me. I was scared, that's partly why I came here, and I hate that I keep making you feel this way. You don't have to prove anything to me. I know you love us. I came here because I need to let go of the past and I thought the best way to do that was by coming here and facing it. I just thought that was the best way for us to move forward. I wasn't running away from us."

"June, I do have to prove myself, and it's okay. I lied to you once, sure my reasons felt justified, but it put insecurities in your heart. I must've failed so far at making sure you know that I'll never do it again, or you wouldn't have felt like you had to go. I'm here, June, right here. I'm here for the long haul. Where you go, I go. If you feel like you need to be here to face the past, then I'm facing it with you. When we get back, I'm not spending another night away from you. I'm with you, June. I'm never letting you go again."

What could I say to that? His words ease so much turmoil. He's right. I shouldn't have come here without him, but I'm so glad I did and that he followed. It's exactly what I needed. Our lips crash together, and in the early morning dawn, we make sweet, sweet love.

"DAD, I CAN'T BELIEVE you're here." Lily lunges onto the bed and plops down between us. Luckily, I threw Jake's t-shirt on after our love making, and he pulled on his boxer briefs.

"Lily, I wouldn't have missed your first trip here," Jake bops her on the nose with his finger and she beams the biggest smile. I have no doubt that Lily is as enamored as me. The sun, now higher in the sky, shines brightly through the window creating a warm glow over the room. I'm warm from the heat. I hug Lily and throw the covers off of me, declaring, "Pancake time!"

"Ooh, Mom makes the best pancakes!" Lily hops off the bed to follow me. I smile. It's just pancakes in a box, but they sure are tasty.

I look over my shoulder one last time before walking out of the room, "Coming?" I flash Jake a bright smile.

"Pancakes with my girls. I wouldn't miss it."

Lily is a pro at helping me make pancakes. She mixes the batter while I start a pot of coffee.

"Coffee smells good," Jake kisses me on the cheek and takes a seat at the country style kitchen table. I watch him suppress a yawn.

"Did you drive all night?"

He shrugs.

"Why don't you sleep for a little while after breakfast and I'll take Lily into town to stock the fridge?"

"Yeah okay, but I don't want to sleep that long. I want to be able to show Lily this place too."

I nod my head agreeing with him. Lily opens a new bottle of syrup and sets it down on the table, while I pour the batter into large circles on the griddle.

The three of us enjoy a nice breakfast and as we finish, Jake yawns again, then heads upstairs to sleep. I send Lily to her room to get ready for the day and I tiptoe into the bedroom and change clothes, throwing on a pair of fitted capri jeans and a flowery peasant blouse finished with a pair of black flats. I kiss his forehead and watch him for a moment listening to him breathe deeply in his sleep.

As Lily and I drive into town, I'm surprised with how much is still how I remember. The ice cream shop Dad used to take me to still has the red and white awning and the barber shop next door still has the red, white, and blue pole out front. A few old men sit outside a restaurant with Styrofoam cups, a gentle steam rises. A man with a full white beard is laughing at another man who's wearing a black Irish trinity cap.

It has an old southern charm to it. Driving through town and pulling into the parking lot of the Piggly-Wiggly, I think about the majestic quality this town carries, too bad it also carries our demons.

We grab a cart and start filling it with fresh fruit.

"Mom, these peaches are huge!" Lily grabs several and tosses them into the cart. I grab a green, plastic produce bag made for fruit, take them out of the cart and show Lily how they go into the bag then continue shopping. She continues to try and put a million items in the cart and I am constantly taking each one out and examining it to decide if we need it.

"We won't be here that long," I tell her for the fourth time taking out a jumbo pack of gummies.

"Alright, I get it," Lily says.

We head over to the butcher and get steaks for dinner tonight burgers for tomorrow. We check out and I put Lily in the SUV. I'm returning the cart when I feel the oddest sensation, like somebody's watching me. I look around as the tiny hairs on my neck raise. I don't see anything suspicious, but this feeling scares me. I hurry back to Lily and start the SUV, backing out of the spot as quickly as possible.

A horn blares at me and I slam on the brakes making Lily lurch forward in her seat. "Mom?" she asks concerned.

"Sorry, baby." I mentally curse myself for almost running into a car. I take a deep breath and decide that I'm overreacting. It's not anything. I'm sure of it, aren't I?

We return to the house and unload the groceries. I shake off my weird feeling and busy myself by cleaning. I ask Lily if she wants to go for a walk and she happily agrees. Outside, the sun is warm and everything is just a little greener than in Ohio. It feels like someone, somehow amplified everything. The grass is like this vivid shade of green that my young mind probably didn't ever fully appreciate. Now though, I revel in its beauty. Wildflowers intermingle between the trees and the sound of flowing water in the distance reminds me just how close I am to everything. I'm not ready to face the river with Lily. Instead, we walk past Jake's old house and I'm surprised when I see a beat up Chevy truck in the driveway. I know it was sold, but it still surprises me. We walk through the clearing that Jake and I first got physical in and I tell her how Daddy and I used to play there.

Lily hangs on my every word. By the time we circle back to the house, she is anxious to wake up Jake. I let her while I start lunch.

"Juniper," Jake says into my neck kissing me while I stand at the counter making sandwiches.

"Mommy and Daddy kissing in a tree," Lily sings.

I laugh, "It's sitting in a tree."

"That's not what I saw," she singsongs.

Jake laughs at us and swipes a sandwich. "This is great," he says between bites.

"So, are you guys going to get married, or what?" Lily asks grabbing a sandwich.

"Lily!" I scold because she shouldn't be going there.

"What?" she asks.

"No, it's okay," Jake says to the both of us, "Lily, that's a smart question."

"It is?" she asks at the same time I think, it is?

"Your mommy and I are definitely going to get married one day, but I get to ask her first and that gets to be a special moment between Mommy and Daddy."

My jaw is slack with how casually he just threw that out there to Lily.

"Are you going to take a long time?" she asks.

He laughs, "Not too long, and I promise you'll be the first to know. Deal?"

"Deal," she sticks out her hand to shake on it.

Although my heart is beating fast, I'm no longer afraid of what the future holds. I'm looking forward to it. Coming here was exactly what we needed. Fear is not ruling me where Jake is concerned.

"Guess what, Lilypad?" I say knowing exactly what will placate my girl.

"What?" she asks taking a bite of her giant peach. Juice from the succulent fruit dribbles out of the side of her mouth.

"Daddy's moving in with us, as soon as we get back." Jake beams at me.

"Decided it needs to happen right away, sweetie," Jake tells her.

"Awesome!" She throws her tiny arms around Jake squishing her head into his cotton t-shirt. I love how natural it is for the two of them.

I sit down and eat my lunch and we talk about what kind of furniture Jake has and what we can use. I can't believe he's moving in and I've yet to see his place.

After lunch, the sky grows dark and it begins to rain, so we stay indoors and play board games until we've let Lily win so many times she's suspicious that we're letting her win.

Jake praises my choice in steaks and cooks them on the grill under the overhang, while Lily and I make a salad.

Our dinner is filled with stories of how I swam up to Jake in the river. The way Jake tells it melts my insides. It's a story of such simple, sweet love. I'm not sure that before this moment I ever truly realized how much Jake loved me right off the bat.

We clean up as a family, each person helping out. Later, in Lily's room, Jake sings Butterfly Kisses. This time, I don't wait in the hallway. I sit down beside him on the bed as his voice radiates beauty throughout the room and listen. Lily's sleepy eyes watch her daddy and I know she is in serious love. As I watch him, my world as I know it ceases. It's no longer Lily and June. It's the three of us. This is what was stolen from us, but we have it now. We've survived and we're a family.

CHAPTER TWENTY

The weather hasn't been so great here over the last few days, that's why when we wake up today and the sun is shining through the window Jake mumbles, "Finally."

"What's that?" I question barely wiping the sleep from my eyes.

"It's finally nice enough that I can take Lily fishing. After breakfast, I'll take her into town and get some new poles."

"She'll love that." I kiss him and then he gets up out of bed with a huge grin on his face. It makes me think that maybe there was a time when Jake's dad took him fishing, and it wasn't all bad. Maybe it was good before his Mom died, and he wants to give his daughter some of the same experiences?

"I'm going to stay here. I want you guys to have this time together."

"You don't have to. I'd love for you to come with us."

I throw on some yoga pants and a gray t-shirt, "No, it's good. You two should have some time together without me. I think it will be good for the both of you." Besides, I need to lay some ghosts to rest that I've been letting follow me around for all too long. I don't tell Jake this. For some reason, it feels like I need to do this by myself and this feels like the perfect time.

Lily, who pretty much is always in a good mood, is exceptionally happy at the idea of spending the day fishing with her dad. We have breakfast together while Lily asks all about what type of fish they might catch, and I pack them a lunch to take with them. They both kiss me goodbye, and I wave to them as they pull out of the driveway.

I grab a pair of Mom's mud boots from the hall closet and slip my feet into them. You never know how slick it's going to be by the river's edge especially with all of the rain we've had as of late. Jake is taking Lily to a spot where the mouth of the river is large and is designated for all kinds of fisherman. I think perhaps he doesn't want to revisit the river down here, but I need to. Something deep within me needs to confront everything and make peace.

Outside, the air is sticky. I'm surprised by the humidity. Although, this far south it should be expected. I take my black hair tie off my wrist and secure my hair into a loose ponytail. I walk the same path that I traveled religiously that summer. It's overgrown with branches jutting out of the ground and thick underbrush mixed with mud covering the path. I'm grateful for the boots. My feet squish with every step, but I barely pay any mind to it. It's like an invisible string is leading me, and I need to follow it.

I pass the barn, and think about my first kiss. My fingers splay over my lips as I remember, then continue on my journey. When I reach the bank, I'm surprised when I see Mike Daniels' boat tethered to the dock. It's worn and rusted. Where it once looked like it was a great fishing vessel, it's now coated with a thick green slime along the bottom. What's left of the seat is torn and frayed. I hate to think what animals have taken up residence on the boat. My skin prickles. I get that same eerie feeling that I got the other day at the grocery store. I look around; I'm alone. I shudder, trying to shake off the heebie-jeebie feeling. I sit down on the small part of the dock that the boat is tied to. A little water splashes against it sprinkling my jeans with tiny dots.

I look at the boat and back to the water, images of the night that changed so much play before my eyes. I have to say what's on my mind and so I give it all to the wind. This isn't about forgiving Mike, it's about forgiving myself and letting go, so that we can move forward. If anything, the last few days have shown me what kind of family we have. Forward is the only direction I want to go after this, no more looking back.

"Jake's a good man. He was a good son, too. He took everything you gave him.

"All the hate."

"All the beatings."

"Everything. He took it all and you just had to go and try to hurt me, didn't you? I was a kid. He was a kid. He didn't deserve anything you did to him and he certainly didn't deserve the aftermath. You know he did time for your death? I'm glad it was me that knocked you overboard. I hated you for everything you did to him. You deserved to drown in this river. The best thing that happened that day was the current taking you away.

"We have a beautiful girl and we love her, in spite of you. You tried to hurt us, but look at where you are. You're gone and we're here, living. Jake is the best dad in the world and he's only just begun. Our family is going to get bigger and you are done. You can't hurt us anymore. Goodbye, Mike Daniels." I release a deep breath, feeling so much lighter. The iron chains that were weighing me down have come loose and let me rise back to the surface. I don't know why coming here has made everything so clear, but it has. Crystal. He can't hurt us. He never really could. Our love has always been so much greater than Mike Daniels.

I stand and turn to leave, but freeze in my tracks when I hear loud clapping coming from in the trees. That prickly sensation is back tenfold as a deep fear takes root.

"Bravo, bravo!" More claps as *that* voice rings through the air. My mind screams run, but my feet are firmly planted, frozen in place, because from out of the trees steps Mike Daniels.

CHAPTER TWENTY-ONE

Mike Daniels looks a lot like I remember him. He's as tall as Jake, but he now has a scar brandishing his cheek. His hair is mostly gray and his clothes, for the most part, look newer. You would think he was an ordinary man at first glance, but you would be wrong. His eyes tell a different story. They are filled with one emotion, hate.

"June, right? Who names their daughter after a month, anyways?" He takes several steps towards me and my feet become unglued letting me step backward keeping the distance.

"You...you're dead."

He laughs at me. It's the most villainous sound I've ever heard. "Tsk. Tsk. So dramatic, June. Nice speech, by the way. Did you get everything off your chest? Did it make you feel better? It sure amused the shit out of me," he snickers and advances another step.

I take another step back and back myself up next to the boat. "How are you here?"

He shakes his head, almost with amusement. "That's not the question you should ask."

I bite the inside of my cheek, "What should I ask?"

"The question you should ask is what am I going to do to you?" His face is the most sinister face I've ever seen. I know his intentions are to hurt me. I can either jump in the boat or into the water. On an impulse, I decide that the water is my best option. I need to get away as quick as I can. I take a leap but I'm painfully yanked backward when his hand snakes into my hair. "Oh, this is going to be fun."

CHAPTER TWENTY-TWO

Since Jake pulled into town he couldn't shake this feeling that something bad was going to happen. He felt it the moment he drove into this town, and he felt it as he pulled away from June to take Lily fishing. He and Lily had talked about fishing for the last two days while they'd been rained in, and he wanted to do this with her. There wasn't a lot that Jake thought he could offer Lily, but this was one thing he'd learned to do with his own dad that wasn't horrible. In fact, it was probably the only good memory he had with *that* man.

As Jake drives Lily to the fish and tackle store, that he hopes no one recognizes him, that was the last thing he needed. He'd made a lot of enemies in this town doing Eli's work but he was also a lot bigger now and knew how to handle himself in ways he never dreamt possible, nor was it a way he was proud of. No, this town held more shame and hurt for Jake than he'd care to admit and as the familiar landscape passes he felt it, every bit of it.

He parks the truck, helps Lily down and walks into the store with Lily's hand in his. It surprises him how different it looks. It used to be a dirty place that reeked of fish guts, but now it looks like a brand new store. It's clean and organized with a fresh coat of paint on the walls.

Jake asks the clerk where the kids rods are and is pointed in the right direction.

"I want this one Dad!" Lily tells him, pointing to the only pink and purple rod they have. Jake smiles at his daughter, "Then it's yours."

They round the corner and Jake finds a graphite rod that has a good bend to it. It's not the most expensive fishing pole, but it will do the trick. Next he shows Lily the cooler filled with worms.

"That's so neat!" she says picking up an eight-inch nightcrawler. He smiles, loving that even though his daughter wants a pink and purple rod, she's not afraid to get dirty by playing with worms.

"I'll show you how to hook it too. Did you know if we cut that worm in half both parts will still wiggle?"

"No way," her jaw is slack as she starts to pull the worm apart.

"We don't want to do that just yet." Jake places his hand on top of hers to stop her from ripping it in two, even though that's something he would've done when he was her age. Minutes later, they check out of the store and begin walking to the truck.

An older woman wearing a thick white shawl around her shoulders, who is naturally leaning forward due to the gravity of old age places her hand on Jake's elbow as they move down the sidewalk. "Jake Daniel's is that you?" Her voice, even though it's ages and has a slight shake to it, is a voice that Jake could never forget.

"Mrs. Jones?" he asks not believing his eyes. Mrs. Jones was old when she taught him about music. He had just assumed that she would not be around anymore. Seeing her again was a shock to him, but it was a good shock; a welcome shock.

"That's my boy. Now come here and give me a hug." Jake wastes no time bending down and wrapping his arms around Mrs. Jones. She was the only good thing in those first years when he was forced to work for Eli and seeing her again somehow makes him feel happier than he'd already been, and Jake had been plenty happy as of late.

"Mrs. Jones, I never thought I'd see you again. This is my daughter, Lily." Lily halfway hides behind her dad and peeks her head around his body, not sure what to make of the stranger.

"I won't bite sugar, let me get a look at you."

Jake puts a hand on Lily's shoulder sensing that she is nervous and he finds it amusing considering Lily has never once come off as shy as long as he's known her.

Lily's dark hair and blue-green eyes that match her daddy's, look up at Mrs. Jones in wonderment, "Hello," she finally says after several long assessing seconds.

"I don't bite. I swear it. Look at her Jake. She's your spitting image, prettier, though." Lily gets a good look at the softness in Mrs. Jones eyes and she smiles thinking that this must be the oldest woman on the planet, and so she asks her, "Are you the oldest woman alive?"

Mrs. Jones laughs, "Oh no, my sister she has five years on me, now she's the oldest woman alive," she says winking.

Lily looks up at Mrs. Jones in wonderment. "Lily, Mrs. Jones taught me all about music. She taught me to play the keyboard, to read and write music and to use my voice."

"That's so cool," Lily smiles and Jake can't help but flash her a huge grin.

"It was so good running into you. I'm sure that June would love to meet you. She's Lily's mom."

"The one you'd sing about?" Mrs. Jones asks shocking Jake that she remembers.

"The one and only. We're only here for another day or so, but we'd love to have you over for dinner. What do you say? Tomorrow night?" Jake asks hopeful, not wanting to lose this connection with Mrs. Jones since she was such a huge influence in his life.

"That'd be real nice Jake."

"Great, June will be so excited. June's family's place is just off Burton St."

"She wasn't related to Merda was she?"

Jake scourers his memory and snaps his finger, "I think you're right. I'm pretty sure that's her aunt. Did you know her?"

"I sure did. I know right where her house is. Is four too early? I'm afraid I can't make it much past eight o'clock these days without falling asleep."

"Four would be great!" Jake says beaming.

"You have fun fishing," Mrs. Jones says, starting to walk away.

"Wait! How'd you know we're going fishing?" Lily asks.

Mrs. Jones taps her temple and smiles and then walks away. Jake smiles again because they were walking out of the Bait and Tackle store carrying fishing poles and it was pretty obvious what they were up too.

Jake and Lily drive to the fishing spot, only to find it overcrowded. Jake was hoping it wouldn't be this bad, but he figures since they're here he might as well make the most of it. Even if they have to eat their lunch in the bed of his truck because the only few picnic tables are already taken.

He teaches Lily how to bait a hook and where some girls would be squeamish, Lily doesn't mind it one bit and then they find a space among the other fishermen and cast their lines.

The men around Jake annoy him. They're cursing and drinking beers, not the type of thing he wants his little girl around. He could say something and put them in their place or he could walk away. Jake shoots the men a glare after he hears the F word being thrown around again and then decides that there is no reason that he needs to put up with this.

"Lil, we're going to go fish somewhere else."

"What's wrong with here?" she asks too caught up in her fishing pole and trying to figure out if she has a bite or not to notice anything else.

"There's too much noise here. It's scaring all the fish," he tells Lily and packs up their things deciding that even though he's not ready to go back to his old home to fish, anything is better than here.

Lily reluctantly hands over her fishing pole and the two load back up the truck and head towards his childhood home. Jake knows the best spot to fish and if he pulls out by the barn he can avoid making eye contact with *that* house. He would do anything to never have to see it again.

Driving past June's family home, Jake is relieved to see June's SUV still parked in the same spot. He still has that feeling deep in the pit of his stomach that he can't explain, but knowing she is home, lessens it some.

Jake pulls down a dirt road that leads towards the river and is glad that his truck is four wheel drive when his truck easily moves through the mud.

He passes the barn and something about the way the door is perched partly open makes his gut churn. He doesn't know what it is about that door, but he doesn't feel like fishing anymore. He feels like turning back to check on June, but one look at Lily and he knew he needed to give her the afternoon. She was already so disappointed that they left the first fishing spot and he wanted to give her this, so he trudges on, ignoring the feeling.

He parks his truck at a small bank. Two huge tree stumps are still perched on the edge of the bank where he rolled them years ago. He always loved this spot. It's dense trees often hid him when he didn't want his old man to know his whereabouts, especially those nights he would sit here with June. The air is warm and smells fresh. It's a smell that calms him. Suddenly, it doesn't feel so bad bringing his Lily to where he used to fish. This wasn't a spot that his dad tainted. This was a place that he shared with June.

"Your Mom and I used to come here."

"You did?"

"We sure did. She was so fearless, still is. I was a few years older than her so I thought she should stay away from me at first, but she wouldn't have it. She swam right up to me in the river once. Just down there," Jake points down the river.

"And what'd you do?" she asks holding on to his every word.

"Splashed her and then the next day she showed up at the barn we passed. She helped me with the chickens."

"You had chickens?"

"We had all kinds of animals. She helped me clean fish too."

"Mom did that? I can't imagine. She doesn't like to get dirty," Lily says casting her rod into the river after her second attempt.

"Good now reel it in nice and slow." He grins at his daughter loving this talk. "She'd clean anything to help me get done early. We were inseparable."

"It's like a fairytale," Lily sighs as she reels her line all the way out and casts it again.

Jake laughs, "Maybe it was. Maybe the best part of the fairytale has yet to come. Don't reel your line so fast this time. Let the water take it a little."

"Like this?" she asks.

"Yeah, baby. You're doing real good."

"Mom would be a good queen and then I could be the princess," Lily says and then her eyes get big as she feels a tug on her line. "Dad!" she whisper yells.

"Reel it slow baby and then let up for a second. You gotta make the fish think it's got a fighting chance. He'll hook himself even more."

She follows his instructions making him proud.

"Fast Lil. Do it fast now," he coaches and is ready to step in if she needs a hand. The fish flies out of the water attached to her hook.

"I did it, Dad! I did it!" A small fish he's going to throw back dangles from the line.

"You sure did!" he says, knowing how good that feels to catch one for the first time and so grateful he's getting to share that with Lily.

A loud bang and then a scream echoes through the trees making Jake freeze in his steps to free the fish. His stomach turns. June, he has to get to June. "Lily listen to me. I need you to get in the truck. Take my phone and call 911 after you lock the doors. Can you do that?" he asks hurriedly shoving the phone into her hands.

"Dad? Was that Mom? I'm scared," she asks.

He grabs her hand leaving the fish to flop on the ground and rushes her to the truck. "Get in. Lock the door. Call 911. Don't open it for anyone, but me, Mom or the police got it?"

Lily doesn't answer she's scared and doesn't understand what's happening. "Lil, it's important. You got it?"

She nods as he hands her the phone. "I love you, kid," he closes her in the truck and rushes towards another scream, his June's scream, a scream he wished like fuck he wasn't hearing.

CHAPTER TWENTY-THREE

Pain rips through my body as I land on the deck. I need to get away from this man. I need to fight. I kick out landing a hit to his leg. It doesn't seem to have much of an impact only to irritate him. I'm rewarded with a hard slap to my face. "No, stop!" I scream.

"Next time, I won't be as nice!" he sneers. The way he says it shoots fear straight to my gut.

"Please," I beg in between cries. "I'm sorry!"

"Heard your speech back there, don't think that you are." His fist tightens on my hair. He's dragging me, pain rips through my head again. "Get up!" he roars.

I scramble to my feet even though his hold on my hair hasn't loosened. I search around me, looking for anything I might be able to use as a weapon, but I don't see anything. I struggle to try and get out of his grasp. Something hard and cold presses at the back of my head.

"Don't fight, or I'll blow your fucking head off." There is a certainty that Mike's voice holds that frightens me even more than I already am. All I can think about is Lily and Jake. I have to do what he says until I can figure out a way to turn the tables on him. My Lil needs me. Jake needs me. What if he kills me, then goes after them? No, I can't let that happen. I'll do anything to make sure it doesn't.

He leads me onto the boat. Another stab of fear runs through me as I fall backward onto the spot where we fought so long ago. I land on the deck, a piece of wet, rotted wood soaks my shirt. "Why are you doing this?" I call out in fear with his gun pointed at me.

"Why? Let's see. You killed me, or so you thought. I guess I should be thanking you, though."

"Why?" I ask before I can stop myself.

I'm met with the evilest laugh. It fills the air and ricochets off the trees making it feel like we're all alone. I don't hear any birds chirping. There are no leaves blowing in the wind. Even the river seems to have stilled. It's just the two of us on this boat that started it all.

"Sit." He motions to the shredded vinyl chair that leans against the wheelhouse. "The time for telling isn't now. First, you have to do your part, and get my boy here."

I sit in the chair not seeing any other option with the gun pointed at me.

I know that if he gets Jake here, he'll kill us both. I can feel it. At least, Lily will have one of her parents. No, I can't think that way. I need to get out of here. I need to figure this out, but I won't lead Jake here. "You're the worst thing to ever happen to Jake. I won't lure him here, you sick fuck."

Whack.

A sharp crack against my face make my eyes hit the back of my head and I fall sideways hitting the deck again. Mike raises the gun towards me and I scream loud as it goes off hitting the wooden rail next to me. I scream again afraid that he's going to kill me. "Noooo!"

"That one was a warning," he approaches me and I want to squirm away, but fear is holding me captive. My face stings from his blow as he leans over me. I can smell his musty body odor. It repulses me. He repulses me.

He reaches into my pocket and pulls out my phone, presses a few buttons and places it on speaker as I watched through a swollen eye. The face of my phone flashes, calling Jake.

It rings, once, twice, three times and then four. I pray that it goes to voicemail.

"Mommy?" my little girl answers and fear coats her voice. Oh, God. Oh, no. Not my Lily.

"Talk," Mike says under his breath. "Get him here!"

"Lily, listen to me!"

"Mom, what's going on? I'm scared," she asks cutting me off.

"Baby, where's Dad?"

"He," she sniffles, "We heard you scream."

"Lily honey, I need…" The phone is ripped away and Mike Daniels hits end, then tosses it again.

"Sounds like my son should be here any second." He grabs me by my hair again lifting me off of the ground and pulls a rope from the side of the boat. I yelp in more pain.

With the gun still trained on me, he points to the chair again and orders me to sit like I'm some feral dog.

"Why should I, you're just going to kill me?" I scream hoping that I can buy some time for Jake.

"Bitch, I'll kill you if you don't," he orders again and shoves me onto the chair.

I'm trembling with fear. I don't want to die, but I don't want anything to happen to Jake or Lily either.

"You're sick!" I spit.

He backhands me again. The pain slices as my lip splits open and blood trickles down my chin.

"Leave her alone!" Jake's voice booms. He comes into view, walking onto the deck and I see a look of disbelief along with anger wash over his features.

"There you are, son. So good to see you again. I was just getting reacquainted with your girlfriend."

"What? How? You're dead!" Jake asks confused but approaching cautiously Jake will get us out of this. He has too. The look on his face tells me he's determined. I don't see a trace of fear.

"I'll get to that, but first why don't you come over here and have a seat next to your pretty little girlfriend? Oh, right. I guess she's not that pretty right now seeing as I've seen to her face," he laughs.

Jake doesn't return his laugh. No, Jake's face twists into something I could've gone my entire life without seeing. "Careful, old man. You keep talking and I'll kill you before you get a chance to reveal how you're still alive."

"Oh, you're feeling brave, are you?" Mike retorts.

"How are you here?" Jake asks again. His voice holds so much power you would think he was the one wielding a gun.

A look of surprise flashes over Mike's face like he can't believe Jake is no longer the scared boy.

My heart is beating wildly.

"Oh, boy. You want answers? Thinking I'll kill your girl first." Mike Daniels raises his gun towards me. The next second happens so fast, I barely register what transpires.

Jake closes the distance and grabs the back of Mike's elbow. He bends his arm backward making the gun fall to the deck and then a split second later he smashes Mike's face into his knee, knocking him out.

Holy shit.

Jake swiftly kicks the gun away and then meets me halfway. I'm out of my seat and falling into his arms, careful to step away from Mike Daniels.

He cups my face, "You okay, Juniper?" I nod my head even though I'm so filled with adrenaline I can hardly breathe. I can't believe Jake just took him down like that. I think I'm in shock. "Jake," my voice wobbles as I say his name.

"God, when I heard you scream. I've never been more scared in my life," Jake kisses my forehead.

"Lily?" I ask.

"She's locked in the truck. I told her to call the police. Go to her. We're parked by the clearing on the bank," he commands. I reach up and kiss him. He's careful not to break my lip apart worse than it already is, and I run like crazy to my girl who must be out of her mind with worry.

I'm so shaken up by everything that I slide on the mud. My knee hits the ground twisting it. "Fuck!" I hiss in pain as I try to lift myself from the thick sludge only to slide down again. I need to get to my baby. I need to make sure she's okay. A dark, moss-covered root sticks out of the mud. I grab a hold and haul myself up. I stand and my knee shouts in protest. Putting my weight on it is hard, but I need to get to her. I limp along as quickly as I can, scrambling to the truck.

I lean on the truck taking the pressure off my knee and throw open the truck door.

"Lily?" I don't see her in the cab of the truck and she doesn't answer me.

"Lily!" I call out again. Using the strength in my arms, I hoist myself inside.

Empty.

Shit.

"Lily!" I call out again.

Silence.

"Lily!"

Nothing.

A flashing light catches my eye on the floorboard. I reach down wincing at the pain in my knee only to find Jake's cell phone laying on the ground. "Lily, where are you?"

I'm afraid that I somehow could've missed Lily and that she headed towards Jake. I scurry back to the boat, moving with my limp as fast as I can.

I approach the boat with caution. I'm not even sure why, just something about the stillness makes me feel like I need to. What I see when the boat is finally in sight has my blood running cold.

Standing up, holding my daughter close to his side, is Mike Daniels with a gun aimed directly at her head. Jake is watching them intently. I can see a gash on his side. His shirt is quickly staining red. My family needs me.

Sirens echo in the stillness. My baby girl followed Jake's order to call the police. I look around me, hoping to find something I can use as a weapon. The only thing I find is a jagged piece of wood with a nail sticking out of it. I pick it up and stick it in the back of my pants then pull my shirt over it. It won't protect me against a bullet, but frankly, I don't care. Mike's already injured, maybe I can use that to my advantage.

I walk down the deck, knowing I'll be seen right away. "Let my daughter go! You need to train a gun on someone? Train it on me, instead." I not so gracefully climb on board the boat.

"Well, isn't this nice. The family all together again," Mike sneers.

Lily is crying hard, "Mommy, Daddy's hurt. He hurt Daddy."

Jake looks at me like what are you doing here and up close I can see how pale his face is. He must be losing a decent amount of blood. "I see that, baby. He's a bad man, but it's all going to be okay." I don't know where my sudden calm is coming from, all I know is that I need to trade places with my daughter.

Mike laughs, "You're just in time for story time. Lily, why don't you tell your Momma the first part of the story."

Lily hiccups between sobs.

"Go on girl," he nudges her with the gun. I don't care about his story, all I care about is Lily, the fact that she's scared out of her mind, and Jake.

"He... he said that you hittin' him gave him the perfect opportunity. Did you hit him, Mommy?"

"Baby, he was hurting your daddy."

Mike cuts me off. I take another step closer. "Stop. Don't move," Mike bellows, "I'll take it from here. So, where was I? Aw yes, you see, when you knocked me overboard I almost drowned. Almost. At the time, I was indebt with Eli. That part was all true, but Jake thinking I was dead gave me the perfect opportunity. I found Eli and told him that we could use this against you. Told him that Jake was so caught up in you that he'd do anything he asked of him. Made a deal with him to stay dead so we could get Jake to do whatever he wanted. It worked out good too. After a while, I was able to get a cut of Eli's profits. See, Jake was so good at collecting and hurting people that it wasn't even always Eli's debts. After a while, word got out to every player in town that Eli had a boy under his thumb that could get anyone to pay up. We sold him. Anytime something needed to be done, we sold him. Paid real good too." Mike laughs and I can see Jake's face tighten.

"Enough!" Jake tries to yell but doesn't have the strength.

"I'm just getting started, son."

I hear sirens getting closer. Mike must hear them too. I can't imagine this speech is going to go on long enough for the police to find us unless the police can't find us. We're not where Lily called them from. Hopefully, they can figure it out.

"Then, Jake left to chase after you, and our money source started to dry up."

"How could you use your son like that? He was a kid," I yell, not liking or really caring to hear the rest. I get it, from what he is saying, he used Jake and had no regard for him, not that I ever really thought he did, but everything he is saying just proves it.

"He was a brat and that woman loved him. Him of all people."

Oh, his cruelty has no bounds, "You mean his mother? Of course, she loved him. He's her son!" I yell and get close. My talking back to him has done the trick. He's taken the gun off of Lily and has aimed it at me. "You didn't deserve either of them, and I'm sure your wife would be disgusted by you. She'd hate you."

"You little bitch." He steps forward and hits the spot on the deck with the rotted wood. It's exactly where I was hoping he'd move.

"Lily, run!" I scream and at the same time Mike's foot goes through the rotted wood. He screams out. Lily doesn't waste any time running to the side of the boat. Mike is caught off guard so I reach behind my back and grab the piece of wood I have shoved in my jeans and swing it with all my might, hitting his hand knocking the gun loose.

"Stupid cunt," Mike yells again. I see Lily run from the boat and safely onto the deck dock. I reach for the gun, but I'm not quick enough. Mike grabs my foot and tries to drag me closer to him. The wood under him splinters more. The pain in my knee radiates down my entire body. Then...

Bang.

The gun goes off. Air swooshes past me as a bullet zooms by and hits Mike Daniels square in the chest. His shirt soaks through with blood. His body instantly goes limp and the rotted wood gives way completely. His entire body falls through the rotted deck and into the river below. This time, there's no current to sweep him away. This time, he's gone for good.

CHAPTER TWENTY-FOUR

It's been five days since everything happened with Mike Daniels. Jake spent the first two days in critical care because of the amount of blood he lost, and since his dad used a rusty piece of the boat to cut him with, the risk of infection was really high.

Mom and Dad drove down as soon as I called them, filling them in on everything and have been helping me with Lily and Jake ever since.

We immediately got Lily into therapy and the therapist tells us that she is doing well with all things considered. We'll go home when it's safe for Jake to travel, which shouldn't be too much longer.

"Mom, two more buttons and we're at Daddy's floor."

I smile down at my girl. She's almost as excited to get Jake home as I am. We step off of the elevator and Lily grabs my hand, the same way she has every time we've been here to see Jake since he moved to this floor; and just like every other time, as soon as we're five feet from the door she drops my hand and runs for his bed. "Daddy!" she screams.

"Hey, baby girl." He kisses her on the head. "You ready to help me break free of this place?"

"Silly, it's the day you get out. You don't have to break out. Mom says we're going to wheel you out."

I laugh and then lean into Jake and give him a kiss. "You ready to go?"

"So ready. Nurse Ratchet should be here any moment with discharge papers."

"She's not that bad." Jake gives me a look that says, oh, really.

"You'll be out of here soon enough," I kiss him again. His soft lips against my own remind me of how much I could've lost. He's here. He's okay, I tell myself every time his lips touch mine, but I can't help feeling haunted by what could've been. I could've lost Jake... again.

"Hey, none of that," Jake says noticing where my thoughts have gone. "I'm coming home, sweet Juniper."

"Juniper, I like it. Can I call you that?" Lily asks.

"No," we both say in unison.

Lily pouts, "C'mon"

"Sorry Lil, that's mine. Besides, you get to call her the most special name."

"What?" she asks innocently.

"Mom. You get to call her Mom."

She huffs out just as the nurse walk in, "Alright, just need you to sign a few places and we'll get you out of here. What do you want to do about all the flowers? I can get someone to help us, but we may need a few carts." I laugh because Liz couldn't get out of work so she overcompensated by sending way too many flowers.

"We're going to go back to Ohio soon. Can you donate them to patients who could use some happiness?" I ask.

"Sure, I don't see why not. Now, sign these, and we'll get you out of here." She hands Jake a clipboard and pen, then points to every spot he needs to sign. "Just remember to follow-up with your primary care physician in Ohio. No heavy lifting. Minimal activity."

Jake gives me a look and nods toward Lily. I understand where his mind is at, so I bring Lily to the window and distract her by asking her to count the birds with me. This always seems to work.

I hear Jake behind me, "So, when can we, you know?"

"Not until your doctor has cleared you for normal activity."

Jake sighs and I know how frustrated he is, it mirrors my own. A few minutes later the nurse is walking with us, wheeling Jake down the hallway. I can tell he isn't happy about it, and that he's staying quiet about it because of Lily.

We climb into my SUV. I'm careful of my knee that was sprained during everything and we wave goodbye to the nurse.

"Got some news today," Jake says once we're on the road.

"What's that?" I ask curiously.

"I found out that Dad's property, including the house, after it was transferred to Eli, it was then transferred to an LLC, which happened to be owned by my dad."

I shake my head, not understanding and then it dawns on me, "You're the next of kin."

"Yup," he says, "Need to decide what to do with it, and I'm thinking that we need to tear the barn down, but maybe the house can be fixed up and sold."

Of course, he'd want to tear the barn down. The police did a search of the house of the property and found a room in the back of the barn that Mike was living in. It wasn't so much that his belongings were there that was worrisome. No, what was really scary was the box of info on Jake, pictures of him walking out of prison, his apartment, him walking out of work, me, Lily, the entire thing screamed stalker. The irony of it is that Mike spent years profiting off of Jake being his enforcer, and in the end, it was that man that Mike turned him into that took him down.

"I think taking the barn down is smart. Let's talk to a realtor and get an idea if it's even worth it to fix it up."

"I'd like to get the most money out of it. I hate that house. I hate everything it represents and I want to be able to give our kids the future they deserve."

"Kids, huh? As in plural?" I ask.

"Well, yeah. I missed you being pregnant. Once we get settled and put this behind us, I plan on making our Lily a sister as many times as you'll let me."

"Seriously?" I laugh.

"Mom! I'm going to be a sister!" Lily shouts from the backseat.

"We should've had this conversation away from listening ears," I say to Jake.

"Why? She's right. You'll be one soon enough, just not yet, baby."

"Humph," she sighs and starts to sing along with the pop song on the radio.

Jake looks like he's being tortured having to listen to the song until it changes to a part where Lily has to actually sing. When she opens up her voice, Jake turns and stares at her in complete awe.

"Oh, yeah, she's got your talent," I laugh.

"You've been holding out on me." I go to slap his shoulder, then stop myself, afraid that I might hit his chest and make it hurt.

We pull up to the summer house rather quickly and Mom and Dad greet us outside. They've been to the hospital a few times, balancing between giving us space and showing concern. Mom gives Jake a hug and Dad pats him on the back. "We have a surprise for you inside," Mom says.

"Is it cookies, Grandma? I hope it's cookies."

Mom shakes her head laughing at Lily, then says, "Let's see what we can find."

I squeeze Jake's hand letting him know it's all good, and we slowly walk inside.

Sitting on the over-sized chaise is Mrs. Jones. She showed up here the day after everything happened and Mom, Dad, and Lily got to meet her. I was still at the hospital with Jake, but once he was moved from critical care, I made the effort to seek her out and introduce myself to her. This is the woman who breathed life into Jake when all he had was bad. She gave him music.

"Mrs. Jones," Jake's voice is soft and caring when his eyes land on hers. The tiny woman stands and wraps her arms around Jake's middle.

"Heard about what happened to you. Wish I'd known what was happening years ago," Mrs. Jones sniffles.

"Oh, no. Don't do that. Don't take what happened on you. It's not on you. You were so good to me. You were such a saving grace."

"My best friend's name is Grace," Lily says changing the tone in the room.

"Why don't you tell me about her, dear?" Mrs. Jones says sitting back down. Mom hands Lily a cookie and my girl curls up next to Mrs. Jones. "Well, Grace and I met when I was three years old. That's a long time ago," Lily says and continues to babble to an all too pleased Mrs. Jones.

"Thank you for bringing her here," Jake whispers in my ear.

"I think this was all you. She's wonderful and I'm so glad you had her."

He kisses behind my ear and I notice him wince from pain as he straightens from the kiss. "You need to get off your feet."

"I'm fine," he says.

I shoot him a look and can tell he doesn't have it in him to fight me. He takes a seat on the other chaise and winces again. I fuss over him, laying a blanket over him even though it's warm, and Mom helps me by getting him pillows.

"Seriously, women." Jake gives Mom and me a death stare which Dad sees.

"Why don't you ladies start dinner, and give that man a break," Dad says to Mom and me. Mom pats me on the shoulder, and I follow her into the kitchen. I help Mom with dinner Every few minutes I peek my head out, only to see Jake laughing with Mrs. Jones and Lily.

"Relax, honey. He's okay," Mom tells me after I look in on him for the fourth time.

I sigh, "I know, Mom. It's just I came so close to losing him… again."

"You can't keep living in what happened. He's safe. Your family is safe, and something about the way that man loves you makes me think that he's never gonna let you go again."

I give one last look into the living room and Jake catches my eye and the way those blue-greens shine back at me, I know she's right.

After a delicious dinner, a goodbye and a promise to keep in touch with Mrs. Jones, we say goodnight to Mom, Dad and Lily. There isn't an extra bedroom, so I find myself nestled close to Jake on the chaise in a darkened house.

"Mom told me you were never gonna let me go again."

"Knew your mom was a smart woman," he whispers while stroking my stomach.

"You know, I'm never going to let you go again, either. I trust you. I trust in us. I love you."

"Juniper," his voice is low and raspy. "I know. I feel it, babe." He places his fingers against my heart and dips his forehead, pressing our heads together, "And I see it. I know it might seem crazy, but we've been fighting so long for us that it feels like we shouldn't be breathing like everything is normal, but it's going to be. You, me, our Lily; we get to have our life. We get to have our happily ever after." He kisses me and it's soft and sweet. We're not rushed; not anymore, because he's right from here on out, it's us living, not looking back, but looking forward. We have right now, and we have tomorrow-without anything standing in our way.

EPILOGUE

Two years later

"Fuck, babe! I missed you!" My fingers dig deep into Jake's ass. "Harder. Oh, fuck yes!" I scream out.

Jake stills, "Are you okay? I'm not hurting you, am I? I know the doctor said you might be sore for a while and we still have a week, but I couldn't wait."

"The only person who is going to be sore is you if you don't hurry up and fuck me before everyone wakes up!"

Jake chuckles and circles his hips making me groan.

"Alright, you sure you can handle it?" he asks huskily, "Cause I need to hear my wife scream."

"Oh yeah," I respond and then sink my teeth into his shoulder.

"So, good. So, tight," He grunts and then he gives me what I need. He moves fast and hard. Hands grope. Bodies slap.

"Lips, babe," he orders and I gladly give them to him. My God, five weeks without him inside of me was way too long.

I'm panting; he takes my breath away. Our lips roam over one another. Mine part for his tongue, and just like every single kiss, it's explosive. Our skin slides over each other, slick with sweat. His hard body presses into me and I groan, breaking the kiss.

He pounds, deep and hard. "Yes! Give it to me!" I say lost in feeling.

And oh, boy does he give it to me.

"You there?" he asks.

I nod as Jake picks up speed and lifts my legs higher. My eyes roll to the back of my head and my legs quiver. He thrusts in once more as I shudder around him and he stills, finding his release.

I'm exhausted and sated, and immediately drift off to sleep, barely conscious when Jake comes into the room, and places tiny lips around my breast.

"She's almost here! She's almost here!" Lily bounces up and down.

"Lil, we still have about twenty minutes until Aunt Liz will be here. Give your Mom a break, would you? She's exhausted."

"I'm fine really. I'm getting used to not sleeping." I yawn and then look down to the tiny bundle of dark hair suckling my breast. Our son was born five weeks ago and he's the most precious little boy. We named him William Lucas Daniels after my dad. I think he might have my dad's nose. I know it's too early to tell, but he looks like a cross between my dad and Jake.

"What do you think the surprise is going to be?" Lily asks.

"I have no idea." I really don't. Liz called at the last minute and said she was coming into town to see the baby and she was bringing a surprise with her.

"Maybe, she's finally decided to settle down," Jake grins.

"Is she moving?" Lily asks.

"No, honey. Settle down means to have a boyfriend."

"Eww," Lily makes a disgusted face and Jake and I laugh.

Will unlatches and I give him a few pats on his back lifting his blue and gray fleece covered body into the air. He's a fast burper, so it only takes a second of patting his back and then I offer him the other side. He doesn't latch and I'm relieved. Maybe I won't smell like breast milk when Liz gets here after all.

Jake notices that Will is done and says, "Here, let me take him." He reaches down and grabs Will from my arms and then gives me a quick kiss on my lips. "Come on, Lil. Let's give your Mom a few minutes." he says as they walk out of the room. I yawn again, climb out of bed and walk into my large, brand new, extremely opulent bathroom.

To say our new home is large is an understatement, but Jake got a deal on it because the builder was going belly up and the large settlement we got for his wrongful imprisonment suit was enough to ensure we have a home large enough to fit our expanding family.

Looking in the mirror, the first thing that stands out to me is the bags under my eyes, the second is my hair. It's tied up in a knot on the top of my head, and not the on purpose kinds of knot, but the I just had sex and haven't slept in weeks kind of knot. I'm a hot mess, and I need to hurry. I quickly strip out of my clothes and hop into the shower, basking in the few minutes I have to myself. I wash my hair and shave in record time and by the time I get out, I decide maybe my eyes aren't that bad.

I spend about thirty whole seconds on make-up; Liz better understand. I sit down on the side of the bed to dress and almost fall over to nap. Dressed in a comfortable pair of yoga pants and a button up blouse that's easy to nurse in, I make it downstairs just in time for the doorbell to ring.

"She's here! She's here!" Lily says throwing open the front door.

"You're beautiful babe," Jake says in my ear.

I smile at Jake, and look over to see Will asleep in the plush Papasan swing. "Come on, let's go see Liz's surprise." Jake grabs my hand and we walk out front to see Liz getting out of the passenger side of a large, white Escalade. My curiosity is peaked even more. Who's driving? Maybe Jake's right, and she's met someone.

"Lily!" Liz squeals and picks my girl up and turns her in a circle. I'm so caught up in my best friend and daughter that I don't notice the man step around the Escalade.

"Bro!" A male voice shouts and rushes towards Jake with wide open arms.

"Holy cow! Dietz!" I shout, breaking up the man hug and heading straight for Dietz. I haven't seen him in years. "You look exactly the same!"

Well, not exactly the same, in the eight years since I saw him last, he has filled out more. His dark hair is still styled, but instead of the baggy jeans in that grunge style he used to wear, he's wearing fitted jeans and... I pause in my perusal and bust out laughing, he's wearing Jake's 'are you looking at my weiner' t-shirt.

"June, look at you! Hotter than ever! Boob job?" His eyes rake over me with amusement and I smile, 'cause it's Dietz, anyone else I'd find offensive.

"Watch it!" Jake says in a playful growl.

"What's a boob job?" Lily asks.

"Oh, sorry kid. It's when...Ouch!" Liz stops Dietz from explaining to my daughter about breast implants by giving Dietz a purple-nurple.

I pull Liz into a tight hug and notice there's something different about her. I can't put my finger on what it is, but there's something. "How are you here with Dietz?" I ask.

"Yeah, what gives?" Jake asks looking at the two of them.

"You going to invite us in before you give us the Spanish inquisition?" Dietz asks throwing his hand around Liz's waist. My eyes widen in shock. They look all too familiar with each other.

I know we need to get in the house in case my little man wakes up, so I gesture towards the front door, "Come on in," and lead everyone inside.

Will is sleeping soundly. "Oh my goodness! Look at him. He's the cutest!" Liz says rushing over. "Can I pick him up?"

"We just got him to sleep, and June hasn't been getting much of a break. Let's let him rest for now. He'll be up before we know it," Jake tells Liz and I watch as she gives him a glare not liking his answer.

"Let's go to the kitchen where it's quieter." I grab Liz by the elbow before she has a chance to protest, and Lily and the guys follow us. "Here Lil, you can have a brownie, now," I offer and she hops up on the stool surrounding the over-sized granite island.

I pour myself a cup of coffee that my husband so thoughtfully brewed for me and take a seat at the table, still completely shocked that Liz is here with Dietz, and it looks like they're together.

"Alright, you two?" I look back and forth between Dietz and Liz who also sit down. Jake leans against the island close to where I'm sitting.

"So," Liz begins, "A few weeks ago, I went to a bar in Greenwich Village. I know, I know. Greenwich Village isn't usually my scene, but I was supposed to meet this co-worker there who ended up having a fight with her boyfriend and she never showed. Anyways, there I was making the best of my night and trying to avoid advances from this really skeevy guy when the door to the bar opened, and in walked Dietz with a bunch of guys."

"And it was love at first sight," Dietz chimes in.

"No, I didn't know who he was, but he approached me almost immediately and said-,"

Dietz takes over the story and I'm getting whiplash going back and forth. "I said I remember you. You're the beautiful blonde that I've never forgotten."

"I racked my brain trying to figure out if I'd ever dated him," Liz huffs then stands and pours herself a cup of coffee.

"She didn't remember me, but not to worry. I told her I knew you and was there the night you met Lucas, I mean Jake." He turns and faces Jake, "Dude,that was some crazy shit. I knew you were innocent."

Jake nods his head in Lily's direction to remind him of her presence.

"Right, kids. Okay, so once I told her I knew you guys, then she remembered. I wasn't lying when I said I never forgot her. She was cute then, but now, my girl's a bombshell."

"We've spent nearly every second together since," Liz says and sips her coffee like she isn't delivering the most amazing news. I'm shocked that the two found each other, but I'm also really happy for her. I only hope that they both have sown all their oats.

"Well, this calls for a celebration," Jake says and he grabs a bottle of amber liquid from a cupboard.

"My man, no more drinking the cheap stuff," Dietz proclaims, slapping Jake on the back.

I refrain from drinking since I'm nursing, instead I order dinner from our favorite takeout place and watch as Lily falls for all that is Dietz.

We have dinner while Dietz entertains Lily with semi-tame stories of Jake. The food is delicious. Before long, Lily's yawning and Jake brings her up to bed.

Liz cuddles William on the couch as Jake and Dietz talk about where everyone from the band is now. Apparently, Dietz is the frontman of his current band and they've recently signed with a major label and will be opening for some big acts this summer.

"Man, I remember you used to have those notebooks and the lyrics you would pull out of them were priceless. We would be writing a song and we'd need something, and you would just pull it from your pocket, and like magic, you had what we needed." Dietz recollects.

"Oh my God!" I stand up from the couch where I was relaxing.

"What is it, babe?" Jake asks.

"All these years, I forgot."

Jake watches me curiously, "What are you talking about?"

"I saved them. I saved them all." I run from the room and down the basement stairs into the storage cubby. I had a bunch of Rubbermaid tubs that I'd been meaning to go through before we moved but with the baby, I never got around to it. I go through the first tub and they're not there. Then, I sort through the next, and there they are under some old keepsakes that I've hung on to for far too long. The black and white composition notebooks look exactly like I remember. I pick them up, counting all five and run back into the room

"Jake, look!" I shove the notebooks at him.

"I can't believe you've had these all these years," Jake kisses me and starts sifting through them.

"Babe, grab my guitar, would you?" Dietz asks Liz.

"I have the baby," she complains, cooing at Will.

"I'll take him." I reach down and grab my baby who is, no doubt, ready to be fed and get comfortable on the couch, covering my breast so Dietz doesn't get an eyeful.

Liz goes outside to the Escalade, and minutes later, returns with Dietz's guitar. Jake sits at his keyboard in the corner of the room as he and Dietz and scour over the lyrics. As they talk quietly, Liz and I watch, mesmerized by our men.

Dietz starts strumming his guitar until he finally settles on a beat he likes. Jake chimes in and the two find a rhythm as if all these years never passed.

Jake begins singing and my world soars when that melodic sound flows from his lips.

(Jake)
Baby, baby
You've been my rock and only
You've loved me since my world was dark and lonely
(Dietz)
Baby, baby
You haven't heard my whole plan
I've loved you since you told me to get gone
(Jake)
Juniper
My sweetest kinda river
You flowed through me and gave me something worth living for
(Dietz)
Izzy Lizzy
My heart keeps beating faster
'Cause I'm dying to know if you'll give me an answer
(Jake)

Juniper
I'll love you for forever
'Cause you're the air I breath
The love like no other
(Dietz)
Isabella
I'm getting kinda antsy
Need to know if you'll wear my ring baby?

Dietz stops playing and Jake drops his music to a slower beat. "What do you say, Liz? I know it's quick, but I feel like I've known you for forever. I've never felt this way and I don't want to ever let you go. Marry me?"

Liz pops up from the couch and throws herself in his arms, "You can't ask me to marry you!"

"I just did baby. Say yes. Be my wife."

"Yes," she whispers and her eyes find mine. I give her a silent nod towards the guest bedroom. I'm stuck on the couch with a baby on my boob, so I can't move. Liz gets my cue and takes his hand leading him away from us.

"Wow, babe!" Jake says sitting next to me and kissing me and then our baby.

"I know!" I squeal, "Can you believe it? The two of them together and they just got engaged in our living room? Our living room!"

Jake chuckles, "Yeah I can believe it. I have you, June, so I know anything is possible."

And there it is. Every day, my man makes me fall in love with him all over again. "I love you," I whisper, careful not to wake William..

"I love you too," he whispers back as he takes my lips.

The End

Other Works by Abby McCarthy

Stand-alones
[Tainted by Crazy][1]
[Current][2]
Series
The Wrecked Series
[Wreck You][3]
[Fight You][4]
[Hurt You][5]
[Stronger Than This – A stand-alone Wrecked Series Spin Off][6]
Bleeding Scars MC
[Cut Wide Open][7]

---

1. http://amzn.to/2i7Ldn7
2. http://amzn.to/1Oqt7W8
3. http://amzn.to/1JQU3wN
4. http://amzn.to/1FgJPFZ
5. http://amzn.to/1HGHi8D
6. https://amzn.to/2HrrmxE
7. https://www.amazon.com/dp/B06XDWYZTP

Aknowledgements

This is that place in a book where I give all my thanks and hope I don't mess up and miss anyone.

Fingers crossed

THANK YOU FIRST TO my family. Steve Harvey says that men are capable of change, but only for that one woman, and God I'm lucky that I'm that one woman for my husband. Our life has only gotten better and I'm so dang grateful. Thank you to my girls for my Lily inspiration. Thank you sisters. Thank you Shana and Jessica for just being you. Thank you Hang Le for another beautiful cover. Thank you Nicole Reid, you always take the time out to let me run a plot twist by you and thank you so much for editing and all that you do. Thank you Louisa for becoming such an integral part of the blog so that I can focus more on writing. Thank you to my blog sisters, Kerry, Jade, Dawn and Kristine. Thank you Cheryl Wilkins and Lisa Hines. Thank you to all of the blogs who have helped support me I understand what a huge role you play! Thank you Emily Smith-Kidman for everything! Thank you Literary Gossip! Thank you to all the women who support me in Abby's Awesome Allies. Lastly, thank you Jimmy Maguire and Debbie Kogok of Toast and Coffee.

To hear original music created with Lyrics from Current please visit, https://m.soundcloud.com/toast-coffee

ABOUT THE AUTHOR

Website
http://abbymccarthyauthor.com/
Twitter
abbyemccarthy[1] (http://www.twitter.com/abbyemccarthy)
Facebook
http://www.facebook.com/abbymccarthyauthor

Abby McCarthy is reader and a lover of words. She is a blogger turned author and released her first novel in May 2014. She is a mother of three, a wife and a dog person. She has always written, sometimes poetry, sometimes just to vent about failed relationships, however in parenthood she has found her voice to help keep her sanity. Words have flowed from her, to review and with the support of amazing friends in the Indie community she has decided to pursue her dream of writing! She loves to write and read romance, because isn't that something we all yearn for? Whether it be flowers and hand holding or just the right tug on your hair. Isn't that what life is about? The human connection?

---

1. http://www.twitter.com/abbyemccarthy

Made in United States
North Haven, CT
14 August 2025